CW00705219

2184 - Twenty-Second Century Man

Green Deal Quartet, Volume 4

Jim Lowe

Published by Jim Lowe, 2022.

This is a work of fiction. Similarities to real people, places, or events are entirely coincidental.

2184 - TWENTY-SECOND CENTURY MAN

First edition. December 27, 2022.

Copyright © 2022 Jim Lowe.

ISBN: 979-8201535995

Written by Jim Lowe.

Also by Jim Lowe

Green Deal Quartet
2084 - New World Man
2100 - Crime of the Century
2142 - The Revealing Science
2184 - Twenty-Second Century Man

New Reform Quartet
New Reform
The O.D.C. - The Online Death Cult
With Two Eyes
Fourth Room

Watch for more at https://jimlowewriting.com/.

1: THE ONE HUNDRED YEAR PLAN

The one good thing to come out of the Green's family planning is I only have one birthday to remember, and it covers all seven of the kids. Brady laughed at his own inner joke.

Brady looked around the dining table on 30 December 2183. It was Tuesday, and Thursday was the start of the New Green Year, the year which promised the fruition of Bodhi Sattva's one-hundred-year plan. His eldest sons, Bill and Rocky, were both forty-one going-on twenty-five in Brady's conversion method for the difference in actual Green years to old Trad year equivalence. Therefore, his next two sons, Wilder and Troy, were thirty-nine going-on twenty-five, and the youngest, Hawk, was thirty-six going-on twenty-five. All Pure Green children - those born post-Revolution, aged as they would have done as Trads until they reached twenty-five. From then, they barely aged even over the decades.

Amie and Helgarth had put up with a few years of Brady calling their own children: *things, its* and other derogatory labels. As Mothers to his five sons and as per their agreement with him to keep his sons' masculinity uninfluenced by the Greens non-binary way of living, they had tried until they couldn't have their children brutalised any longer. Brady begrudgingly called the goys and eventually even called them by their real names Lucy-Ian - Amie named xem after her stepfather Lucian - and Raelynn. They were allowed two children of their own, and Brady didn't want any more children in the home, and he funded the Green cost of having children. In the last twenty years, the cost of bringing children into the world to consume Her resources had risen considerably. If they could have had one more, then it would have been Amie's turn to name her and Helgarth's child, and she would have called her goy Mary-Louis, after her Moms; maybe she should have done this with their first baby, but xe looked like Lucian, irrespective of the lack of a direct bloodline.

Brady looked at Lucy-Ian, who was indeterminate in appearance - he had no say in how Amie and Helgarth raised their own - he kept his bargain with them. Raelynn was dressed in her ever-present Goth gear, complete with black hair with white lightning streaks. They were both thirty going-on twenty-five. Lucy-Ian had a Hodgson boy look, which Brady never uttered - as no good would be done by bringing his old hoodlum neighbours' lineage into a discussion. He could see something in the eyes which might have made Amie think of Lucian, his late best friend. He referred to Raelynn as *her*, as a concession to his Trad ideals. Brady wouldn't countenance using xe as a pronoun. He also viewed Lucy-Ian as female to distinguish between Amie and Helgarth's daughters and his own sons.

His boys looked like variations of Brady - a point which made him proud. They were all above six feet tall, and his iron rule that they had to work out in the gym for a minimum of an hour a day had built them up. He ignored all protestations that they could have any appearance they desired courtesy of the YellowSuits™ and explained that the Greens were weaklings inside their shells. The vision of Mrs Wilson in her grave and Rhea Laidlaw's words about *dying inside* still haunted him. He needed the reassurance that beneath their NanoSuits™, they were as healthy as Trad athletes.

The only variations in their natural state were that Amie's children by him, Bill, Wilder and Hawk, had black hair and brown eyes. Whereas Helgarth's Scandinavian looks gave Rocky and Troy her blonde hair but they still had Brady's brown eyes, and all of them had his Polynesian colouring.

And as for Brady, he was well aware that he was at an impossible age of one-hundred and forty-one years old. He guessed that his birthday was probably on January 1st. He used to think of this as John Kane's sick joke, as he went to great lengths to have Xavier Kane the first child to be born in the Millennium. He dwelled on the thought of Xavier Kane or Bodhi Sattva as he rebranded himself, and Brady wondered if he knew or guessed that Brady was his clone. Glenarvon Cole, his other cloned brother, who may or may not know the truth about the relationship between the three of them, like Brady, didn't know precisely when he was born. *It's gotta be the same. That's the way that sick fuck thinks.* Brady didn't think it was the same thing at all, that he should have seven children in his home, five of his own, all celebrating the same birthday. *That's just convenience - is all.*

There was a roar of laughter around the dinner table as Troy delivered the punchline to his anecdote. Brady smiled broadly, even though he hadn't been listening. Hunter, his old servant, brought Brady his dessert. Brady played with it while he drifted away. His family had got used to this and put it down to his old age. He let them think that - it was easier, but he knew he still felt as good as he was in his Trad forties - which meant he felt like the same person he was when he was still in Ridgecrest Supermax on the eve of the Revolution, almost a hundred years ago.

Brady loved the way his boys looked. They were big and robust and unmistakably out of Brady Mahone's stock. He also bred into them the ethics of competition and winning at all costs, but something about them unnerved him. They had sharp and cunning minds, which was to be welcomed, but it was in business - again, something he could put down to something they inherited from Brady Mahone. After all, with business booming under the stewardship and drive of his sons, he was indisputably the richest man in the world outside of Boulder Creek and Sattva Systems™. He should have been reassured as this business was named after him, named by him, Brady Mahone Entertainment Enterprises. However, it was the way they did business which troubled him. His sons were ruthless winners, but in a corporate way, sometimes they even sounded a bit scientific to Brady's ears, and one thing Brady wasn't - was a scientist.

He disliked the science of Sattva Systems™ with their Nano-everythings, and he disliked Tia Cassandra and the way she treated her crew. Sending her on the last mission to Mars later in the year was the best place for her. Tyrone Beardon, the Bear's nephew once, informed him that Mars was a hostile and freezing desert, and he remembered the delightful laughter from his buddy when Brady said *I can see why she loves it so much.'*

The memory of Tyrone's laughter merged and then was subsumed by the laughter around the table, and then the word his mind was reaching for emerged, it was summoned by the laughter of his sons. It had a timbre and a tone that could only be described as *corporate.*

Is this what I'm on this planet for?

Brady didn't dismiss this question, and he had every right to be concerned. His biological father was a monster. Bodhi and Glenarvon hadn't had children. The John Kane line would come to an end if it was left up to them. Whereas with the man's man Brady Mahone, he would have five Grandchildren ready to rule the world. Brady thought of himself as merely a racehorse put out to stud.

He listened to the heated business discussions around the table. He watched the servants taking away the dishes and cleaning up around the family. Amie and Helgarth excused themselves from the table. *That reminds me, I must get Amie to trim my hair tomorrow. It reminds me of when Mary-Lou used to cut my hair.* He recalled the last time she did it when she showed him the first flecks of grey growing under his black hair. It also reminded him of the 2160s, where he tried growing his hair long and experimenting with all kinds of beards and moustaches. *What is it about the 60s decades which makes men want to be long hairs? The 1960s, 2060s and then 2160s, always with the fucking 60s.*

He had gone through a phase of wondering whether he was losing concentration because he was getting old, but then he decided this was bullshit. It was just a case that the conversation was getting boring - just like math at school.

Brady's sons carried on debating and planning and were no longer paying attention to Brady at the head of the dining table. Wilder had taken up the theme. He kept thumping the table to make his point. 'Glenarvon stated clearly that there would be 26.5 million Disciples and devout followers by no later than June next year. Therefore, out of a worldwide population of 900 million, that still leaves us a potential new customer reach of 18.5 million. That's a helluva lot of Green Credits still left on the table.'

Troy said, 'Hang on a minute. How do you work that out?'

Wilder shook his head in disgust at having to spell it out, 'We currently have a market penetration of the global BMEE brand of 95%, which is great, don't get me wrong. However, the likelihood of selling to the Green zealots is zero, so that is 2.94% of the population we will never reach.'

Bill joined in, 'And why's that. We can sell to anybody; they might take a little more persuasion...'

'No chance. Glenarvon has got them under pain of death or something...'

Hawk said, 'Or on a promise...' Rocky laughed loudly. He loved his youngest brother. Brady laughed along with them.

Wilder continued with his analysis. 'Assuming, there are 5% of potential customers still to exploit, but 2.94% are out of reach, for now...' He conceded. 'Then that means there are 2.06% of winnables. In customer numbers, this converts to 18.5 million potential new customers to reach. There are five of us, so I propose that we agree to sell to a further 3.7 million each.'

The boys quietened for a moment, and Brady observed them, even though Wilder had nearly lost him with his numbers. Rocky said, 'I can easily get more than that out of my Asian base. We have been booming with Traditional Chinese music, and the fashionable Indian Greens can't be seen without their cache of Bollywood movies.'

Hawk said, 'Oceania has a much smaller population...'

Rocky smiled, 'How many can you do?'

'About 1.2 million at a pinch.'

Rocky said to the group, 'Put me down for Hawk's shortfall. It's the least a brother can do.' He slapped Hawk on the back.

Bill said, 'If Wilder puts forward what he can do with Africa, and Troy does the same with Europe, then I'll take up the rest with the Americas.' He pronounced, 'The home of Brady Mahone's Entertainment Enterprises.' They raised their glasses to Brady. He had an image in his mind that he would struggle to shake off - were they raising a glass to him, or were they raising their glasses to the Grandfather, John Kane? Not that he had ever told them about John Kane. He said to them that Archie Mahone was their Grandfather after finally convincing Amie to back his story.

Wilder added, 'I'll meet my 3.7 million targets in Africa before June. What do you say, boys?'

They all shouted, 'Hell yes!' and banged their big fists on the table repeatedly. Brady was making a note in his sketchbook of the targets his sons had agreed.

Brady looked at his boys with dismay, he loved his boys and was satisfied with Amie's and Helgarth's efforts in raising them in his own image, but they still seemed a bit too Green for his liking. He thumped the table to grab their attention. Amie had just walked in, and it made her jump. She looked at Brady and gave him a look which asked if it was really necessary to do that. Brady announced to his boys, 'I'm going to add a little competition to the mix. The first one to hit their sales targets will receive their own private FusionPassengerJet™ from me.'

Hawk smiled for a split second - aware that his target now appeared easy before the yelling erupted...*I would never have agreed...It's a fucking fix...you're bound to win it now, you little...*

Brady laughed as he got out of his chair and headed out of the room and on to his study. He added, 'You can't start until January 2nd. That's a rule. After that, you can win by any means possible which the Security Protocols™ will allow.' Amie grabbed him by the arm and said, 'Why did you do that?'

'Don't worry, I've got a more pleasant surprise for them on my best-guess-birthday. I just want them to feel like a Trad. That's what they would have done in the old days. It will make men of them.' He kissed her on the cheek and grinned before walking away.

Brady went to his study and flicked through the books where he had marked off all the plants and animals he had ever seen. There was still many more to find. *I need a break from my hobbies and so I might complete a little bit of life admin this year.* His fingers stroked over a glossy photo of a Polar bear. *This is an excellent year to plan for the future, especially as the Greens come to the end of their hundred-year plan. You never know, maybe after they've completed their work, I might share my thoughts with Bodhi and Glenarvon Cole. I wonder if they've guessed that we are all brothers?* He carried on examining the one creature he couldn't see up close. *Y'know, I don't think they do. They woulda said something by now.*

2: ONE HUNDRED AND FORTY-TWO, NOT OUT.

The New Green Year's Eve party was lavish but spoiled by the acrimonious atmosphere between the brothers. Brady watched on with pleasure as he spotted clandestine meetings between pairs of his sons. He was transported back to his old prison days when prisoners would try and suss each other out, forging alliances, and working out what the other was planning, and all the time thinking where the double-crosses were in the agreements.

One thing which still united the boys was the Green influence on everybody in the world. When the obsession with the FusionPassengerJet™ competition subsided briefly, then all talk turned to the last of the Green's NanoSuits™ upgrades. Sattva Systems™ had kept it sworn to secrecy from anybody outside the Disciples' circle. There was talk that the Security Protocols™ had been set to silence them if they merely *thought* about spilling the secret. And if the Security Protocols™ detected this, then they would be ejected from the Disciple-hood.

The only pieces of information which had been released from Sattva Systems™ HQ was that it was to be called UltraViolet™ and that it would be released in two phases, the first for the Disciples on the 25 June 2184 - the Centenary of the Green Revolution, and the rest would receive the UltraViolet™ on the 31 December 2184, just in time to fulfil the Bodhi Sattva promise for the end of the hundred-year plan to save the planet.

Brady laughed as his boys bickered at the realisation that many of their potential customers would now have a decision to make. If they chose to spend their Green Credits on Brady Mahone's Entertainment products before June, would they risk missing out on the UltraViolet™ upgrade - as nobody knew exactly how much the UltraViolet™ would cost? There was the possibility that the payments would be due in June, even though there was a delay in receiving the upgrades for the ordinary Greens.

Bill approached Brady, and the others were not going to be outmanoeuvred, so the remaining sons hurried to follow him before he could steal an advantage. Bill looked around his gathering of brothers and then asked Brady, 'What would you do?'

'About what?'

'Come on, Pops. I know you've been watching and listening to us all night.'

'So, it's noisy in here. I can't hear everything, not over the noise of Amie, Helgarth and Debrock's crowd of hangers-on. What's the problem?'

'If the Greens who haven't bought our products before are waiting for the UltraViolet™ upgrade, then why would they risk missing out on the upgrade to start using our product now? I mean, I would get the UltraViolet™ first and then think about the upsides of our product offering.'

Brady looked at his sons, 'What's the deal with this UltraViolet™?'

'We don't know. Nobody does. Well. The Disciples and the Devout know, but they aren't telling.'

'There's your way in.' Brady looked at his bemused sons' faces. He was disappointed at their lack of perception of the art of deception. 'If they won't say, then you can make up anything you want. They can't deny it, or that could give their game away.' He watched them think out the opportunities, but he could see they were struggling.

He knew they could only think of the exciting possibilities of the UltraViolet™. 'Make it not worth waiting for. The UltraViolet™ is a boring upgrade...' He thought on it for a second, 'Remember the InfraRed™, it was nothing more than a primer, it didn't do anything interesting, it was an undercoat. Well, make the UltraViolet™ as boring as that. To get around the Security Protocols™, just suggest that it is nothing more than a gloss finish, a topcoat, nothing special...of ceremonial use only.'

Bill smiled, 'That could work...it really could, thanks, Pops.'

Brady said, 'I know you boys are mad at me right now, but at my pretend-birthday party tomorrow, I've got something to share that I know you'll like. Now, get back to your competition and may the best man win.' He grinned mischievously and watched them re-join the party. He was proud of his boys.

The following day he watched his sons pack as they were treating his competition with the utmost urgency. He walked down to the Mahone Fleet Parking Lot in his extensive Malibu grounds and saw his boys loading up, ready for departure at the earliest possible point. He wondered if he should have let those with the longest distances to travel have a head start if seemingly, every minute counted, but he wasn't going to change the rules now. He smiled as he considered that he would have his Malibu home back to himself for the next few months. As his USA leader, he had told Bill that he would have to live elsewhere for the duration in case the others thought he would use his Pop's counsel for an unfair advantage.

He took a birthday walk down to the bottom of the Malibu cliff, where his home was perched upon. It was a glorious Californian day, with azure skies, wispy clouds and the bright yellow sun casting its sparkling rays across the Pacific. It was breezy and cold, but this refreshed him. He walked along the shoreline for a couple of peaceful hours before returning to the home.

Hunter had some lunch prepared for him. Hunter said, 'I wanted to book a holiday for the end of June, sir.'

'I'm guessing you are one of these Devout Greens, and you want the time off to get your UltraVioletSuit™.'

'Yes, sir.'

'Tell me something. You were a wannabee Hollywood actor before you worked for Libby Skye. How come you've never shown an interest in my entertainment products. I woulda thought they would have been right up your street.'

'I saw, very early on, that John Kane and his son, Xavier, were sticklers for rules. I would never break them lightly. I suppose that's what they could see in me when I joined their employ.'

Brady said, 'I suppose so. How old are you, now?'

'I confess, I lose track.' Brady watched Hunter working it out in his mind. Hunter said, 'Two-hundred and twelve, sir.'

'Two hundred and twelve going-on ninety. Amazing. Don't you worry about dying in service? Do you ever wonder if you've wasted your life?'

'No, sir. Not on either point.'

Brady ate up his lunch and went over to the main lounge to check how Amie and Helgarth were getting on with their preparations for his maybe, one hundred and forty-second birthday party. The dining table was already laid out, hours before the actual evening dinner. Helgarth had rounded up some of Debrock's friends to assist - well, those that weren't already stoned out of their minds. They were fixing up banners, and giant numbers had been found in Libby Skye's stores of unrecyclable plastic partyware from a long-gone age. One thing about taking over the house and contents of a rich Hollywood actresses' home was, if you needed something, you could probably find it somewhere in this sprawling palace.

The giant gold numbers of one, four and two were being pinned up and checked for the straightness of their positioning, while

Helgarth was issuing instructions of...*down a bit...an inch lower on the left-hand side...*

Brady went to see Amie. He had noticed her frustration in recent weeks that she and Helgarth had to maintain their female appearance while he was there. 'I'm going on a bit of a road trip for the next few weeks, maybe longer. I don't plan on going too far because if I turned up on another continent, the boys would think I'm influencing the competition...'

Amie had already zoned out, as she couldn't wait to inform Helgarth so that they could both relax into being who they wanted to be. She nodded along, distractedly.

Brady continued, '...I might even stay at the Mahone Ranch in McFarland for a while. I'm feeling a bit nostalgic for the old days. Anyway, I want to ask you a favour.'

Amie returned from her daydream. 'Yes, anything. What can I do for you, Brady?'

'I'm going to do a little speech tonight, but it's got some numbers and math stuff in it, and you know I'm not good with that kinda thing.'

'Ok.'

'I know you are good with that. I don't just want you to help me write it. I'd like you to speak out the bit with the numbers. Could you do that?'

'I'd be happy to. I could hardly refuse you, it being your birthday and all. I'll go and fetch a pen and some paper, and we'll work on it together.'

At the evening celebrations, he noticed his sons were quieter than usual. *The private FusionPassengerJet™ incentive has really got my boys focused.* He thought. Brady was hardly the life and soul of his party, as he now wished he hadn't planned a speech. *Brady Mahone ain't afraid of anything...except speaking in public, it seems...gotta get a grip here.* Fortunately, the rest of his stoned attendees were making a lot of noise to make up for the ordinarily loud guest of honour and his usually raucous sons - their infectious giggling providing a surreal backdrop to the birthday party celebrations.

He knew the Christmas, New Year, and Brady's birthday celebrations usually disrupted the routine of the resident Greens at the Malibu home. The IndigoSuits™ meant that non-Disciples were advised to sleep from 11pm to 2am. While the Disciples slept from 2am to 5am. Brady chuckled to himself. *The kids are going to be up way past their bedtime.* He shuffled in his chair and played with his food as he thought about his speech. Unlike the competition, he wanted this to land in a positive way. He wanted his boys to understand the need to protect himself and the company. He looked over his notes, and he spotted Amie doing the same. *She looks as nervous as I feel. At least we won't need microphones now that they've got super-hearing and super-everything-else for that matter.*

Amie left her seat and went over to Brady. She whispered, 'Are you ready?'

'I think so.'

'You've got nothing to worry about. You are thinking like a Trad, whereas we are Green.' She kissed him on the cheek, and he noticed the curious looks on the diners who were spread across five large tables in the grand room. He took this as his cue to make a start. He tapped the glass containing the non-alcoholic fruit cocktail, which had been christened a Bradysnapp for the special occasion.

'Thank you for celebrating my one-hundred and forty-second birthday with me.'

The boys shouted, 'Happy birthday, Pops.'

Brady was glad of the interruption, he smiled, as he took these moments to compose himself, 'I'm a Trad. I've already lived well past my allocated Trad years, and yet, here I still am.' His audience laughed along, like any other family with an elderly relative giving a speech. 'I don't know how many years I have left, but I have to make contingency plans for, y'know, death and all.'

Bill shouted, 'You ain't gonna die, Pops - and anybody who says you are is gonna have me to deal with.' There was laughter as Brady nodded in Bill's direction and grinned.

'I know you boys weren't happy with my competition idea, but I want you to keep the Trad values alive. It troubles me that you follow the leaders so blindly. It's dangerous to behave too predictably...' *That's how they get ya, son.* His audience listened to him with the good grace to acknowledge that it was Brady's party, and he could preach if he wanted to. 'Anyway, I didn't want to die and risk that the Brady Mahone Entertainment Enterprises would be lost to Sattva Systems™, and more specifically left for Bodhi Sattva and Glenarvon Cole to do with as they wished.'

Troy said, 'What claim would they have on your company, Pops?'

'It's complicated. That's why I'm doing something about it now. Later in the year, I'm going to sit down with Bodhi and make a Last Will and Testament. Now, I know you might not know what that is, as you Greens don't pass on material possessions and assets after death, but I'm a Trad, and I'm going to leave my worldly goods to the family. They owe me that much.'

Raelynn was stoned and looked out of step with the other guests; as she was in a gender-neutral state but dressed in a high camp Gothic outfit, she stood up shakily, and Amie looked across at Helgarth as if priming her to intervene if necessary. She said, 'If we inherit this place...' She spun around dreamily with her arms open wide as if she was a flight attendant from the underworld. 'Then we wouldn't be allowed to live in this place all alone. We would have to fill the rooms with other Greens. This means all our friends could live here. That would be so cool.'

Lucy-Ian and Raelynn's friends let out stoned cheers and giggles. Debrock shouted, 'We love you, Raelynn.' Helgarth gestured for Raelynn to sit and be quiet. Raelynn flopped on her dining chair.

Brady wasn't going to be flustered or derailed, 'When I'm dead and gone, that will be the least of my worries.' He grinned at Raelynn and then at Helgarth to indicate that no harm was done. He continued, 'I've drawn up a proposal, which will come into effect from my next birthday. I want you to honour my wishes and not challenge the details.' He looked at each one of his sons intently and in turn - and then he looked at Amie, Helgarth, and their children, Lucy-Ian and Raelynn. 'Now, you know I'm not too hot with math, and so I'm going to hand over to Amie to give you the details.'

Brady sat down as Amie stood up next to him. Her shaky hands held her crib sheet. She said nervously and quietly. Brady could hear her as he was beside her. But he knew the rest of the room would be utilising their VioletSuits™ to listen to her. 'From January 1, 2085, Brady Mahone Entertainment Enterprises will be split as follows...' She took a moment to ensure she got her figures right. '...Brady will retain 51% of the company. His five sons, Bill, Rocky, Wilder, Troy and Hawk, will each be given an 8% stake, and Lucy-Ian and Raelynn will receive a stake of 4.5%.' She waited for them to grasp the implications of Brady's decision. She continued, 'Brady's has 2.1 billion Green Credits, which means each son's stake is a gift to the value of 168 million Green Credits and Raelynn and Lucy-Ian's share is be valued at 94.5 million Green Credits.' She looked over at Helgarth, who already knew the contents of her speech.

Brady said, 'This takes place at the turn of next year. I also want Amie to tell you what will happen with my 51% should anything happens to me.'

Amy said, 'In the event of Brady's death, the boys share would rise to 16% each, and Raelynn and Lucy-Ian's would rise to 10%.'

Brady said, 'As for the Malibu home and all the contents and vehicles, I am giving these to Amie and Helgarth. I want this to be their home, to do with as they see fit.' He looked over at Raelynn and then at Helgarth and Amie, as he hadn't told them of this plan.

'Thanks, Pops. Will Bodhi allow this?' Bill said.

'He made an exception for his Mother in leaving Libby Skye this place after the Revolution. I don't think he would risk being called out as a hypocrite if he refused me the same courtesy. I know you see him as some kinda God or guru, but he is just a businessman in my eyes. He will make the deal. I know he doesn't want me as an enemy. I can tell by the lengths he goes to keep me as a friend.'

Helgarth came over to Brady and kissed him on the cheek and held both his hands. 'Thank you for the gift of this home and thank you for your generosity to our children.'

3: BOULDER CREEK
RENDEZVOUS

B rady had a sort out in his Pop's old bunker. The tinned food was over a century old and taking up a lot of space on the racks, and he had come to the decision that if the world came to such a state that he would have to rely on this, then he'd rather not bother. He'd called over a couple of Greens from McFarland to give him a hand on emptying the bunker of surplus tins and other perishables from the Trad days. It felt good for his body to be doing some hard physical labour and good for his mind to be organising the space. He dwelled on the fact that even he called the town simply McFarland again, now that there was no trace at all left that they'd ever been an East McFarland.

He kept Archie's old tech. It gave the place a feeling of a private museum to Brady - not that Brady ever visited museums even when such sites were found in nearly every town. He scrubbed, cleaned, and swept the whole bunker, and he had left the doors wide open to encourage the fresh Californian air to come and visit the old place - it seemed to be afraid of being trapped down here forever. He took time out to watch the billowing dust roll up the steps as if it had the power to defy gravity. He thought the thousands of dust particles glinting against the sunlight up the concrete steps looked *real pretty*.

As he sat on the bottom step with his Thermos of coffee - he didn't want the temptation of the homestead luring him to stay and stop working - he looked around at Archie's newspaper cuttings on the wall, and he desperately wanted to tell him everything that had happened. *Pops would have been amazed and would have wallowed in the horror of it all. He would have abhorred the domination of the Liberal-Lefties.* Brady spied a cutting of a UFO and laughed. *Pops would rather have had the alien overlords than this lot.*

Brady screwed his plastic cup back on his old Thermos flask and muttered, 'This ain't gonna buy the baby a new bonnet.' He had prepared the racking to store documents and evidence. He looked at the assorted pile of dozens of boxes of different shapes and sizes. Some of these were his own stash, but most were the ones he'd retrieved from East McFarland after Judge Audre Jefferson had died but before the final throes of the Operation Clean-Up of East McFarland. He took rolls of industrial shrink-wrap and covered the boxes thoroughly but left Judge Jefferson's neat filing labels showing through. He picked them up one-by-one and placed them on the racks. As he went, he kept re-sorting them if he spotted a sequence of numbers and dates. He found the whole experience therapeutic, even if he had no apparent use for these any longer. He seemed to find the same thrill as a child involved in the burial of a time capsule.

After his work was done, he inspected his Los Banos Police Department filing system, and grinned broadly. He traced his fingers across the plastic wrapping. *They were right - this stuff will last for a thousand years - that's a good thing, isn't it?*

Brady left the bunker, and for a minute, he considered sealing it up and camouflaging the entrance, but he couldn't see the point. *The Greens have known about Pops' bunker all this time and the stuff we kept down there. If they'd have wanted to do anything about it, they woulda done it by now. Maybe it's a stealing deal which the Security Protocols™ would get involved in.*

Over his well-earned lunch, Brady perused his ad-hoc Last Will and Testament, which Amie had drawn up for him. He also checked over the divestment of his business interests to his family. *Amie has done a fine job of these. I don't want to get bamboozled by all those numbers and percentages - not in front of Bodhi and his cronies.* He laughed. *Hell, the older I get, the more I'm starting to sound like my old man.*

Brady got a taste for tidying and cleaning, and for the next few weeks, he cleared out every room of unloved junk, not only in the Mahone Ranch but also the Lopez Ranch. He only kept the items that brought back strong emotional memories, everything else he dealt with ruthlessly. It helped him think; each tidied room seemed to lead to a tidied section of his mind. He imagined his sons flying to all parts of the world, pushing and consulting with their reps - his reps - and strategizing on how they could win the FusionPassengerJet™. *Wilder is the numbers guy, but my money would be on Troy winning - he really understands the Asian market. I'll have to think of a good idea for the presentation ceremony.* Finally, he reached a point where every room in both ranches was cleaned and tidied.

He considered taking a FusionCar™ up to Boulder Creek for a moment, but the roads were always full of Green Tourists. *Shame, I woulda liked that. I miss those times when the roads were always empty, and nobody but me could afford something like my old Hearse. It seems like everyone owns a piece of the Brady Highway these days.* He boarded his FusionPlane™ with its cream-coloured livery and its moss-green Sattva Systems™ logo and flew to Boulder Creek. Brady was probably the only person on the planet who didn't ever need to make an appointment to see Bodhi Sattva.

When he arrived, he had his usual chat with Marjorie - Fleet Captain Marjorie Hampton - about HeavyLoaders™ and LeviathanLifters™ and since the 2150s, the Cassandra rocket launches to Mars. He never tired of attending the frequent lift-offs from the Cape Cassandra FusionPads™ in Florida. Marjorie said,

'This is the last year for the rocket launches, Brady. I know you'll miss them.'

'Yeah, I know. My buddy Tyrone would love to be a part of that. He's had his head in the clouds from the first moment I met him.'

'There's still a chance - but he has to enrol in the last call for volunteers by May at the latest. They will have the UltraViolet™ before anybody else, seeing as they will be moving to another planet.'

'What is this UltraViolet™?'

'I'm not at liberty to say, other than that it will be incredibly beneficial for them in their hostile new environment.'

'Fair enough. Anyway, there is no way on Earth that Samuel would let him go.'

'Is that a pun there, Brady?' She nudged him playfully, and Brady laughed when he realised what he had just said. She added - because she didn't want to appear to exclude Brady from the HQ's plans, 'Most of the equipment is on Mars and assembled. The FusionSpaceShuttles™ are returning the astronauts over the coming months for them to get the new and final NanoSuits™ - by mid-June, the last ever transports will leave Earth, and they will never be allowed to return.'

Brady said, 'Not even if they get ill?'

'No. It's the Green Deal with Tia Cassandra. The rocket launches and the Earth's resources have been allowed to be plundered within Bodhi and Glen's one-hundred-year plan; beyond that, it is all about preserving Mother Earth. There are no more compromises to be made.'

Brady was worried for a moment. 'What about any deals I have made or will make with Bodhi?'

'You will always be an exceptional case. He will always honour his deals with you. In fairness, he has with Tia Cassandra. She accepted the deal with her eyes open, Tia has not been fooled.' She added, 'Anyway, Tia will make it work - she drove a hard bargain.'

She thought about Brady's question a little deeper and then offered him her best advice. 'Everything will be different from 1st January 2185, more than you can ever imagine. They are even changing the units of time for the next phase of Green Science Discovery. With that in mind, I would make sure you have your personal dealings laid down before then. It's getting hectic around here as we are closing in on the end-of-year deadline.'

Brady felt like he was back in his old criminal underworld dealings, 'He can't claim he was busy, and he forgot...'

'No, he wouldn't do that. His word and his integrity are beyond reproach. I'm just saying if you've got business to be concluded with Bodhi, Glenarvon and Sissy - then do it, soon.' Marjorie walked and talked with her old friend, Brady, as she went with him to the main entrance. Sissy and a man - to Brady's eyes in a gender-neutral Green world - met them both. Marjorie said, 'I'll leave you with Sissy and Century. I know you haven't met before, but Century has the same middle name as you.' Marjorie smiled and headed back to her work.

Brady shook Century's hand. 'Really, how come?'

Sissy said, 'Long story, maybe later. Anyway, Century Brady Garcia wanted to meet his namesake, and seeing as I spoil my children...'

'Mops, I'm eighty-four...'

Brady said, 'Eighty-four going-on twenty-five - I'm Brady, Brady Mahone, pleased to meetcha.'

Century shook his hand with a firm grip, 'Likewise, and an honour.' He added before Sissy could interrupt, 'Love your products, man. They are so cool.'

'Now, Century, I believe you have work to attend to.' Sissy said.

Century turned on his heels and strode away. Brady said, 'I want to see Bodhi. I might need you around because you handle the administration stuff, y'know paperwork - I know it's not his strong point...'

Sissy laughed, 'Paperwork, such a quaint term.' She added, 'Not many people criticise Bodhi's talents or lack of them, but when you're right - you're right.' She walked with Brady to Bodhi's drab office.

Bodhi was in a quiet discussion with Glenarvon Cole. They looked up at Brady, and the office fell silent for a brief moment as they all faced each other. Brady thought he had wandered into a delicate moment of negotiations between Bodhi and Glenarvon, but Brady wasn't interested in the future planning of the Greens. He gestured to indicate the office space, with its Sattva cream-coloured walls and joked by way of breaking the ice, 'I think I woulda got myself something a little swankier by now.'

Glen smiled and reached out a hand. Brady gripped it firmly. Glen said, 'Good to see you, man. How have you been keeping?'

'Is all good, man. I'm glad you're here as well, as I need to discuss some private business, y'know, put my affairs in order.'

'Pull up a chair.'

Brady grabbed a chair from the stack against the wall and put it down for Sissy, almost as a statement of his out-of-date Trad values. He then pulled one over for himself. He pulled out his paper notes written in Amie's neat handwriting.

Bodhi smiled a warm smile, 'We are at your disposal, my friend. What is it you wish to discuss?'

'You are all Green, and you don't seem to worry about dying anytime soon. However, I am a Trad, and I gotta go sometime. I'm already well past my sell-by date.' He laughed at his own joke. 'Anyways, even I can work out that you, Bodhi, are one-hundred and eighty-four years old, Glen is in his hundred and sixties, and as for Sissy...' Again, Brady teased, 'But you must never ask a lady her age...' Brady laughed while Sissy, Bodhi and Glen humoured him. Brady continued, 'Bearing in mind I'm very old for a Trad, I am making some changes to the structure of Brady Mahone Entertainment

Enterprises before you start your roll-out of UltraViolet™, so, I'm thinking of May this year.'

Sissy said, puzzled, 'Ok.'

'I've made a Last Will and Testament that I want to come into force from 1ˢᵗ January 2185.'

She said, 'Why not straightaway?'

'Because I don't want any small print clauses to surprise me with the end of your one-hundred-year plan. It's spooking me, maybe it's my criminal background, but I want your word that my wishes will be taken into account after that date.' He watched Bodhi and Glen glance at each other. He handed his papers to Bodhi. Glen, and Sissy leaned in to read them alongside him.

Bodhi said, 'You are the only person left on the planet who is allowed to pass on property to another after death. You are the exception - as you are the only Trad left alive. You are a non-Green. I will give you my word that your property will remain in your family's hands from 2185 and in perpetuity.'

'Is that the same as forever?'

'Yes.'

Brady was troubled with the mention of the word *family*. His puzzled head tipped to his right, and he grimaced. Glen said, 'What troubles you, friend? Something's off, I can tell.'

Brady stood up and paced the room before he returned to his seat. He looked from Glen to Bodhi and back again. 'By family, you mean the people named in these documents. It doesn't mean anybody who isn't named who comes out of the woodwork to make a claim on my company - does it?' He suddenly felt as if he was in the biggest poker game of his life, as he studied every minor twitch in their expressions, but they revealed little. Bodhi and Glen looked at Brady as if this subject meant a lot to him, but they had more urgent business to attend to. Bodhi and Glen gave each other a bewildered glance, and then they both looked to Sissy for a hint of revelation.

Sissy said, 'A Green can't become pregnant with you without an arrangement in place. There aren't any little Brady Mahones scampering around the planet waiting to stake a claim on your wealth.' She laughed, and then Bodhi and Glen laughed along with her as if she had reached the heart of Brady's dilemma. He still peered closely into their facial features, looking for signs of deception, but he couldn't detect any. The only thing he picked up on was Bodhi's grip on his Will.

Bodhi said, 'If Sissy doesn't mind, she could travel down to my Mother's old home in Malibu and carry out the group Distor™ Distribution for you.'

Sissy said, 'My pleasure.'

At first, he thought there was a clue in Bodhi choosing to refer to the Malibu home as *his mother's* old home. It sounded like the sort of thing an enemy would say to Brady's ears, but with the emphasis on *my* Mother and not even the hint of the more accurate *our* Mother. Brady concluded that even if Bodhi had given this thought at some point in his long life, then he had long since discarded it as a possibility. Glen showed no signs at all, of knowing. *All I am to them is a Trad curiosity. If the Greens had museums, then they would probably stuff me and display me as an exhibit when I'm gone. King Brady, the last Trad that walked the Earth - only ten Greenbacks for a look-see.*

4: SCIENCE FICTION MOVIES

The Greens seemed to retain their adolescence and young adulthood throughout their entire lives if they were young enough at the Green Revolution or born since that time. Tyrone was no exception. He greeted Brady's arrival at his home in San Martin like Brady was a conquering hero. 'Hey, Brady. I'm so glad you could make it.'

'Wouldn't miss it for the world, kid. It looks like you got me slumming it, again.'

'You know, Uncle Sam. Ever since that Space Station incident and the trouble you ran into, he won't let you take me anywhere. That's why we are flying with Sattva Systems™ - still, the PassengerFusionJets™ are all the same...'

'Except that, I have to sit next to a load of spaced-out Greens.' He laughed. He teased Tyrone, 'Why do you still wear those glasses? One, you can use the Yellow™ to imitate them, and two, I thought you are all supposed to have enhanced sight, now that you've had the VioletSuits™ and all.'

Tyrone slipped into a character he had seen on one of the old movies, 'Hey, it's my thing, my brand, and they are tortoiseshell...'

'Whatever.' Brady reached into his pocket and pulled out a dozen entertainment files. 'I'm out of selling action at the moment, I've got my boys in a competition with each other, and I can't take sides - but here is that series from the 2060s you asked me to keep an eye out for. They are unofficial recordings as the series was streamed at the time, but the quality's ok.'

Tyrone grabbed them off him, 'Wow!' He flicked through them all, examining the tiny writing under the BMEE logos with the Diamondback rattlesnake weaving through the letters. '25th Century Ezekiel Rovers - this is now a cult classic for all of us space geeks. Thanks, Brady.'

Brady mocked, 'Anything to keep a brother happy.'

'I cannot wait to watch these when I come back.' He looked at his watch. 'We better get going; otherwise, we'll miss the FusionCoach™ to the FusionPort™.'

'I guess this will be the last FusionSpaceShuttle™ launch you'll get to see.'

Tyrone sighed, 'Yeah, this is the only holiday I can get, which coincides with a launch day. It's a shame because there are only three more left after this, and then that will be it, forever. It seems such a shame to me.'

'So, you didn't manage to get the Bear to change his mind and let you volunteer to be an astronaut then?'

'You know what he's like. He pulled in a favour from Bodhi and blocked me. Uncle Sam's a nobody - just a sprayer, and yet he seems to have a hold over the Big Man.'

Brady said, 'The History of the Beardons and the Kanes go back a long way. That's loyalty for you.'

When they reached the FusionPort™, Brady expected to be annoyed by the hustle and bustle of the other Green passengers, especially as they all adopted weird space or Martian alien appearances, but he had to admit he immensely enjoyed being just another tourist. If anybody recognised Brady Mahone in the flesh, they put it down to a Green adopting an appearance of Brady Mahone, as he was the Trad who brought Science Fiction Movies and TV series back to the Green space freaks. Towards the rear of the FusionPassengerJet™, he spotted a carbon copy of himself. *This is fucked up but kinda funny.*

He sat next to Tyrone, and for the next few hours, he let Tyrone babble away about today's launch and what a hostile planet Mars was compared to Earth. Brady didn't mind, some of this seeped into his brain, but mostly, he just liked being in the company of an old and cheerful friend. Brady let the hours drift by, he looked out of the window to watch the banks of white clouds below him, and as the FusionPassengerJet's™ only sound was the sub-sonic hum of its engine, then he could close his eyes at times and listen into the conversations around him. In the old days, he would have hated these geeks dressing up and going to their conventions, but now, the very reminder of those old Trad days was intoxicating. His fellow passengers were giving their critiques of all the Science Fiction shows and movies they had ever seen and pulled them to pieces if they missed out on out crucial scientific details or made the crime of not predicting the future from the long-distance run-around of the past. He smiled as what they were actually doing was disseminating the cultural impact of Brady Mahone and his exclusive Entertainment Enterprises. *I made this happen, me, Brady Mahone. If it wasn't for me, they would have died of boredom in this dull Green world. If there was a God in Heaven, then he must be real proud of Brady Mahone. I have brought happiness and entertainment to the people.*

After the FusionPassengerJet™ had vertically landed, they boarded the FusionCoach™ to take the hour-long drive to Cape Cassandra. There seemed to be a competition to see who could catch the first glimpse of the FusionSpaceShuttle™ ready to leave this Earth from its FusionPad™ on its last logistical trip to send machinery to Mars. The return trip would bring Mars' construction workers back to receive the UltraViolet™. Tyrone scoffed at the crawling progress of the old space missions of the past, and how the months had turned to days with Sattva Systems'™ development of zero-gravity FusionBoosters™.

The FusionCoach™ pulled up within a few hundred yards from the launch pad. Brady said, 'I'm a Trad, and the heat of the blast could kill me. I'm heading back about half a mile.' He looked up at the giant tipped up spacecraft, and it still staggered him how it was about four times bigger than the vine-wrapped rocket at Cape Canaveral. He recalled Glenarvon Cole scampering up to the top of that rocket like a kid playing hooky from school. He smiled at the recollection. He cocked his head and wondered how they secured the equipment, as they were tipped up at the moment, and presumably, they would level up later. He shrugged. *They probably got some Nanostraps or Nano-Blu-Tack knowing those Green fuckers.*

Tyrone said, 'I'll go with you. I keep forgetting, you always seem like a Green to me.'

Brady laughed and put a big hand on Tyrone's skinny shoulder. 'Wash that mouth out, boy.' Tyrone laughed as well, but Brady added, 'You stay up front with your buddies. It must be one helluva rush up there.'

Tyrone didn't protest, 'The heat and the sub-sonic boom is stupendous...thanks, Brady.'

'No problem, kid. I still get a heavy dose of it from my vantage point. Now shoo, I don't want you to miss it.' Brady watched Tyrone rush to join his friends. They were all old in Trad terms, but for these Greens, it seemed they remained like children for the whole of their lives. He headed back to a nearby hill. He had attended many of these launches over the last few decades, but usually, he travelled alone, in his own FusionPlane™ and rarely had the opportunity came along to travel with Tyrone, either because of lining up Tyrone's vacations or the objections from Samuel Beardon the Third. *It seems that these Forever Children have Forever Parents and Forever Family.* Brady thought of his own family and how they were all frozen in their shells, which made them appear and act like they were in their early twenties. *It seems I'm going to be their Forever Daddy.* He liked that idea.

He had an hour to wait for the launch, and he studied the panoramic views of virtual nothingness all around him. It was almost a desert. He figured it was chosen because of the damage a sub-sonic boom could do to any buildings within miles of here. He thought of the natural habitat and what the sub-sonic booms could do to the creatures that lived here. He knew this was why Bodhi and Glen would have been so coy about surrendering to Tia Cassandra's demands. He also knew that this is why they had put a time limit on the Space Program. He agreed with them. As much as Brady loved the big machines, he loved the animals more.

Brady heard the distant cheers of Tyrone and his buddies drift in the air, and he guessed that the launch sequence had begun. He hoped the ascent would go without a hitch, but when the rescue of Tia Cassandra's people in Cima had brought death and destruction to so many Greens that day, all these events now had a sense of jeopardy that wasn't there before when he used to believe that the RedSuits™ made them indestructible. They were difficult to kill, but not impossible. This knowledge added frisson to the excitement of this day.

He lay down as he knew the shock wave would knock him off his feet from bitter experience. Under his prostrate body and with his head peeking over the hill, he felt the first tremors under him, which indicated that the FusionCells™ had been activated. The vibrations in the ground made his skin tingle all over. He then experienced the massive waves of the opening sub-sonic pulses, force pressure waves over his head. He watched the crowd leap up and down, and some were sent flying backwards by the sub-sonic boom - this was a game they played like teenagers on a theme park ride. The sub-sonic boom zoomed the hill and lifted Brady up a couple of feet above the ground before dumping him unceremoniously back down. He was winded but exhilarated by this immense power. He then watched the FusionSpaceShuttle™ leave the ground slowly and then, with each new sub-sonic pulse, climb ever faster into the skies. It shone like the Sun as it soared out of the atmosphere and into the heavens and onto Mars.

He laughed loudly to himself as he watched the bodies of the sprawled Green geeks pick themselves up from wherever the sonic booms had dumped them. They were pointing and laughing at each other. It brought back powerful memories of being a hyper-active and thrill-seeking teenager. He loved Tyrone. Some of the best days he had ever had, had been with this skinny nephew of Samuel Beardon the Third, aka the Bear - his oldest and dearest friend since Lucian had departed this world. He noticed that the Greens were returning to the FusionCoach™, but Tyrone hadn't joined them. Brady strolled over to Tyrone, and he was looking around in the dirt.

Brady said, 'What's the matter, kid?'

'I've lost my glasses.' He looked up, and Brady noticed they were gone. Tyrone added, 'Man, that was one helluva blast - the best ever.'

'Sure was. It all went without a hitch as far as I could tell.' He looked at Tyrone, 'Can't you just make up some glasses, y'know, with the Yellow™ and all?'

'They are my lucky glasses. It's a superstitious thing.'

'You and all your science talk, and now you've got superstitions.'

Tyrone shrugged, 'I know, it's stupid, but...'

Brady remembered how superstitious his fellow criminals were. His buddy got shot to death on the last jewellery heist he committed - the one that got him sent to Ridgecrest. He had lost his lucky chain that very day, and the stories in Ridgecrest often revolved around being caught because of a superstitious error of judgment. 'No problem. I'll be your extra pair of eyes.' They both scrambled around in the dirt, but it was difficult because the sub-sonic booms had rearranged the ground.

Minutes passed by until the FusionCoach™ driver had told them they had to leave or else they would miss the connecting flight. Brady asked for help but couldn't convince him to look for a pair of Trad spectacles without them even having lenses in, as Tyrone hadn't needed the lenses since receiving the Violet™. The driver gave them the ultimatum of two more minutes, and after that, he would be gone. Brady expanded the search and frantically rubbed away the ground, and then he saw a glint of brown from a few yards away. He pushed away from the mound of dirt, and the frame emerged. 'I got it. I found them.'

Tyrone shouted, 'Yay! Brady, you rock. Thank you so much.'

The driver yelled, 'It's now or never, boys.'

They both raced to the FusionCoach™. Some of the passengers cheered ironically, while others gave them dirty looks. Brady glared back at them, and Tyrone barely noticed as he was cleaning the dust and dirt from his lucky glasses.

5: CRIMES AND MISDEMEANOURS

It was night-time in San Martin when Tyrone and Brady arrived at the Beardon home. Most of the occupants had already gone to bed as they had Green work in the morning - even the now ancient old woman Shako. The Bear heard his nephew and Brady arrive and made his way downstairs to greet them. 'I trust you had a good time.'

'It was the best, Uncle Sam. I hope you didn't mind me bringing Brady home. It's been a long day, and I thought he could camp down here for the night.'

The Bear slapped Brady on the back, 'Of course. How are you keeping, brother?'

Brady smiled, 'I'm good. I've been organising things for the future, and I gave the ranches a real good sorting out.'

'That all sounds positive. It reminds me of something my Grandfather, the mighty fine Samuel Beardon, used to say. I tidied my room today - it made me think - should I tidy my mind today - Mmm, I'll think about it.' The Bear laughed as he watched Brady figure it out.

'Very funny. Do you people ever talk straight, or is it all riddles with you guys?'

The Bear moved next to Tyrone and put a big protective arm around him. He said to them both, 'I'll fix you up some supper. Would you like a fruit juice or a coffee to go with it?'

Tyrone interrupted, 'I'll do it, Uncle Sam.'

32

'Now, now, boy. It's the Division of Labour, and you are on vacation. You are not allowed to work this week - now sit down, and I'll bring it over.'

Tyrone sat down, and Brady noticed that he appeared tired. Brady said, 'You lot go to sleep between 11pm, and 2am with your Suits™, so you get your beauty sleep if you want?'

Tyrone yawned, 'Is a good idea. Thanks, Brady.' He headed to the stairs and then to bed.

The Bear said, 'My sleep shift isn't until 2am.'

Brady said, 'This Division of Labour malarkey doesn't apply to me, so let me give you a hand, old friend.' He followed the Bear into the kitchen. Brady made the coffee and chopped up a few vegetables. The Bear seemed hungry as he insisted on making a fruit cocktail for a late-night feast.

They sat down to eat, and they caught up on recent events and old times. Brady asked, 'How come you sleep at different times to everyone else - you're not a Disciple - even though you should be, in my opinion, you are ten times the man that Siddha is.'

'I'm classed as Devout. I'm not hungry for another man's respect and titles. The knowledge that the Lord loves me is all the affirmation I need.' The Bear changed the subject. 'What are your plans, brother?'

'I don't know, I think it's what they call a transitional phase. My business kinda runs itself, which is why I'm gradually handing it over to my boys to run. My mind is planning for the end, y'know, I ain't gonna live forever, but my body is still in real good shape, and I don't think I'm losing my mind unless you're hinting with that tidying my mind story, I never can tell with your twisty fables. Remember that shark story of yours when we first met?'

'That was just taking your theme and running with it, just a little scary old tale, is all.'

Brady laughed, 'You can't half tell 'em - it freaked me out for years.'

The Bear gave Brady's comment a lot of thought. He wanted to make his old friend feel better, 'I think I may have tapped into something inside you. In your old life, your worst fear was probably being locked up forever.'

I don't have no fears, and once behind bars, it just became another home from home for me, albeit the accommodation was lousier. 'Yeah, that's probably it.'

A Satt™ rang out. Brady headed to his coat pocket, not expecting it to be his, as he hardly ever switched it on. In his criminal Trad days pre-Revolution, he knew the Feds loved mobiles for tracking the movements of people like him, and the habit had remained for a Century since. *Maybe I'm as paranoid as Pops after all.* The Bear struggled to locate the ringing Satt™ as well until he found it buried in a drawer with old materials which were waiting to be recycled one day - for these useless bits and bobs that day may never come. The Bear answered clumsily as he was out of practice at using this ancient FusionPowered™ tech. 'Hi, who is this...Oh...yes, he is...' He looked across at Brady, 'It's Sissy, she says she's up to her eyes in work, but she could do your business redistribution ceremony tomorrow...' He held out the Satt™, 'Do you want to talk to her?'

'Yeah, go on then.'

Sissy asked, 'Is that you, Brady?'

'Yes. Tomorrow is too short notice. I'd have to contact my boys, and they are spread over the world. It's Tuesday today, is there any chance we could do it on Saturday?'

There was silence. Brady then heard a muffled conversation on the other end of the line, which he interpreted that she was checking or rearranging her schedule. 'It's my fault...I should have thought...yes...Saturday...evening. Would that work for you?'

'I can do that.' *I've bought me some thinking time. I still don't trust these fuckers.*

'This is a complex ceremony for us, as it's something we need to mock-up as a one-off...just for you. It would help if we had some senior Greens at the Distor™ Distribution Ceremony to act as conduits...it's the only way we can get it to work.'

'How come?'

'It's the power required to overcome a Trad such as yourself in the chain. You are a potential circuit-breaker. If you don't want to convert to Green which would make this a simple procedure...'

'No. It's ok, I get it. Who have you got in mind?'

'There would be myself, and Glen and Cain have volunteered...I thought Samuel would come along, as I know you trust him...'

Brady thought for a moment, and he looked at the Bear. Brady said, 'Hey, old buddy, I need your help.'

The Bear smiled warmly, 'How could I refuse a brother? What can I do for you?'

'I need you to come over to my home in Malibu for a distribution ceremony...maybe we could travel down together. I know my place is a bit fancy pants for your liking...'

'I'd love to. I've always been curious to see the Brady palace.' The Bear spoke the words, but Brady was doubtful that he meant them.

Brady said to Sissy, who was waiting patiently on her Satt™. 'Yeah, the Bear will be there. I'll see you Saturday evening.'

He hung up the Satt™ and hugged the Bear, 'Thanks, man - much appreciated. I've got some calls to make.'

The Bear went to do the washing-up while Brady called his sons. He knew they would pick up, as he knew his number would flash on the screen. He made so few calls in his life that he knew it would be deemed to be urgent.

After a while he glanced at his watch, he saw that it was 2am. He thought it strange that the Bear was already most likely fast-asleep in his bed while Tyrone emerged looking wide awake. Alicia was with him, and she made Tyrone his breakfast as he was still on vacation, and this was her Division of Labour obligation to him - a reward and a show of respect for his Green work he completed through the rest of the year.

Alicia said, 'Hi, Brady. Do you want some breakfast?'

Brady laughed, 'I've only just had supper.' He added, 'Hey Kids...' He said to the youngsters in their hundreds - but going on thirty. 'The Bear is coming over to my place in Malibu this weekend - do ya wanna come along?'

Alicia said, 'Normally, I'd love to, but I'm working.'

'Fair enough.'

Tyrone said, 'Absolutely. I can't wait.'

'Great. We'll head over on Thursday. We'll make a long weekend of it. I'm sure the Bear won't mind you riding along, seeing as he will be your chaperone and all. It's about time you saw the place, and it will give me a chance to return the hospitality.'

'It will be nice to see Amie and Helgarth again - it's been too long.'

6: THE YEARS BETWEEN US

The flight down to Malibu was a pleasant affair with Tyrone and the Bear treating it as if Brady was taking them on vacation. There was a lot of light-hearted ribbing of the Bear for behaving like a scaredy-cat as he grumbled about Brady flying his FusionPlane™ too fast. Brady ignored him as he swooped, banked, and pushed the FusionPlane™ to its limit. Tyrone loved it and kept talking of the top speeds of FusionRockets™. By the end of the flight, the Bear played up his role of the cautious back seat driver because it made Tyrone laugh.

Tyrone was still laughing loudly as he alighted the FusionPlane™ until he was stopped in his tracks by a vision that appeared before him. It wasn't the sight of Brady's mansion on the clifftops or the array of every kind of FusionVehicle™ in Brady's parking lot, and it wasn't even the sweeping vistas of the Pacific. It was the floating figure in the ethereal Gothic form of Raelynn. She drifted toward the new arrivals as if she was in a dream. For no apparent reason, she even twirled as if this was completely normal. She approached Brady and kissed him on the cheek. 'Hi, Brady.' She turned very slowly to take in Brady's guests, 'Hi, Brady's friends.' To Tyrone, it appeared that she even smiled in slow motion.

Brady said to Raelynn, 'These are probably the two best friends I have in the world.' The Bear smiled broadly. Brady continued, 'This is the Bear, as I call him, but his real name is Samuel Beardon the Third. I met him way back, not long after the Green's took over the world...'

Raelynn held out a soft hand, and the Bear shook it as if it might break if he held it too firmly. 'Any friend of Brady's is a friend of mine.'

Brady said, 'And this is Tyrone, his nephew, we've had some great times together...'

Raelynn kissed him on the cheek, and her face brushed his lens-less spectacles. 'You are real. I love Trad accessories. Maybe we could have some great times together.' She pulled slowly away from him, and her quiet laugh had a timeless quality to it.

If the attraction was evident to Tyrone and Raelynn, then for the moment, it bypassed Brady as he completed the formalities. 'Raelynn is Helgarth and Amie's kid.'

Tyrone said, 'Helgarth and Amie are your Moppas?'

Raelynn giggled, 'I prefer Maddies - don't you think that is so much funnier?'

'I do now.' Tyrone chuckled.

It was then that he noticed the spark between them, and he suggested, 'Raelynn?'

She took her eyes away from the lanky visitor from San Martin, 'Yes.'

'Perhaps you could give Tyrone the grand tour while I look after the Bear?'

'Love too.' She grabbed Tyrone's hand. 'Come with me.'

Brady and the Bear watched bewildered by the speed and the turn of events. Raelynn seemed to infect Tyrone with her Gothic slowness as they drifted off like ghosts toward the shoreline. He had expected her to give him a guided tour of the Brady Mahone residence, first. Brady said, 'That was weird. You don't think...'

'Yes, I do. I think your Raelynn has made quite an impression on Tyrone.'

'She's not my Raelynn, but yeah.' He strode off up to the clifftops to his Malibu home, and the Bear followed. Brady said, 'You don't think we should be concerned, do you?'

The Bear laughed, 'She sounds like she's *yours.*'

Brady laughed, 'No. No, I suppose I do kinda sound responsible for her. I love her like one of my own, but there must be an eighty-year age difference, even if it looks like about five, or maybe ten, on the surface.'

'You have a point, my friend, but nothing could happen that both sides weren't comfortable with. The Security Protocols™ would intervene at the first signs of exploitation, but you know that...'

'Yeah. I suppose it's the Trad side of me that thinks it ain't right.' He added, 'It's the taking of people at face value. If they look thirty, then they are thirty, even though my mind is always trying to work out how old everybody really is, even myself. I mean, I should be dead and long gone by now, and yet, here I still am.'

'Don't question the Lord's blessing, brother. If he gives, then it must be for His reason.'

Brady was careful not to brag about his home as he knew it wouldn't impress his friend. He described every room and facility as if he was taking his friend on a tour of John Kane and Libby Skye's old home, and he was given it as part of a deal with Xavier Kane, aka Bodhi Sattva. For his part, the Bear knew what Brady was doing and appreciated the effort of Brady to be humble, as he knew this wasn't Brady's usual style. The exception to Brady's rule was to show the Bear to the best Guest room in the place, and he ensured he had staff on hand to look after the Bear's every need.

Over the next few days, it became apparent to everyone that Raelynn and Tyrone had become inseparable. There had been no point in showing Tyrone to his guest room as Raelynn had insisted that he was sharing her room.

One by one, his sons returned from their far-off lands. Even Bill, as the North America Director, had to travel from Vancouver. And then, on Saturday evening, the delegation from the Sattva Systems™ HQ arrived, without fanfare.

Brady had gathered his family and his staff to greet them. The formality of the situation was unusual for Brady, but he believed the occasion and his intentions warranted it. He announced, 'I know you will know my guests, but maybe you've not had the opportunity to meet them.' He cleared his throat, 'This is Genesis Garcia - she used to be the Governor of California in the old days...I'm sorry, I don't know the name of your role for Sattva Systems™...'

Sissy smiled, 'I'm the Marketing Disciple and Chief Advisor to Bodhi Sattva. It's a pleasure to meet you.' She shook the hands of everybody.

Brady said, 'This is Cain. Since the first day after the Green Revolution, I've known him as he was the Disciple of my hometown of McFarland back then. Now he is the Regional Disciple of the Western Seaboard of the USA.' Cain seemed to entrance the gathering as he gazed at each one with his crystal green eyes. 'And this is Glenarvon Cole, the leader of the GreenRevs.'

Brady was shocked to see his sons break ranks and reach out hands for shaking and hugging him. Hawk shouted, 'You are a fucking hero, man.' Bill said, 'A true legend.' Glen looked at Brady apologetically.

Brady looked at his three guests from Boulder Creek and said, 'Hunter will show you to your rooms. It will give you time to freshen up, and we've got some food and drink as a buffet in an hour. It will give you a chance to meet my family and make any arrangements you need for the ceremony - if that's ok with you?'

'That's great.' Sissy said 'Thank you, Brady.'

Brady watched in bemusement as Hunter came over, and Sissy hugged him, 'My dear Hunter, it's been so long, how are you?' Cain and even Glen treated Hunter as a long-lost friend. *I really should have got to know Hunter better - the sly old fox.* Sissy hooked arms with Hunter as the group headed towards the stairs.

At the buffet, Brady was strangely quiet, while others mingled agreeably. Amie and Helgarth chatted with the Bear while smiling together at the sight of the two love birds Tyrone and Raelynn. Brady had taken the precaution of having Debrock and his stoner friends have their fun at the other end of the building. It seemed as if Helgarth and Amie had arranged that they didn't need to do Green work anymore. He guessed that their exceptional circumstances would be paid for out of their share of his business. He could have got angry about that, but he was reassured by a certain Trad-ness in their thinking - plenty of his old criminal buddies would have partied their proceeds of crime away.

He was more perturbed by the hero-worship his own sons were bestowing on Glenarvon Cole. *I dread to think what they'd be like if they realised that he was their biological uncle.* It gave him comfort that he was the only one who knew this secret, for now. It gave him a sense of leverage and power. When his boys did come over and chat with their Pops, one-by-one, they all had similar stories to tell. These included how they were going to win the competition for the FusionPassengerJet™ because they were miles ahead of their targets, and also, Brady's idea of rubbishing the potential benefits of the UltraVioletSuits™ was a stroke of marketing genius.

Sissy and Cain worked closely together as they pulled out various Distors™ and primed them for use. He also noticed them rehearsing their lines and consulting his notes. He put his hand to his pocket to seek the reassurance that he had his own Distor™ on him. He took it out and wondered if, after today, he would ever bring the figure back to the 2.1 billion Green credits he had now. He wondered what had possessed him to make him want to give nearly a half of all these away within an hour from now. *I'll still have more than a billion Green credits, and like they say, I can't take them with me when I'm gone.* He urged himself to remember that his primary reason for giving them away was to ensure that the Greens didn't take them or put them out of reach of his kin.

Glen came over and spoke to Brady. He seemed warm and trustworthy, but Brady thought of him as a warrior just as his sons did. 'This is a big day for you. You've achieved so much - you must be very proud.'

'Yeah, I suppose. It just seems the right thing to do. I'm getting older - even if I don't feel it, and I need to think about other's futures and not just my own.' Brady didn't want to talk about personal and family stuff with Glen. He viewed Glen as a man first, and not a Green, possibly influenced that Brady knew he was his cloned brother, or maybe that's the same as a real brother. 'Enough about me. What have you been up to lately?'

'I've overseen the project to select 24,642,756 Disciples and the Devout as part of my one-hundred-year part of the Green Deal.'

Glen watched Brady's puzzled frown with amusement. Brady said, 'That's a lot of people...and why that number?'

'I had help. It was like an old pyramid scheme, I recruit three, who each recruit three, which means I've now recruited twelve - three and nine.'

'That still doesn't explain that number.' *What have I got myself into now? This is going to be worse than Tyrone and his long numbers.*

Glen said, 'It's something which means more to Bodhi than me. Apparently, John Kane had a thing about the number three. He always liked to have a number divisible by three or nine in it somewhere whenever he conducted a scientific project. However, Bodhi wanted one Devout or Disciple for every square mile of hospitable land on Earth. This was so that all of Mother Earth could be monitored and looked after. The number 24,642,756 is the number of square miles, and it is a number divisible by nine and three.'

'You lot are fucking insane - you know that - don't you?' Brady looked to the heavens.

Glen roared with laughter and slapped Brady on the back. Brady could see that his sons were impressed by Glen's camaraderie with their Pops. He smiled at this show of respect. He then saw Sissy gesture to Glen to prepare. Glen got the boys to remove the table and chairs to the edges of the room to leave space for the participants to form a large circle.

Cain announced, 'We are ready for the Division of Brady Mahone's Entertainment Enterprises. Glenarvon Cole will show you to your positions.'

He went over to Brady first. 'Follow me, man.' He led Brady to the top of the circle. The huge window framed the sun setting over the ocean in a blaze of reds, oranges, and pinks. He placed Bill to his left and then skipped a place. He took a smiling Wilder next. Next, he approached Samuel Beardon the Third. Cain clasped hands with him and then encouraged him to take up the next slot. Then it was Hawk's turn, and then at the bottom of the circle, he smiled as he persuaded Raelynn to leave Tyrone's side and take her place. She floated dreamily onto her spot, and the skies fire seemed to light up her Goth features. Next to Raelynn, he placed Lucy-Ian, and the two goys giggled like schoolchildren sitting next to each other in class. Cain moved without prompting to stand next to Lucy-Ian as Glen led Troy into position. Like Cain, Sissy moved to her spot and then, as the circle was nearly complete, Rocky was placed at Brady's right-hand side.

Glen retrieved the slightly larger translucent moss green Distors™ and handed these to Samuel Beardon the Third, Cain, Sissy, and then retained the last one for himself. Glen made one final check - before moving into his position between Bill and Wilder.

As he passed Brady on the way anti-clockwise around the circle to his slot, Brady grabbed him by the arm. He hissed, 'Hey, tell me I'm not about to get screwed over here.'

Glen put a hand on Brady's shoulder, 'Everything is being done to respect your wishes - I promise.'

Sissy waited until Glenarvon Cole signalled that he was ready. She announced, 'Welcome to the ceremony to complete the Division of Brady Mahone's Entertainment Enterprises as per the wishes of Brady Mahone, and with the authority of Sattva Systems™ and the Word of Bodhi Sattva. Please hold out your Distors™.' They all held out their Distors™. 'Brady, if you set yours to freely give...' She then named his family going clockwise from Brady. 'And Rocky, Troy, Lucy-Ian, Raelynn, Hawk, Wilder and Bill, please set your Distors™ to freely receive.' They set themselves in a relaxed pose. 'Cain, could you please check the status of these Distors™ before we continue.'

Cain glided around the room in his white robe like a butterfly settling on each flower. When he returned to his position, he said, 'They are ready to give and receive.'

Sissy called Amie into the room, and she came in with Helgarth. 'Amie, could you confirm the distribution details as laid out in the documents and verify that these are the figures Brady Mahone gave you.'

'Yes, they are correct.'

Brady began to worry that Amie could double-cross him and change the amounts, but he reasoned that the Security Protocols™ could kick in, and then he realised that she wasn't in the circle and didn't have her own Distor™ in the game.

Sissy's Distor™ opened, and she tapped in instructions, and this took a few minutes. Then she said to Amie, 'Amie, please confirm that the figures and instructions set in the Master Distor™ are the same as the written notes you gave unto me.'

Amie said in the direction of Brady and then looked around the rest of the participants, 'The details are correct and fulfil the wishes and intentions of Brady Mahone.'

Brady wondered why they didn't check them with him, but numbers weren't his strong suit, and it was probably better to leave this to the experts. He equated this to letting his Defence Lawyers do the talking in the old days - not that that stopped him going to jail anyway.

Sissy said, 'Cain, Glen and Samuel Beardon the Third, please activate the DistorBoosters™ in your possession.' They all switched on their Distors™ and muttered, 'May the additional energy and information pass through me freely.'

She looked around the circle, 'We are nearly ready. I will be the last to complete the chain. I want you all to extend your hands and reach and hold onto the Distor™ next to you.' The circle complied. Brady was unexpectedly nervous, and he retreated into his mind to imagine drawing a seagull he could hear screeching outside. It was his go-to method to stay calm.

Then Sissy connected with Rocky to her right and Troy to her left and chanted, 'Let the Division of Brady Mahone's Entertainment Enterprises commence.' Brady noticed the room's walls turn Green, and then he spotted a Green glow around every person in the circle. He observed that the glow came from the Distors™. He looked down on himself, and he was reassured that he wasn't emanating Green, and he then spotted that Amie and Helgarth were not touched by the Green glow.

The process took about a minute, but it felt much longer than that to Brady. Then Sissy announced, 'The first part of the process is completed. Now, if I could ask Amie and Helgarth to join the circle, either side of Brady. The rest of you may have to spread out a little, and you can let go of your Distors™ for a moment.'

Amie moved into Brady's right while Helgarth moved to his left. Cain came over to check the status of their Distors™. He nodded his approval to Sissy. Brady looked at the other family members who were reviewing the newly replenished Green credits within their Distor™ displays, and they were delighted. The only exception was Raelynn, who didn't check at all. She looked as if she was on another planet, or maybe in another room, her room with Tyrone. Brady thought this made her look cool, and he admired her for that.

Sissy called for quiet and calm as the mutterings had increased as the realisation that they were independently wealthy sunk in. She said, 'Now we come onto the matter of the Last Will and Testament of Brady Mahone in the style pertaining to the Traditional Culture of said, Brady Mahone. Amie has already confirmed the details. However, I must point out to you all that it is Brady's wish that this comes into effect on the day after the Green's one-hundred-year plan has been completed, which at this moment means January 1st, 2085.' She joked, 'So, you better take good care of him until then.'

His sons laughed. Brady smiled. *Just like the old days when I made a deal with my fellow criminals, it's a half now, and half on completion kinda deal.*

Sissy said, 'Just as before - if you could reach out and hold the Distor™ of the person next to you...' She waited, and then when she was satisfied, she continued, 'Let the Last Will and Testament of Brady Mahone be enacted with the authority of Sattva Systems™ and the Word of Bodhi Sattva.' As before, everybody glowed Green, including Amie and Helgarth this time, but again Brady was unaffected. Again, it seemed to take a minute to complete, but it seemed a little quicker this time to Brady.

When it was over, they all released their Distors™, and the circle broke. Brady shouted, 'Let's party.' And as if this was a cue, Brady's servants and Debrock and his hangers-on came into the room. Non-binary and non-stereotype music, or Green Tunes as they were lamely called, blared out - the reintroduction of music had been considered safe, and a concession to the disgruntled young Green protestors which had sprung up in recent times. The Security Protocols™ monitored it for signs of binary, race, colonialism, imperialism, and most important of all, Trad influences. Of course, Trad music had been widely distributed courtesy of Brady Mahone Entertainment Enterprises, but he had the Green elite to consider at this party.

Debrock handed out his dabs to anyone who wanted them, oblivious to the upper echelons of Sattva Systems™ being present in the room.

Brady quietly checked his Distor™ which glowed green with the figure of 1,421,237,285 Green credits, it was still a telephone number to him, but he knew it was slightly more than he had expected. He guessed that Sissy had included his latest earnings in the figure - and he knew his boys had produced a record surge in orders. He was a little disappointed that this string of numbers didn't commence with a 2, but he also felt a sense of relief that the ceremonies were over and that he was a big enough man to give so much away to his family.

7: HUNTED

While his guests partied, Brady sought out Hunter. He found him in his own room with Sissy, Glen and Cain. Even though this was Brady's home, they still appeared shocked when Brady knocked at the door and strode in. Brady said, 'I want to talk with Hunter alone.' There were no idle pleasantries. 'You can continue your little catch-up later. This won't take long.'

Sissy placed a hand on Hunter's and said softly and just beyond Brady's range, one of the benefits of the Violet™ was the acuteness of his hearing. 'Have no fear. I have your back.' She looked at Brady, 'Of course. We shall join the others at your celebration. You have provided generously, and we are grateful.' Glen and Cain stood up to join Sissy, but as they left the room, Glen hung back, 'I'm going to listen in, and I'll report back later.'

Cain asked, 'What concerns you, friend?'

'I don't want any surprises now that we are so close to completing the hundred-year plan. I've got the Disciples and the Devout. Bodhi has been UltraViolet™ for five years with no side effects. The only person who may not fulfil the promise is Brady. I want to put my mind at ease.'

'He has behaved predictably for the most part - within the erratic parameters of a Trad.'

Sissy said, 'Ok, Glen. Just don't get caught listening in. We don't want to arouse his suspicions needlessly.'

Glen said, 'They are talking. I need to listen now. I can handle this.'

Sissy and Cain headed off as Glen listened in at the crack of the door, which he had left slightly ajar.

Brady wasn't a skilled interrogator, and Hunter had already spotted that this conversation was heading for a trawl of information, as Brady always began with discussions about his extreme old age. Brady then started to probe further, 'Who employed you? I don't think it was Libby. I think you are much higher up in this Green infrastructure than you are letting on.'

'John Kane employed me, sir.'

The one thing that annoyed Brady about his extended length of years in this world was that working out dates started to feel like complex math. 'He employed you to win the trust of Libby and spy on her.'

'I loved and respected Libby. She was an immensely talented actor, but yes, I reported back on her, just as I have reported back to Bodhi on you. In my defence, sir, you have always known that you were not my employer.'

'And the rest of the staff?'

'Yes. I am their Disciple in this tiny Green Community. They report to me, and then I report back to Sattva Systems™ - often it is to Bodhi, personally.' Hunter sat up straight and with almost regal dignity, and for the first time, he viewed Hunter as a figure of power and authority and not as a humble servant. Hunter continued, 'You cannot fire me or my team. You do not have the authority. I am a Disciple, and this is my area of responsibility. I am the Disciple of this area of Green Malibu land, even if your home no longer existed. My duty is here.'

Brady put his hand to his face to conceal his concern. He then removed his hand to reveal his brown eyes, which studied his potential adversary. He left his hand still covering his mouth. He shook his head and then shrugged and put both hands on the arms of the chair. He said, 'Well played. I didn't have a clue.' He laughed, 'What a brilliant con, you got me.'

Glen smiled at the door but was troubled.

Hunter said, 'I haven't been unhappy working here. You have been a pleasure to work with, and I am happy to continue in this role.'

'Apparently, I don't have a say in it, but yes, that's fine by me. I won't treat you any differently. I mean, I won't get nasty or play games with you. I'll just treat you as if you've got a job to do. However, it's gonna be real hard to see you as the old Hunter.'

Hunter nodded an acknowledgement.

'Ok, I'm gonna take a moment here. I don't know what to ask you as you've taken me by surprise - not many people do that to Brady Mahone.' He looked into Hunter's eyes, 'There is more to learn from you, of that, I'm damned sure.'

Hunter flinched.

Brady struggled to find the right question to open his interrogation. He drifted back to a century ago. It was apparent now that he was tricked into visiting Libby Skye. The person who made that first approach was Hunter. 'Was it Libby who asked to see me? Or was it Bodhi? Y'know, when you first approached me.'

'Bodhi ordered Libby to entertain you, but it was Cain who relayed the order to me to locate and bring you to her.' He looked away as if saddened by the memory. 'He asked too much of her...'

'The bit where she gave me access to her stuff. Yeah, I remember, she tricked me. No, wait a minute, it was you who tricked me. I'm still bloody annoyed about that.' He then realised he had taken everything in the end, but he didn't like the thought of being outplayed.

'That wasn't me, precisely. Libby issued me an order, and I was duty-bound to obey. I begged forgiveness from Bodhi, and he granted it.'

'But he didn't forgive Libby. I'm guessing that she should have lived as long as you. What happened? Was she allowed to die like a Trad for behaving like a Trad?'

Hunter said after a short pause, 'She self-selected her path. She knew what she had to do but couldn't comply. Her Suits™ were allowed to degrade at her natural Trad rate.'

'I don't understand these weird terms you Greens use. I'm guessing she was allowed to die like any other - one-hundred and fourteen-year-old.'

'Technically speaking.'

Brady scoffed, 'That's real cold, man - and I'm a killer!' He said, 'What we have here is that the great Bodhi Sattva failed to protect his Mother. In fact, he wilfully neglected her.'

Glen winced and shook his head.

Hunter said, 'I suppose you could choose to put it like that.'

Brady asked, 'Could you do that to your mother?'

'My Mother was a Trad who died eighteen months after the Green Revolution, as did the rest of my family. They never listened when I tried to get them to go Green. They treated me like a crackpot conspiracy theorist. They only have themselves to blame.'

Brady shook his head in disbelief. 'Why did Bodhi forgive you? It appears to me that you were as guilty as she was. You could have ignored her instructions.'

'He forgave me because I gave away the most precious item in my possession. When Xavier changed his name to Bodhi and to eschew all the trappings of material success to embark on a journey to save the planet, he gave to me...'

Brady pulled out the Sattva Ring, which hung on a chain around his neck. The emeralds and diamonds sparkled.

'...Yes. By giving you that ring, in place of Libby's most precious items, I had proven my worth to Bodhi.'

'Do you want it back?'

'No. Never. You are welcome to it. I give it to you freely and make no claim to it.'

Brady looked at the Sattva ring and then put it back inside his T-shirt. 'So, we've established that you did the leg work to get me to see Libby. You cheated me, you let Libby die...'

'I object. She brought it upon herself If I had intervened...'

'Ok. I'll let it pass. What else have you done?'

'Just reports. Comings and goings, life events, new acquisitions...'

'Tell me something which will make me believe you.'

'Like what, sir?'

Brady was getting frustrated. He knew he should be asking more searching questions than this, 'I don't know. Is there anybody who came to visit me, who rang alarm bells with your superiors - or whatever you call them?'

'Fleet Captain Marjorie Hampton. She visited you in an unauthorised capacity.'

Brady shrugged, 'She didn't tell me anything. She just wanted to make sure I stayed safe. That's what your job is - isn't it?'

'Yes, sir.'

'Drop the sir, shit. I don't want to hear you do that anymore. Is that clear?'

'Yes.'

'Good.' Brady went back through the years, his business, this home and his fortune - he struggled to articulate his concerns, 'Did I achieve all this?' He gestured all around him, 'Or was it given to me to keep me happy, for some purpose or other?'

Hunter smiled, 'This is all your own work. You are solely responsible for the success of the Brady Mahone Entertainment Enterprises. It was your idea before Bodhi was even aware of your presence and ability to traverse between the Trad and Green world. You own this, and now your family has its share of the burden.'

Brady folded his arms and nodded with pride. 'What skills did my predecessors have when they built their businesses? Y'know Kane Industries™, Sattva Systems™.'

Hunter looked to one side as if searching a long-misplaced memory. 'Mr Kane's head was in the right place, but he had no humanity. He was cold and ruthless. His one redeeming feature was that he made his money from Green technology.'

Brady said, 'He was an utter bastard as far as I can tell. If he'd have been in Ridgecrest Supermax, where he belonged, I would have torn him limb from limb for what he did. He was in a different league from the nonces I've had to live and survive alongside.'

Glen was puzzled as this wasn't the picture he had when he had dealings with John Kane. He had been his partner and environmental mentor. He had funded all of his projects in his war to save the planet from climate change disaster.

Brady said, 'What about Bodhi?'

'Bodhi is a saint, a prophet and a saviour. He was raised to be like John Kane, but he found compassion for all living creatures from somewhere. He has sacrificed so much personal pleasure for the evolution of mankind. He believes in a race that will always put the welfare of the planet first. He has watched over you, Brady Mahone. Your welfare is of deep concern to him. A man can sow seeds in the field, but he needs a beast to plough the field.'

'I ain't no man's beast. Is that all I am to you, a beast?' Brady jumped up angrily.

Hunter drew himself up to face his interrogator. He showed no fear. 'No. You have immense qualities of your own. You inspire doubt like no other living creature. You are the Temptation we must avoid. You carry death with you to every corner of the Earth. You

are Corruption. You are the Corrupter, the Deceiver and
Death-Bringer...'

Glen knocked on the door and marched in. 'Hi guys, everybody
is wondering where the guest of honour is.' He flashed a look at
Hunter and ordered, 'Could you check everybody is happy in the
main hall? That's if Brady agrees.' He looked at Brady, 'Is that ok with
you?' He added, 'Are you feeling ok, man? You look tired.'

'No. I'm fine.' Brady physically and mentally shook himself out
of his trance. He began to wonder if Hunter had actually said those
things about him. He looked at Glen, whose smiling face reassured
him enough for him to say, 'It's been a stressful day. Maybe I need to
let my hair down.'

Glen rubbed Brady's head hard, 'There's not much to let down
on there. Come on, let's party. Show me what a good time looks like
at Chateau Mahone.'

Brady responded meekly to the challenge, 'Yeah, sure. Have you
had some of Debrock's dib-dabs?'

Glen usually refused Nature's highs on the grounds of keeping
his senses alert, but this felt like a potential emergency. 'I haven't
touched the stuff in decades. It will go straight to my head, and you'll
think I'm such a lame-ass - but if you promise not to laugh at me...'

Brady said, 'Just, shut the fuck up, brother.' Still, Glenarvon Cole
showed no response to this teasing statement. Brady yelled as if he
had rediscovered his masculinity in the company of a fellow soldier,
'Come on. Let's get wrecked.'

8: GRAND DESIGNS

Tyrone nudged Brady awake. 'Hey, Brady, you said you'd give us a lift back to San Martin. You also said that Raelynn could come with me.'

Brady rubbed his eyes and tried to orientate himself. He was in his bedroom at his Malibu home. 'What day is it?'

'It's Sunday. I'm back at work tomorrow. Raelynn wants to stay at my house for a week or so. Uncle Sam says it's ok.' Tyrone smiled.

'You're God knows how old, and you still need the Bear's permission?'

'I don't mind. It's a respect thing. You'd like your boys to be like that, wouldn't you?'

Brady shuffled around in bed without escaping the warm pull of his blankets, 'What do you mean?'

'Still wanting to hear their Father's advice, even if they are a hundred years old.'

Brady grunted, 'No.' But then he thought about it from his muddled stoned haze. 'Yeah, I suppose so. I wouldn't want them to ignore me - that's for sure.' His head cleared for a moment, 'Where is the Bear?'

Tyrone smiled, 'He headed back to Sattva Systems™ with Glenarvon Cole, Genesis Garcia and Cain. He said to tell you that he had a lovely time, and he thanks you for your generous hospitality.'

Brady stretched. Tyrone smelled the body odour wafting in the air, and it took him back to the time before the RedSuits™ when everybody used to smell like this. Brady said, 'Was the Bear being sarcastic?'

'I don't think so. We were all laughing our heads off at you and Glenarvon Cole. You were like a comedy double act, with all those funny Trad stories. You were brilliant with all your convict tales. Raelynn thought you were so cool.'

Brady slapped his forehead as if he were kick-starting his memory cells. 'Fuck, I don't remember a God-damn thing. It sounds really embarrassing.'

Tyrone said, 'No. It wasn't. Your boys lapped it up, and Amie was sweet when you and she told stories about what it was like for you on the Mahone Ranch. Cain was getting quite emotional as it brought a lot of memories of those old days for him.'

Fuck, Debrock's stuff must have been the bomb. I don't remember anything at all. The last thing I remember was Hunter going all-out biblical on me. I musta pushed him too hard.

Brady sat up in bed - this was his first achievement of the day. 'Where is everybody else?'

'Your boys were up early and in the gym, but now they've all headed off to win some competition you set them. They didn't want to disturb you.'

'Why? What time is it?'

'10:30. That's why I didn't want to leave it any longer.'

'And the others?'

'Lucy-Ian, Amie, Helgarth, Debrock and xyr friends are still on the beach. They've been out there since Sunup.' He had a faraway smile, 'Raelynn is waiting for me.'

Brady asked, 'Have you seen Hunter?'

'Yes. He's outside in the corridor.'

'Hunter!' Brady shouted.

Hunter came in, 'How can I help you, sir?'

'I'm gonna have a quick wash and get changed. I won't be having breakfast; I'll eat on the way.' He looked at Hunter for a reaction, but he was acting the same as he had for the last eighty-four years in Brady's employ. 'Can you get the kitchen staff to knock-up a hamper for three? I'll need it within thirty minutes.'

'Certainly, sir.' He turned away sharply.

Brady thought he had said that he didn't want to be addressed as *sir* anymore, but he wasn't sure. 'If you give me a few minutes to get freshened up, then I'll meet you at my FusionPlane™. Tell Raelynn I'll take you on a scenic route and make a day of it. She doesn't get out enough. I'm thinking of flying over the Grand Canyon. Does that work for you?'

'Absolutely, I can't wait to tell Raelynn.' Tyrone beamed.

'Off you go, then.'

Brady showered and dressed in his favourite NanoProtected™ jeans, a white T-shirt and a pair of Xavier's old designer sneakers. He put on his sunglasses even while still inside, as he knew when he left the building, he wouldn't be able to cope with the Californian sunshine in his present hazy state.

He relayed messages to the staff to let them know that Raelynn was with him today, and then she would be stopping over in San Martin for the foreseeable future. Helgarth would worry about her more than Amie.

In the distance, he saw Tyrone and Raelynn kissing, but they stopped when they saw Brady approaching the FusionPlane™. Raelynn raced up to greet Brady extravagantly, she leapt into him, and he caught her, and she hugged him. 'You are the best, Brady Mahone. I love you so much.'

'I love you too, honey. Now, let me give you the guided tour.'

They got in the FusionPlane™, and as soon as Brady completed the vertical lift-off, he set the SattNav™ to go to San Martin but with several diversions. He wasn't feeling fully functional to fly manually, so he put the FusionPlane™ on autopilot. He was ravenously hungry, and his staff had already left a considerable picnic hamper for him and his guests. He opened it up, 'Let's take a look-see shall we.' He pulled out sandwiches and a thermos of coffee for himself, 'Watcha waiting for - tuck in.'

Brady slowly began to feel like his old self. He looked out of the window, 'Hey Raelynn, that's San Francisco below. It used to have buildings called skyscrapers - they were called that because they were so tall, they touched the sky - and there were loads of them.' Brady laughed as he realised, he wasn't going to the most eloquent of tour guides.

Raelynn played along good-naturedly, she might have adopted the image of a Goth, but she had no idea of the mannerisms and the eternal disdain needed to complement this appearance. 'You mean the buildings were as high as we are now?'

'Sure thing, hun. And all those grids you can see were the Highways. I mean, some of the vegetation looks ok, but I'm not so sure about the brown and dust holes.'

Tyrone said, 'Some of the most heavily polluted and damaged areas are taking longer than expected to recover. They may be permanently scarred. Of course, the world is just going back to its natural state. Not all the land was beautiful, even in the beginning.'

After a short while, Brady said, 'Wow, look at that, the Golden Gate Bridge. Except it's Green - I shoulda guessed.' He laughed. 'Hey, Tyrone, of all the old Trad structures, why do they leave these standing.'

'It's as you'd guess - some infrastructure is useful - even we have to travel conveniently.'

Raelynn said dreamily, 'I would have loved to have seen it in gold.'

Brady said, 'It was always more of a red to me, except when it was lit up at night, then it kinda had a golden glow about it.'

Tyrone said, 'It's called the Green Gate Bridge now. It's turned that colour because it's been NanoProtected™.'

Brady had the FusionPlane™ head over in the direction of Phoenix. He didn't want the journey to be solely over forests and wildernesses before getting to the Grand Canyon. He wanted Raelynn to have a variation of landscapes to take in on the Brady tour.

They flew in peace for a while. Tyrone and Raelynn murmured together while Brady tried to recover his lost memories from the night before. The last thing he recalled with any clarity was Hunter taking on the role of a preacher in much the same way as the Bear would do. He tried to square up how the people of God, and not just the Christians - it was the same with all the spiritual types he had met - could be on the side of the Greens. They had stood meekly aside as churches and temples of every faith had been dissolved into nothing. They didn't even seem to want to build Green communities in the same areas of the most significant buildings. It didn't make any sense to him.

He waited for a pause in the conversation between Raelynn and Tyrone to ask his question. 'Hey, Tyrone, you know me, I don't like to talk about things that get heavy and all - and you being all into the science stuff - can I ask your opinion on a few things?'

'Sure, what do you want to know?'

'I don't want a lot of technical detail - I can't cope with that.' He knew he had to get to the point, 'You're kinda neutral on all the religious aspect of this Green thing, that's why I want to see how it all fits together...I know I ain't putting this too well. I don't want to ask your Uncle Sam as he's biased, and plus once you get him started, he don't stop.'

'Ok. I'm an atheist. I don't believe in religion, I'm not even particularly spiritual, but I know how it works because I've had Uncle Sam preaching it to me my whole life. You ask me anything,

Brady. I will give you the best answer I can, but it is my personal view - the Greens don't have a position on this. They are predominantly ecologists, environmentalists and all the other scientific branches which emanate from these studies.'

Brady was reassured. He could tell that Tyrone was taking his request seriously, and he didn't feel threatened by humiliation if he asked a stupid question. He noticed Raelynn watch over the both of them as if this subject pricked her interest. Brady said, 'Why doesn't the Bear get angry when he sees all these churches destroyed. Why doesn't he fight to keep them open?'

'Remember these are my personal opinions. Uncle Sam would never agree with my theories. The more spiritual Greens have conflated Saving the Planet with doing God's will. Bodhi has rationalised it as organised religion is capitalism with spiritual marketing. They were treasure hoarders and held vast lands at their disposal for thousands of years. They let people suffer instead of selling off their treasures to help them. Obviously, the Trad believers hated this idea, but those who were Green and who understood the imminent danger of runaway climate change were stuck between two opposing world views.'

'I kinda get that, but surely once the Greens had won, then you'd think they'd change their minds and ask to keep the temples for themselves. I know I would.' *But then again, I'm a criminal who wouldn't trouble myself over renegotiating a deal.*

'Who would you ask?'

Because the question was short, Brady suspected it was a trick question, 'Bodhi, I suppose.'

Tyrone looked down at the forests and then looked back up into the clouds. 'The Greens have different factions, with different mindsets but one common goal - to save the Earth. People like me study and follow the science. Others just want to work for the greater good. They used to be the volunteers and the activists in the old days.

People like Uncle Sam and religious and spiritual people across the globe have many things in common in their teachings - if you apply a little lateral thinking in some cases.'

'Like what?'

'There is usually a catastrophe foretold, some kind of cataclysmic event, an end-of-days kind of deal, and this is accompanied by a saviour, a prophet of some kind, or a second coming, a son of God. If you turn away from him, you are doomed for all eternity, but if you follow, then you can be saved and live out your days in paradise, heaven, a rapture, or maybe even a Heaven on Earth.'

'Are you telling me that Bodhi thinks he is the next Jesus Christ?'

'Not exactly. Bodhi doesn't come out and say that. I don't think he is even religious. I believe he is a scientist and a businessman. However, all of the ingredients of the prophecies are there for people like my Uncle Sam to believe. He believes that Bodhi is the Second Coming of Christ.' Tyrone joked, 'And people like my Uncle Sam like structures and strict rules - all religious followers do. He follows the rules - if churches have to go - then so be it.'

Tyrone rewound the subject as he didn't like where this was going, and he needed time to think about the inevitable follow-up question. He looked to Raelynn for help, but she was mentally and metaphorically in the clouds. Tyrone chose an action story to divert Brady's attention. He smiled as he realised this was a tactic his Uncle Sam had used on him many times before. He said, 'One of the most ferocious battles took place in the early days when the GreenShells™ encircled the Vatican City. The Trads protecting it threw everything they had in attempting to fight off the Greens. They threw rocks, gathered swords which they believed carried the power of God within them to slash uselessly at the Shells™. They even used blood sacrifices to try and lift the perceived curses. This went on for months after the Revolution until they decided to place people around the perimeter to stop the encroachment for as long as they could.'

Brady said, 'They did something like that at mASSIVE™ Park in Cupertino.'

Tyrone laughed, 'That was a time when science nearly became a religion for many.' He added, 'But, eventually, they died out. But here's the thing - many of the Christian Greens wanted to preserve the City, and particularly the treasures in the St Peter's Basilica and masterpieces of art like the Sistine Chapel, but they were denied.'

Brady hadn't heard of any of these things but let it pass. He asked, 'Why?'

'Because it held the power of nostalgia, and it held the power of the Trads in its wonders. This could tempt people to go back to the old ways. Only the roads of the Vatican City remain. Everything else is gone. The same can be said of the Pyramids, the ancient buildings of Greece...I do remember there was a discussion about whether the Great Wall of China was infrastructure or nostalgia, but at the end, that went as well.'

Raelynn may have just been thinking over how to help Tyrone because she chose this moment to intervene. 'Brady. You know when you said you couldn't remember anything from last night because of your dab blackout?'

Brady looked at her. She was smiling softly, 'Yes.'

'Do you remember seeing me when you were in Libby's room?'

'No. What was I doing in there?'

'You were with Glenarvon Cole. You kept going on about how beautiful this movie poster was.' She added, 'You and Glen were having your big male bonding moment.' She paused and gazed into his face, 'You really don't remember, do you?'

Brady searched for something to remind him. He had a split-second flashback of Glen putting his arms around him and consoling him. 'Was I being soppy?' He changed his wording, 'I mean, being stupid stoned?'

'I thought it was nice. Anyway, you both left when you saw me. You went off giggling together.' She added, 'What was it about that poster, that you wanted to show it off to Glenarvon Cole? I wouldn't have thought it was his thing.'

It was the most beautiful item I have ever seen, and I've stolen some fantastic jewellery in my time. She was my real Moms, and she never even knew I existed. She was Glenarvon Cole's Moms. How would our lives had turned out if she had known the truth?

Brady felt a surge of strong emotions. He didn't speak for a moment out of fear that his voice would crack. He looked out of the window and spotted the remains of Phoenix coming into view. He nodded in the general direction of Phoenix, hoping Tyrone would pick up the reins of the appointed Tour Guide.

Tyrone looked ahead and understood, 'Raelynn, look, that's Phoenix, Arizona.'

They looked out at the vast gridlines which marked out the blocks. There were dozens of FusionCars™ on the virtually deserted roads. They looked like cream-coloured ceramic boxes using the road network to head out of the city, as there were no buildings left to visit. To Brady, it looked like an old arcade game from up here. While Tyrone and Raelynn held hands and watched Phoenix drift slowly by, beneath them. Brady took a deep swig of water and brought his emotions back under control.

Once they were clear of Phoenix, the autopilot headed north to the Grand Canyon. The conversation returned to the small talk between tourists and fellow travellers. Brady struggled to assimilate the events of last night with the troubling theories of Tyrone. The one thing that gave him comfort was the genuine affection that Tyrone demonstrated towards him - he had always been a friend to Brady Mahone. He thought, *if I was that bad, surely the Beardons would have avoided me like the plague.*

The sense of awe as they flew over the Grand Canyon restored Brady's spirits. He felt like they had entered a neutral zone. The Grand Canyon was just as magnificent now as it was in the time of the Trads. The Greens couldn't take the credit for this. Brady took the FusionPlane™ out of autopilot and swooped and explored the area from as many viewpoints as he could. He had never seen Raelynn look so happy as she raced through every superlative in her vocabulary. Tyrone being right next to her, completed her perfect day. Brady resolved not to spoil this with his heavy talk.

Once he had had his fun manually flying the FusionPlane™, he set it back to autopilot but on a course to circle the Grand Canyon while they all indulged in their picnic in the sky.

9: HOME FROM HOME

Brady needed company. He had thought about heading off to Boulder Creek after the Distor™ Distribution Ceremony had been completed, as he wanted to collect his latest instalments of Green Credits from the proceeds of his business, but even though his math work was limited, he concluded that he had already been paid. He had changed his mind, not only after his confrontational interview with Hunter but also because he was embarrassed by his stoned behaviour in the evening. He believed they would look down on him, and he couldn't face Glenarvon Cole in case he started to get over-friendly.

He decided that if Boulder Creek was temporarily off-limits, then maybe the Bear would let him stay awhile in San Martin. He knew the Bear would forgive him his transgressions, and he always felt at home in the Beardon homestead. It was the kind of family feeling he could never recreate in his own Malibu home - he thought of Malibu as being more of a party palace than a home, not just because Debrock and his friends had taken up semi-permanent residence there, but Amie and Helgarth seemed to be on a never-ending mid-life crisis since Lucy-Ian and Raelynn were born. He saw Raelynn in a whole new light since she had found Tyrone, and he felt that the Beardon influence might be good for her.

The Bear greeted them all with his customary warmth when he landed his FusionPlane™ and the Beardon home, and he had no objections at all in putting up his old friend. He surprised Brady with his relaxed attitude when Tyrone insisted that Raelynn should share his room. Samuel Beardon the Third seemed as delighted as everybody else in seeing the joy these two had found in each other.

Brady handed over the remains of the picnic hamper, as it had been supplied with enough food for ten instead of the intended three. The gift was received graciously and in the spirit of recycling and reducing food waste.

Once everybody had settled in, Brady and the Bear took a stroll together into the centre of San Martin. Brady soon understood the warmth of the welcome the Bear had offered to Raelynn. He said, 'She is a Godsend. Tyrone only had eyes for enrolling as a volunteer to colonise Mars. I had to pull in a favour from Sissy to stop his application, but now Raelynn has come onto the scene. I believe he will finally put all that nonsense behind him. What do you think?'

'They've definitely fallen for each other. I wouldn't be surprised if they want to enter one of those arrangements you have. How would you feel about that?'

They strolled past the park where a bandstand was being decked out for the Centenary Celebrations - even though these were still a few months away. The Bear said, 'I would be happy for them.'

Brady smiled, 'Raelynn is not technically my family, but she has Green Credits of her own now. She has her independence - she can come and go as she pleases.'

'You are correct, my friend. Raelynn is Pure Green, and if she gives freely, it will be accepted in that spirit.'

People came over to the Bear to offer their congratulations, 'You must be so proud...you'll have to tell us what it's like...you've earned the right...I'm so happy for you...pass on my congratulations to Alicia...'

Brady said, 'What's that all about?'

'I have been chosen as one of the Devout and the Disciples to receive the UltraViolet™ in June, on the Centenary of the Green Revolution - so has Alicia...'

Brady said, 'But not Tyrone?'

'No, Not yet. I think his application to the Mars project has confused things.'

'Why is that?'

'If he were accepted into that, then he would get the UltraViolet™ first. I think he's been missed off the Devout List because he was on the astronaut's list. I'm sure Sissy will sort it out.'

Still, more of the townsfolk of San Martin came up to congratulate their preacher, Samuel Beardon the Third, 'Well done...What is the UltraViolet™, I'm dying to know...Will you let us into the secret?'

The Bear responded to them with a mixture of thanks, accompanied by warm smiles, 'You know it's forbidden to share with you, if I was of that mindset, I wouldn't be one of the Devout, now, would I?' He laughed loudly.

Brady said, 'I've been doing a lot of thinking lately.'

'That will be because of all the chatter about the Centenary celebrations, my friend. It has a different resonance for you, as you are considering a lost way of life, whereas we are honouring all we have achieved.' He put his arm on Brady's shoulder. 'Naturally, it should cause you to reflect, and with your Last Will and Testament, you have started the difficult process of considering your mortality. You are thinking about a time beyond your death.'

Brady sighed, 'Yeah, you're right. Lately, I've been considering all the people I have known who have died, and what they left behind. I don't want to be all self-important like, but many of these people only live on in my memories. I feel that when I die I'm kinda killing them all over again, as if I'm taking their spirits with me.' Brady laughed, trying to disguise his fear, 'Trouble is, I don't think they are going to like the place where Brady Mahone is going.' He pointed at the ground, and the Bear understood that this was a gesture that he wasn't going to be moving heavenwards. Brady said, 'Can I ask you a personal question, and I don't want it to sound offensive...'

'Ask away, my friend.'

'Underneath that Suit™ of yours, are you whole? Are you a young shell over an ancient body?' He was thinking about Rhea, but he didn't want to discuss her. It wasn't that he didn't want to appear stalker-ish. He sensed that he might put her under a threat he couldn't perceive. He had a similar instinct about Fleet Captain Marjorie Hampton. He knew their clandestine operations were to protect him, he assumed, but also, he sensed that the Bear and the rest of the Boulder Creek crew hadn't authorised their operation.

'I am older than I appear, but with each new Suit™, I am repaired and renewed. Without these, I would have died many years earlier.'

'And if you know you are dying between Suits™, then there's nothing you can do about it?'

'The Orange™ informs you of precisely how long you have left so that you can make your arrangements to die.' He added, 'I don't wish to be controversial, brother, but the Trads couldn't have risked that. An old Trad knowing he had only a couple of weeks left to live, might have harmed others - to settle old scores. We have the Security Protocols™ and the RedSuits™, one Green cannot harm another, even if they wanted to.'

As much as he loved the Bear, he had the paranoia of a criminal to hold back this information. He chose a different person to explore his theory. 'Bodhi's Mother, Libby Skye, died at one-hundred and fourteen years old. At the time, I thought that was ancient, but now, that was young for a Green - wouldn't you agree?'

The Bear was puzzled. He hadn't expected Brady to discuss Bodhi Sattva's Mother. 'I believe the promise was that we would all live, in good health, until a minimum age of one-hundred.'

'Whatever - but Bodhi had cheated these rules with Libby because she was his Mother. I know Cain would have told you this at the time.'

'Yes. I remember. You are skilled in the art of spreading doubt. Where are you going with this?' He looked troubled. He barely acknowledged another batch of congratulatory comments and pats on the back from his well-wishers.

'I think Bodhi let her die instead of helping her to live. He has form. You could say he has a history of neglect. It was well within Bodhi's power to save his own Mother, but he chose to let her die.' *She was my Mother.* 'What kind of a man could do that? I know I couldn't have done that to my Foster Moms, never mind my real Moms. And yet here he is, the great Bodhi Sattva, putting himself out there like some kinda Second Coming of Christ while he makes me out to be the other guy. I don't get it, and I certainly ain't loving it.'

The Bear hustled Brady into a side street. 'You can't go around suggesting things like that. You aren't looking at the bigger picture.'

'Sounds like the sort of thing that Bodhi would say.'

'We all have choices. Libby Skye self-selected...' The Bear looked fearful. He looked down as if he half-expected the ground to open up beneath him.

'Are you saying she chose to die? She looked full of life and had every intention of living life to the full the last time I saw her. I'm just saying, man - I knows what I sees.'

'We are creating heaven on Earth...'

Brady barked, 'You're changing the subject. Bodhi withdrew his support; he killed his own Mother for your bigger picture. You even suspect that he had your own Father killed, the great Samuel Beardon the Second...'

'Please, don't mock my Father.'

'But you do suspect...'

The Bear broke down and fell to his knees, 'Yes. Yes, I fear that he ordered my Father's death to keep the Green Deal alive. I admit it.'

'So, why am I the bad guy in all this? As far as I can tell, I've been good to you. I helped you uncover the truth about your family. You do remember how much that used to eat you up. It troubled you bad enough for you to befriend me, who you considered to be some kinda Trad demon - or worse.'

'Because it was ordained. It was prophesied. You are the beast of burden.'

'Prophesised by Bodhi - that's what you're saying. He killed your Father, his own Mother and yet you let him because you think he's a God.'

'A Son of God.'

'Well, I ain't as well versed in the Bible as you are, and I can't tell you none of your fancy stories, but I know enough to know that Jesus didn't kill Mary...' He added, 'He's just a man, more like a Godfather, who will stop at nothing to get what he wants. Just because you agree with his desires doesn't change a thing in my book.'

The Bear pleaded, 'Stop it...stop it, please. What do you want from me?'

Brady smiled and lifted the Bear up. Samuel Beardon the Third was the same height and build as Brady, but he seemed somehow diminished. Brady said, 'It would be kinda nice for you to stop treating me as the enemy. I don't think I've done anything to deserve this disrespect from you. Am I really that bad?'

The Bear searched Brady's face for signs of who he really was. He couldn't discover anything which dispelled the thought that Brady was a friend. 'No, not wholly.'

Brady laughed, 'A ringing endorsement. I suppose beggars can't be choosers. Let me ask another - is Bodhi really that good?'

The Bear smiled thinly, 'No. Not wholly.'

'There you go. That wasn't so difficult, was it?' Brady added, 'Let me reiterate, y'know, get my facts straight. I know you like your truth, well, so do I - it can be a powerful thing to have on your side, wouldn't you agree?'

'Yes. Always.'

'So, I have your agreement in my assessment of the facts. Hey, that sounds like something Judge Jefferson would say...' Brady laughed, '...That Bodhi Sattva killed Libby Skye and Samuel Beardon the Second...I'm being kind here by not mentioning the billions of Trads because they don't count to you...and Samuel Beardon the Third swears to Almighty God that this is the truth - the whole truth...'

'Yes, Brady. So, help me, God.'

10: LAST CALLS

Fleet Captain Marjorie Hampton was surrounded by HeavyLoaders™, and the multiple sub-sonic booms merged into a permanent loud hum. Rhea Laidlaw parked her FusionCar™ and walked over to meet her. She said, 'You needed to see me? It sounded urgent.'

'I'm off the Devout list. What about you?'

Rhea was puzzled, 'I'm still on it - the Disciple list - but I don't know what they're planning. Do you?'

'No. I think they know about me. I've made a decision.'

'What are you going to do?'

'I've applied for the Mars mission. I'm going to see Bodhi, but I wanted you to know.'

Rhea checked to see if anybody was watching before hugging Marjorie. A HeavyLoader™ from across the vast parking lot ascended vertically into the sky. They waited for it to speed away and scanned the parking lot for prying eyes. Rhea said, 'What's your reasoning?'

'It's a sense. I always worry when companies secretly compile lists. If anybody asks, they always offer reassurances and tell you how valuable you are to the organisation, but deep down, you know that if you are not on the right list, then your time is up.' A technician in cream-coloured Sattva Systems™ overalls came over to Marjorie with documentation. She signed it and thanked him. She was careful to make sure he was out of earshot before continuing. 'My best workers are receiving the UltraViolet™ in the June celebrations. I've made discreet checks - they all believe I'm on it, I've said nothing to change this assumption.'

'What's your plan?'

'There are three missions to Mars left before the operation ceases. I plan to be on the next one. I'm hoping Bodhi allows me to leave because of all the work I've done for the Greens over the years.' She added, 'It will be instructive to see how he handles my request.'

Rhea said, 'I'm going to miss you, but you know I have to stay...'

'Of course, you do, especially after all this time...'

'How are you going to cope - up there?' She pointed at the sky.

Marjorie stood almost to attention, 'The UltraViolet™ is a fantastic addition to an astronaut's armoury, as the final upgrade will prevent degradation - and my engineering and flight knowledge is desperately needed, especially as we will be in a low-gravity environment.'

Rhea looked into the brown eyes of her old friend, 'But there's not much up there, and it's beyond freezing cold...'

'My husband died in a desert in Iraq courtesy of the Green Revolution, he had uncovered significant intel as part of his mission for the CIA, but it was too late. I will go to a desert of my own - just the temperature will be different, and I will build a new world, seeing as I failed to protect the Traditional Cultures in this one.' She looked away briefly.

Rhea said, 'They had a clandestine department based within the Los Banos Police Department Headquarters. I know it reached there, but like you say, it was too late. I searched the place, but the Greens had taken everything. We can't do anything about it now. Ever since I've wondered if they knew we were part of the investigation into Sattva Systems™ - if they did, then we must be the enemies you keep closer.'

'I didn't think they did know until recently,' Marjorie said. 'They are onto me, which is why I'm out of here. I can almost hear the cutting of ties everywhere. They are planning something huge for the end of the hundred-year plan. I know it.'

Rhea shrugged, 'We can't arrest or prosecute. All we can do is keep the flame of truth, freedom and liberty alive - no matter what it takes.'

Marjorie said, 'I'm smuggling communications devices onboard.'

'There are plenty of devices already on Mars - aren't there?'

Marjorie looked all around her again, 'When I was in Glenarvon's inner sanctum, I was privy to his plans. The communication systems between the Mars Colony and us are set to degrade on January 2, 2185. He wants them to be cut adrift and forgotten about - forever. I might be able to squeeze another few days of comms out of them until they track these down.' She passed over a SpaceSatt™ to Rhea. 'Keep it safe. Don't let anyone know you've got it.'

Rhea pocketed it away expertly.

Marjorie said, 'What are you planning to do next?'

'What I always do, double deal and be everybody's go-to girl for discreet information.'

Marjorie laughed, 'Who'd have thought that a child TV star would end up being a spy.'

'Daddy was in Homeland Security. Most of his people were watching the extreme right, but then the CIA informed him of a radical left plot. It seemed crazy, but Daddy took it seriously enough to recruit me into the FBI - the days of pure nepotism - I know.'

'But they would have known who you were. You were all over social media.'

'That's why it worked. I put out lots of posts on environmental issues, and then I applied for a job on their news channel. It was a disastrous career move in media, but I loved being a special agent. My brief was to gather information and if I could identify the leadership. Fuck me if I didn't do exactly that, except it was on the day of their victory speech, which as we know was too late.'

Marjorie said, 'Must be the knowledge that I'm planning to leave which is making me all nostalgic for the old days. I'll never forget your final TV appearance - you got Glenarvon Cole to show himself for the first and last time...'

'Don't forget the guy who shouted, "We did it, Bodhi." I hope my Daddy got to see that.'

Marjorie hugged her and then stepped back. They were friends, but she didn't want her body language to give them away. Rhea said, 'So, here's my next moves. I need to flush out whether they know about me. You're right. I think your cover has been busted. I'm going to confirm that you can't be trusted, and my recommendation is to let you go to Mars.'

'Ok. That should build trust.'

'Bodhi has me spying on Tia Cassandra, but you know I'm doing the same for her. I will ask her to accept your application - you will be a fabulous addition. I will also inform her that you are a part of my team. She trusts me as she helped me find out about the inner workings of Sattva Systems™ back in the day. I shared what I found so that she could have an advantage over her rival - but that didn't pan out. We totally under-estimated Bodhi Sattva and Glenarvon Cole.'

Marjorie said, 'They had Genesis Garcia covering their backs. It's handy when you've got the Governor of California and, by default Silicon Valley in your back pocket. Oh, and we mustn't forget Cain, the Head of Deep Mind and Siddha at the Treasury...'

'...And other well-placed Greens across the world. I'm sure Tia will want to know everything. She will love having you working alongside her. You'll get along with Dagny - she's an engineering and logistical genius if she ever gets from out of the shadow of her legendary Mother.' Rhea added, 'It would help me if you are challenged by any of those people, that you feel betrayed by me. It will reinforce my cover.' She saw a couple of technicians approaching. 'Gotta go. You be safe up there. I'll always be thinking of you.'

Rhea looked behind her at Fleet Captain Marjorie Hampton and then strode on to the Main Entrance of Sattva Systems™ HQ to find Bodhi. In the cafeteria at his reserved table - one of the few trappings of success he allowed himself - she found him.

Bodhi said, 'Hello, Rhea. Would you care to join me for dinner?'

Rhea put on a winning smile, 'I'd love to.' A staffer came over in a cream-coloured Sattva Systems™ overall. Rhea said, 'I'll have the same as Bodhi.' She looked at his meal. He was eating the same evening meal as he always did. It stopped him from wasting mental energy, and a surfeit of choices was an irritating trait of the capitalists. The same reasoning was why he had a table reserved in the same spot in the Sattva Systems™ Cafeteria. He had tempeh bacon with sauteed mushrooms, avocado and wilted arugula for breakfast. At lunch, he ate whole-grain pasta with lentil *meatballs* and a side salad. And the meal he had this evening with Rhea consisted of cauliflower and chickpea tacos with guacamole and pico de gallo. She said, 'Have you ever been tempted to have a place of your own?'

He smiled as their food was delivered and thanked the member of staff. 'Not at all. This is my home, and all of my family are here.' Rhea knew that what he meant was not family but colleagues. She also knew that he slept in a basic sleeping pod, and he washed in the communal showers. He looked up from his meal, 'The naughtiest things I do are my little conversations with you. What news is there from the outside world?'

'Fleet Captain Marjorie Hampton has applied for the Mars Mission, as have thirty-seven of your employees.' She handed him over the list she had written. He perused it between mouthfuls of food - he might have the same meals, but he still appeared to enjoy them.

He smiled, and his eyes widened occasionally. 'There are many that I might have suspected, but there are one or two which have surprised me. Thank you, this is excellent work.'

'Does Marjorie shock you?'

'No. She visited Brady Mahone's private residence without our knowledge or permission. She is protecting him in some way, or maybe passing on information.'

Rhea laughed, 'I think it's the former. Brady wouldn't know what to do with the kind of technical information which Marjorie deals with.'

'When did she switch allegiances - in your opinion?'

Rhea pretended to think about it, 'I think it was the Colony rescue mission and the destruction of Cima back in '42. Many Greens lost their faith when they discovered that their loved ones were killed.' She added more positively, 'Also, it's the pull of the new. Your project is coming to its conclusion, but Mars is a whole new beginning for mankind.'

Bodhi took a swig from his black vegan coffee. 'Were you tempted to join them?'

'No. I'm a home bird, a proper little bird of paradise.'

Bodhi laughed at the paradise reference. 'Do you think I should let them go?'

Rhea took back the list and re-examined it, 'There is a helluva lot of experience and expertise here. I can see how these people could be invaluable to Tia. However, they've done their bit for you, and you'll never see them again...' This was her test to see if Bodhi would confirm or deny Glenarvon's plan to cut off their comms.

'Yes. The easiest way for me to think about the future is not to have to consider the past. I will never see them again because this will enable me to not have to think about them again.'

Rhea considered the flaw in this logic - she would never see her Daddy again, but she would never forget him. 'I think you should let them leave because they have self-selected to do so.'

'You are right.' He smiled. 'Tia Cassandra has returned for her UltraViolet™ ceremony. Are you going to visit her?'

'Yes. I'm heading to Florida in the morning.'

'I want to know about any contingency plans she has if it all goes horribly wrong up there. I don't want any surprise visitors in the future. I've got the next thousand-year plan to consider.'

Rhea drained her black coffee. 'Don't worry. She trusts me, and she loves bragging about all her achievements.' She stood up and left. She walked past the thirteen-point pledge in the Main Hall and studied every point on it. *It's funny how something that big just gets ignored. It's true - familiarity does breed contempt.* Glenarvon Cole had written it. Bodhi Sattva had endorsed it, and Genesis Garcia had marketed it for Green public consumption.

The end to capitalism. End materialism. The most destructive ideology against nature.

Equal rights and opportunity for all citizens.

An end to all weaponry so that our people can live in harmony with nature without being threatened.

To protect all Green spaces across the globe and bring an end to the exploitation of the land.

To protect all living creatures. Stop the killing.

End intensive farming.

Reduce the population of the planet by peaceful means and self-selection.

Improve education, with a more prominent focus on ecology, environmental sciences, and ethics.

To repair the damage brought on by the Industrial and Technological Revolutions.

To bring an era of peace, harmony, and tranquillity to those that help to save the planet.

And finally, to the three requests outside of the top ten primary goals. The goals of the GreenRevs, the army that changed the world:

End hate thoughts and crimes, including gender identity and discrimination.

Remove all traces of Imperialism and Colonialism.

Improve mental health by establishing kinder societies.

Rhea uttered, 'It doesn't say by how many.'

11: CAPE CASSANDRA

Rhea picked up her Rental FusionPlane™ - as a Disciple, she could have had one of her own, but she knew Bodhi would appreciate her refusal of ownership. She stopped off at San Martin to complete her Disciple administrative duties. As she flew over the Beardon house, she slowed down. She noticed Brady Mahone's FusionPlane™ parked up nearby. *I will have to be careful not to bump into him - far too risky.* She noted that Tyrone was passionately kissing a girl. She circled and watched as he pulled away from her embrace and headed off to work. She recognised Raelynn.

She set the FusionPlane™ next to her Disciple's office, and she soon was quickly surrounded by well-wishers on her being approved of being an early adopter of the UltraVioletSuits™. The people were hungry for news and gossip, and it made her feel like an old-fashioned politician when she didn't give them an ounce of new information. She maintained a cheery persona before heading for the relative calm of her office.

These people are so needy.

Once at her desk, she went through her notices. There were the usual vacation applications and arrangement proposals. But because she hadn't been around for a while, there were many of them. She read them through, plotted them on her charts, entered them into diaries and authorised them with her Green Stamper.

Rhea then opened the old recycled safe - it was the original safe - but anything which continued to be of use in the post-Trad environment was re-assigned as recycled. She took out the San Martin Devout Approvals. All the usual suspects were there, including Samuel Beardon the Third and his daughter Alicia, but where was Tyrone? She picked up the applications for the Cassandra Mission. She knew Tyrone was a likely candidate. She went through the few names - it wasn't a popular choice as to why a Green would forego Heaven on Earth and trade it for hell on another planet? She thought sadly of Marjorie - who sensed that she might not be left with a choice by the end of the year.

She found Tyrone's name, and it had been marked - *rejected*. His was the only refusal, and in the *comments* column, it had the initials *SB*. She guessed that Samuel Beardon had pulled some strings. She didn't understand the strong influence he had with Bodhi. She had uncovered information on Samuel Beardon the First and Second, but he seemed to be a humble labourer in the Green scheme of things. She then looked at the long list of the rest of the population of San Martin, which ran into several thousand. She found Tyrone on this list. She didn't understand the potential consequences of this, but deep within her gut, she felt that this was bad news. She sensed they were up to something. She didn't like the secrecy of the chosen, and one or two of the inner sanctums around Bodhi seemed delighted with Brady's sons spreading the word that the UltraViolet™ was nothing special. They were excited by the prospect of the UltraViolet™, which was at odds with the Mahone Boys' theories. She pondered on this dichotomy.

Rhea looked at her watch and decided that she would think about this while she travelled to Florida.

She waited her turn to leave the Sattva Systems™ FusionPassengerJet™ on arrival at Cape Cassandra. The plane was full of Green tourists, as today was the largest payload ever transported into space. Many of these Green tourists were Sonic Boom Surfers here for the most giant wave in history. Tia Cassandra had been allowed to take whatever she could to Mars - as long as she had completed this before the end of the year. Therefore, she was going to exploit this to its limits.

It was a way of working which suited Bodhi. He wasn't interested in possessions or even the intellectual talent. He was only concerned with keeping to his own one-hundred-year plan - everything else was an interruption or a distraction. He had used this tactic in the significant dealings leading up to the Revolution - his rivals couldn't believe the generosity of this gentle man. He also used this in lesser events, as in the Christmas offerings to Brady Mahone by his Mother, Libby Skye - except that she had tried to cheat Brady. It was the ultimate sin in Bodhi's eyes - she behaved like a Trad would when given the same instructions.

Tia didn't greet many people in person, she usually far too busy, but she made an exception for Rhea. 'Welcome, Special Agent Rhea Laidlaw. What news do you have from the other side of the tracks?' Tia said this as in the phrase as if she had precisely chosen it. Rhea always liked the precision of this giant of old tech.

Rhea hugged her and smiled, 'Who'd have thought it would have come to this when we thought we had Sattva Systems™ on the ropes almost a hundred years ago.'

Tia said, 'At least we are still alive and still have skin in the game. He is my rival - not my enemy. I don't mind being beaten by the better opponent. I'll just have to do better in the next game.' She paused, 'What's he planning?'

'He's going to cut you all adrift. There will certainly be no comms, and I suspect the infrastructure of your space missions will be dismantled. He wants you to be gone - and stay gone.'

'I'm not surprised. I was the last person he wanted to see again from the old days. If it wasn't for the fact his self-replicating nanobots and enzymes were threatening the whole planet by attacking my space materials, he would have left us there in the desert. I understand his rationale.' She looked at Rhea and smiled, 'What's his end date?'

'No later than the New Year, maybe even before the Centenary celebrations on 25 June. - sorry.'

'Walk with me. I want you to see this.'

Rhea had seen rockets before, but none the size of this. 'Are you sure it can even get off the ground?'

Tia said, 'I have to say I admire his technology. If we had joined forces, there's no telling what we could have achieved in the old world. The NanoSuits™ have transformed our astronaut's experience on the planet - all we need to do is provide oxygen - and even that in far smaller quantities than we could ever have envisaged. It's a shame he doesn't want to stay in touch because we have already developed their FusionPowered™ SpaceSatts™ with our Super-Fast-Data Laser delivery system. The time-lapse in comms has been reduced from minutes to seconds.'

'I'm planning to keep in touch - until they discover the comms link.' She paused before asking, 'I want you to do me a favour.'

'Go on.'

'I want you to take Fleet Captain Marjorie Hampton with you. She will be useful to your project, and she was my Military Intelligence source from the old days.'

'Agreed. I never turn my back on talent.'

'And I want to have a couple of reserve slots for last-minute applications. There will be little time for you to vet them. I need you to trust me. If you see my personal authorisation...'

'I can do that.'

Rhea always liked the decisiveness of Tia - time was a resource too precious to waste - a feature she had in common with Bodhi. 'I have some better news.'

Tia laughed, 'I'm always in the market for good news from our celebrity reporter. What is it?'

'Take whatever you can. When he said there was nothing off the table, he meant it. I've known him long enough to know that his word is of utmost importance to him and his followers. He will not trick you. If anybody tries to cheat you - *they* will be punished - not you.'

Tia laughed, 'It's gone to his head - I've seen it before with some of the old tech moguls - he's got himself a fluffy little God complex.'

Rhea thought that maybe Tia could be accused at the time, especially as she was designing a whole planet in her own image. She looked at the enormous FusionSpaceShuttle™, which was about six times larger than any flown before. Even though this was technically Tia's mission, the livery was still in the Sattva Systems™ cream with a giant Sattva *S* in moss green. It seemed that even if Bodhi Sattva had no interest in Mars, he was still going to leave his brand on the planet. Rhea knew the NanoRepair™ coatings wouldn't allow it to be redesigned at a later date. The Ceramic outer shell of the vehicle glistened dully against the storm clouds in the Florida sky. She said, 'What have you got in there?'

Tia laughed, 'I thought you'd never ask. I have a complete FusionTrain™ engine. I'm pushing the FusionRockets™ to the limits.' She explained, 'In the lower atmosphere and rocky terrain, a railroad network will be immensely useful. What's more, there are no inhabitants on Mars, which means no planning permission, neighbourhood protests and no need to bribe corrupt politicians. The only limits will be our imagination.'

'Aren't you concerned that the rocket launch might fail - y'know, explode under the strain.'

'Of course. It will be a massive setback. However, I believe in my heroes. If anybody can make it work, then Commander Rocky Fitzpatrick can do it.' She stood with her arms folded proudly. She had the demeanour of a woman who assumed success until failure made her reassess. 'I know we are probably too close. What do you think?'

Rhea sensed her consternation and remembered that Tia had little experience of NanoSuits™. She said, 'Imagine your feet reach hundreds of feet into the ground. This will give you the stability of rock. Don't be alarmed if you see some of the tourists literally flying past you - they will rest on the surface until the shockwave blasts them away - the Green tourists call it Sonic Boom Surfing.' She watched Tia concentrate as the countdown began. 'Are you ready?'

'Yes. I'm ready.' She smiled at Rhea and then turned her head to take in her view of the launch. The first small shock waves of the primer sub-sonic booms pulsed past them. The Green tourists wobbled and cheered. Tia looked down at the ground and looked impressed. Then a massive boom rumbled and whooshed, and crowds of whooping and hollering Green tourists were flung far and wide. Tia watched them land heavily and even crashed onto jagged rocks, but not one was in the slightest bit injured. She assessed this usefulness on the Martian surface.

The giant rocket seemed to barely leave the ground. For a moment, it seemed as likely that it would fall as rise. Another massive sub-sonic blast ripped across the land, and the Green tourists had quickly got to their feet again in time to ride the next wave. Rhea laughed at the antics of the tourists, but Tia's attention had turned to the fate of the lift-off. The rocket rose glacially, but it was now heading in the right direction, and then the final sub-sonic surge, the loudest there had ever been or would ever be heard on Earth. The rocket surged upwards at breakneck speed. She knew the NanoStructure™ would survive the outward trajectory through the Earth's atmosphere and beyond into space. Tia cheered and shouted, 'Dagny, we did it.'

Tia said, 'I can't wait to turbo-charge the Martian Project. We are the new pioneers.'

'I imagine there are going to be huge challenges...'

'I know. It's going to be marvellous - we are going to be pushed to the limits of human endurance, but also, we will continuously learn and achieve. What are these Greens going to do with their Heaven on Earth?'

Rhea laughed, 'Enjoy it. I think that's it.'

Tia said, 'I would have little use for these Green drones with their low-level labour and idle dreams. Give me the strivers and the heroes - they are welcome to the leftovers.' She looked at Rhea, 'I know you have much to do down here, but there is a place for you if you want to join us.'

Rhea stroked her chin and gave the offer serious thought. 'We need to keep our spirit flickering on Earth. We don't deserve to be forgotten - I won't let it happen.'

Tia clasped Rhea's shoulders and said, 'Good for you.'

12: THE WINNER IS.

Brady's sons had returned from far and wide to hear the results of the competition. As they landed at their Malibu home, they couldn't have failed to see the gleaming PassengerFusionJet™ in pride of place in the Mahone Vehicle Parking Lot. Soon, one of his sons would take ownership of it.

Amie had received the sales figures from Hunter, who no longer felt the need to hide his close association with Bodhi. In the start-up years of his business, sales figures were as simple as how many Files had Brady sold, but handing over the reins to the accountants at Sattva Systems™ meant there were spreadsheets and weighting allowances on many different types of sales - from freebies to pre-orders and series commitments. If he let Amie do the analysis, she could at least deal with the queries if one of his boys decided to challenge his decision. Brady thought of Mary-Lou and her cataloguing ideas at the beginning of his business journey and how Amie must have inherited her analytical mind.

Soon the Malibu home was full of noise and laughter as the back-slapping sons greeted each other and tried to suss out who was the most likely winner. They were welcomed lovingly by their Maddies Amie and Helgarth, and Brady's staffers dealt efficiently with their whims. They had guessed that the competition announcement would take place in the evening, but Brady always kept his boys on their toes, and the winner would be announced at the buffet. He wanted this to be an informal and fun affair and not sitting around a table as a bunch of businessmen at a meeting.

He called his boys together, along with Amie, Helgarth and Lucy-Ian. He felt the loss of Raelynn not being here - she had become a favourite to him in recent times, but she was happily ensconced in San Martin with Tyrone, and the thought of the two lovebirds added to his sense of joy of today. He had taken the precaution of taking Bill to one side - as he was the eldest - and asked him to ensure that the result was final and that when it was announced, he wanted the others to accept this graciously and cheer the winner whole-heartedly. He confirmed that he didn't know who'd won, and as a carrot, he put out the prospect of new competitions if this one was a success. Bill understood, and Brady watched him work the room.

Amie tapped a cut-crystal glass repeatedly with a silver spoon to bring the room to order. She handed Brady an envelope like an old-fashioned award ceremony. Brady thought that Libby Skye, his Mother, and the previous owner of this home, would have approved. He strode to the head of the gathering and said, 'You've all done remarkably well - many of you smashed your targets. You rock, boys.' They cheered Brady and each other. 'The reason we are doing this early, today, is because the winner is going to fly us to a place in their territory. I have five of my favourite Reps on standby to greet us, and when I have announced the winner, I will Satt™ them, and we'll head straight on over.' Brady deliberately took his time and built up the tension like a game show host from the old days. 'When we get there, I will do a meet and greet and hand out a few free samples while you enjoy yourselves. You've earned a break.' He looked around his hushed audience. Amie looked out of the window as she had noticed each of Brady's sons had searched her facial expressions for clues. Lucy-Ian and Helgarth joined her, and each held her hand.

Brady announced loudly, 'And the winner is...Troy with 4.3 million accredited sales.'

The boys cheered. If they had reservations, then they didn't show it, as they knew they had the chance of winning many other competitions to come. Troy walked up to Brady and received his congratulatory hug from his Pops. Brady shouted, 'Get your bags packed, we are going to the Green Quartiere Aurelio in Rome, Italy. My old friend Marco will ensure we are well looked after. Now let's put Troy's new FusionPassengerJet™ through its paces. I'll have the staff bring your things.'

As Troy wandered back to his brothers - clutching his envelope - Bill had planned a surprise from the others. The four boys rushed Troy and lifted him high in the air and carried him like pallbearers all the way through the grounds of their Malibu home and all the way to the steps leading up to his private jet. Troy welcomed everyone on board and thanked his Pops again as he was the last one passenger. To Brady, this recalled some of the old stag parties he used to go to when one of his criminal buddies used to fall for the idea of going straight and settling down - it never used to last long, but the stag parties were fun. None of the girls was accompanying them to Rome.

Brady sat at the rear of the FusionPassengerJet™ and took a back seat in the raucous conversations the boys were having. He didn't know why he felt disappointed in their sales tactics. Brady had always given free samples to the children to win over hearts and minds and then homed in on one woman to sleep with later in the day - it felt like a reward for his good works. *I'm not going to do this tomorrow. I need to set the boys a good example.* His sons were telling ever more grotesque stories about orgies, but even more concerning to Brady was the crossing over the gender lines to greedily exploit every pleasure conceivable from these days and nights of debauchery. They shamelessly told of only targeting the attractive Greens for free samples, and that giving out free samples to the elderly or the young, was just a complete waste of product. He noticed that Troy didn't pilot the vehicle long as these conversations enamoured him more than his new toy.

The boys were still in high spirits by the time they landed at Green Quartiere Aurelio. Brady told them to go and settle in while he dealt with Marco. He knew they were already planning to re-enact the roles of the ancient Roman Emperors. He thought uncomfortably of John Kane playing Emperor Tiberius in his sickening movie production. He also thought of Archie, his Foster Pops, and this both sickened and saddened him. He shook himself out of his reverie. *There's no point in doing all this for my boys just to end up being the party-pooper. I just gotta let them have their fun.*

Marco greeted him. 'Hello, my old friend, Brady. It's been many years - much too long.'

'Hi, Marco. How's it hanging?'

'It's good. Very good. Your boy Troy - he works very hard to win. I like him.'

Brady said, 'I'm pleased to hear that.'

Marco ushered Brady to his FusionCar™, 'Come, come. We have a lot planned for tomorrow. You honour us with bringing all of your sons, but you reward us mostly with your own visitation.'

Brady said, 'I want to choose a place to give away lots of free samples, but I don't want to cause any bad feelings.'

'You can trust me. What is it you request?'

'There's a funny named place, or rather there used to be - it's called St Peter's Basil...'

'St Peter's Basilica, yes, yes...why?'

'I'm still a Trad, and someone told me a story once, about that was where some of the fiercest battles against the Greens took place - you don't have to tell anybody why I chose it...'

Marco looked at him from his position as the driver before returning his eyes to the road. 'It's only been a hundred years, friend, they will know - but don't you concern yourself, I will arrange it for you. Is there anything else I can do for you?'

'Yes. I want lots of children to be present. Let it be known that I am only giving away kids' samples tomorrow.'

Marco looked troubled but didn't say anything further on the subject of children. Instead, he asked, 'Do you need a companion for this evening?'

Brady smiled, 'Normally, that would be a given, but tonight I want to set a good example for my boys.'

'Good for you. I'd better not let you know what Troy has planned for his brothers then - it might make your hair go curly.' Marco laughed. 'What are you going to do instead?'

'I'm going to walk the area and get a feel for the place.'

'There's not a lot to see that you couldn't see everywhere else in Italy. It is but meadow and vineyard. There are no traces of trad existence any longer - sorry, my friend.'

Brady nodded, but he wasn't going to amend his plans. 'If you could drive me there and maybe give me an hour to myself and then pick me up later - that would be cool.'

They drove in relative silence to the site where St Peter's Square used to be, and Marco dropped Brady off in this deserted space. The Greens didn't visit the area in case they were being viewed as overtly nostalgic. This was strictly forbidden, whereas Brady's Entertainment products were a more furtive pastime and therefore seemed to be semi-permitted or overlooked if not overtly allowed. Brady had little knowledge of this almost sacred space. He had no more insight into the Catholic Church's hierarchy as he would on Islam or Buddhism - but he did understand that the old Trads used to put a lot of store in special places - even if it was sports arenas in many of his criminal buddies' instances. He wouldn't have realised that he was now standing on the same ground as where the Pope would give his Papal addresses to the faithful. Brady might have added a religious dimension to his sudden state of deep thinking about his journey to here and his current circumstances if he had.

He ambled through the old grounds of St Peter's Basilica, and he thought of all the treasures which had dissolved and seeped back into the ground. He equated it to losing his Malibu home with its own artworks on the wall - bought with John Kane's wealth and Libby Skye's taste and considered this a waste. He would never have been able to comprehend the drop in the ocean of his own art collection compared to the hundreds of thousands of priceless treasures housed here. Now there was nothing but long grass and weeds.

HUNTER WAS THE ONE person who shook Brady out of his one-hundred-year dream state. His accusations of Deceiver and Corrupter felt like a religious key driven through his flesh and unlocking his heart. It felt like a spiritual assault. He could have batted off and rationalised any physical assault on him, but he had a deep sense of injustice about Hunter's tirade. Brady continued his walk and headed to where he thought the first GreenShell™ had been erected within days of the Green Revolution. He imagined being a pious Trad being confronted by this almost supernatural force.

Tyrone's story came back to him vividly. He imagined all the holy people using the power of prayer to destroy this invisible Green wall. And the ordinary folk would have pounded at it with their fists or clawed at it with their fingernails. His Pops would have been convinced this was an alien invasion and he would have told everybody around him how he was right all along. *Pops woulda liked that.* Others would have claimed that this was the End of Days. *They woulda been damn right about that.*

Brady guessed the breakthrough moment would have come when somebody in the crowd decided that the most Holy of relics should be looted and used against this implacable enemy.

Brady was lost in this adventure - he was the hero, fighting off the defenders of the treasure to get his hands on holy swords, daggers and spears, and Brady would be victorious and head back to the Vatican City walls with his weapons. Priests and nuns would gather around Brady, putting their most heartfelt prayers into the holy armaments which Brady retrieved. And Brady would raise them high and plunge them into the GreenShell™ and destroy them and bring down the walls. Except...he knew what would have really happened.

He would have stabbed and flung them at the wall as uselessly as the Hodgson Boys throwing their rocks at Mrs Wilson's car. He wondered what he might have done next. *I wouldn't have slumped to my knees; that would be admitting defeat - and Brady ain't no loser. I woulda held my head up and walked right outta there. I woulda left the others to their crying and wailing.*

A crow flew past and cawed at Brady. He shouted, 'Shut the fuck up.' He usually loved animals and birds, but he irrationally felt that this bird was taunting him. It had also lost him his train of thought. *I'm guessing Bodhi only gets interrupted by doves, but me, let's just say I know when I'm being set up.* He was a criminal, he was always paranoid about being played, but Brady's paranoia had only increased since he involved Bodhi and his team in the making of his will. The doubts gnawed at him. He used his quiet time to think deeply about what they had in store for him. As he wandered back to St Peter's Square, he was ever more convinced that the end of Bodhi's one-hundred-year plan could only bring him bad news for his business. He was sure he had signed his life away, but he couldn't figure out how and why. He was late for his rendezvous with Marco, but that didn't trouble Brady. He knew Marco would wait all night for him to return if required. Brady was troubled, angry even, but he only had one strategy in his armoury, and that was to play it cool.

The following morning, Brady returned to St Peter's Square, but this time in a FusionCoach™ driven by Marco, and his five sons were fellow passengers. Brady looked at the wrecked visages of his boys and joked, 'It appears that none of you had your Green beauty sleep last night.'

Troy said blearily, 'We had to celebrate, Pops.'

'Yeah, whatever. I don't need the gory details. Just pay attention and watch the master at work.'

As they pulled up into the spot where the St Peter's Square used to be, Brady was dismayed at the paltry size of the crowd. There appeared to be no more than forty children accompanied by their parents. Brady growled, 'What's this, Marco? Are you trying to show me up in front of my boys?'

'No. Honestly. It was your request to bring only children. There aren't many kids. They cost so much money to raise - it's the temporary hyper-inflationary Green credit increases - only the exceptionally hard-working and dedicated can afford to raise children. Some of these people have travelled for hours...'

'Ok. I get it.' Brady shouted to the boys. 'I asked for only kids to attend, y'know the children are our future and all that crap. Is it the same everywhere? Y'know, hardly any kids?'

They all nodded and uttered, 'Yeah.'

Bill added. 'That's why none of us is in a hurry to give you Grandkids, Pops - they cost a fucking fortune.'

Brady shook his head. 'Ok. Forget that for now. I just want you to know that this is why we've got a small crowd.'

Troy said, assuming he had to in this situation as technically the host, 'No problem, Pops. Everybody here knows how much your customers love you.'

They all traipsed out of the FusionCoach™ and whatever the sons had been taking last night weakened them so much that they seemed withered by the sunlight. Brady smiled ruefully as he watched his boys stagger behind him. The small crowd cheered as loudly as they could to make Brady feel welcomed. They also put on a show of gratitude for the products, hopefully, rare and sought after, that he might shower upon their children. Brady played to the crowd. He picked up the youngest ones and talked to them just like the old days when kids used to traipse along to see Santa Claus in his grotto. Brady smiled, as he would have been shoplifting while everybody was distracted.

He gave them fistfuls of children's entertainment products, as he had brought along enough to satisfy a much larger gathering. Some parents proudly proclaimed that these were the first BMEE products in their child's lives, and it meant so much to them that the great Brady Mahone had given them to their young ones personally.

It touched Brady when one young girl he picked up and flung into the air before catching her safely squealed with delight and said, 'Thank you for my lovely present. I love you, Brady Mahone.'

He answered, 'I love you too, sweetheart. What's your name, little one?'

'My name is Sofia.'

'That's such a pretty name for a beautiful little girl.' He looked at the parents but said to Sofia, 'Do you want your Moms and Pops to pick you some more from my samples' case?'

'What's Moms and Pops?'

Sofia's parents looked with consternation, fearing that Brady might be offended. Brady smiled, 'What do you call them?' He pointed at her parents.

'They are my Mappas.'

Brady laughed, 'Why, of course, they are. Silly old Brady.'

'Silly old Brady.' Sofia teased. Her parents laughed with relief as they picked through his sample case and picked out the most popular entertainment products for Green Italian children.

13: THE SERMON AND DISCOVERY

S amuel Beardon the Third was working on his final sermon before his own private UltraViolet™ ceremony. Across the globe, just over 26.5 million others would take part on Friday, 25 June 2184 - it was nicknamed Green Friday - but he was chosen to represent one of the thirteen commandments at Bodhi Sattva's personal invitation. It was both an honour and a curse because the twelve knew - and only the twelve - why the thirteenth was missing.

His sermon was on the gratitude for the life of good health which God had given them.

Alicia came into his room at the Beardon home. 'Dinner will be ready soon - it's one of Shako's traditional recipes.'

'Thank you, daughter. I shall be along shortly. The Good Lord provides for us all.'

'I'm guessing that's the theme for your sermon. You always talk about the theme before the day. I guess it's your way of mentally getting into the role.'

'I suppose it is - and for His guidance may he make me eternally grateful.' He laughed to indicate he was joking with her. He stood up and went downstairs with Alicia. He wasn't surprised to hear that Tyrone and Raelynn had taken a packed lunch out with them. They only seemed to want to be exclusively in each other's company.

The lunch was a pleasant affair, as everybody speculated on what the unique functions of the UltraViolet™ might be. Samuel knew but was sworn to secrecy. He wasn't going to throw away one hundred years of work and servitude now. All around the table had qualified for the early adoption of the UltraVioletSuit™, and he hoped the administrative error would soon be straightened out for Tyrone. He was saddened that Raelynn would be missing out, he had grown to like her, but hopefully, this relationship would run itself out in due course - six months is a long time in new love.

Many of the guesses of what the new Suit™ could do were wide of the mark, which made the Bear laugh at inappropriate moments. However, some came very close and fearful he might give the game away, he laughed at these also, but then he double-checked the expressions of his fellow diners to ensure he had kept the secret secure. He also listened sadly, but not outwardly so, to stories of the other San Martin residents' frustration at having to wait until the New Year to receive theirs. This had never happened before, but it was put down to Bodhi being ill all those years ago, and that this had pushed the final date back by these crucial six months.

Then there was the bitter talk among some of the residents that Brady's son, Bill Mahone, had been going around, telling anybody who would listen that the UltraVioletSuits™ were a load of horseshit and wouldn't do anything but add a slightly protective gloss on everything. And being Bill Mahone, who was in the know, and he had all the previous Suits™ himself, this seemed plausible. There was much talk of him doing brisk business for the Brady Mahone Entertainment Enterprises. They also speculated on why Bill Mahone hadn't stayed for very long in San Martin until Alicia gave the definitive answer, 'Debrock and his cronies have taken their stash of weed to Malibu.'

This was before Samuel Beardon the Third was informed that Brady Mahone had taken all his hoodlum sons to visit the Vatican City, of all places. He was deeply affronted by this knowledge, but like everything else in this last year of the hundred-year plan, he had to treat it as a test of his faith in God and in his chosen one, Bodhi Sattva. He resolved to ride out the bumpy road of his emotional highway. He knew for sure that more tests would follow and that the Lord would test Samuel Beardon the Third to his limits. He was also confident that he would have the fortitude to succeed.

After the dining table had been cleared, Samuel returned to his room to complete his sermon. He had to finish it quickly as his Disciple Rhea Laidlaw needed to check it, even if this meant delivering it to her at night. She was busy and had many meetings to attend in the next few days meaning she would miss the sermon. There was too much at stake to let Samuel stray from the message either in words or tone. Before he left, he got down on his knees and prayed for God to give him strength. He went to check on Tyrone, he went into his room, but there was no sign of either Tyrone or Raelynn.

Samuel Beardon meandered through the quiet streets of San Martin and breathed in the fresh night air. He remembered the old days of smog, frequent forest fires and other climate catastrophes, and these recollections restored his faith. He was in a relaxed frame of mind when Rhea greeted him. She was still in her office working through her backlog of administrative duties.

'Hello, Samuel. How are you holding up?'

'I cannot lie to you - it's difficult. At the dawn of the Green Revolution, I had to harden my mind to the Traditional Cultures - and I did, with the help of Almighty God. But I found that easier to do because the planet was at risk by letting them survive and multiply. However, I'm struggling to grasp the reasoning behind this.'

Rhea nodded and looked at him sadly. 'It seems to me that the only things you have are your belief in Bodhi Sattva and the science...'

'I've always been a man of faith.'

'Ok. Has Bodhi ever not told the truth or broken his word?'

Samuel thought about his Father and Grandfather, he also thought about John Kane, and then he thought about Brady Mahone and how he unravelled the dark truths connecting them all. There had been times, long ago when he wondered if Bodhi could have had his Father killed in prison, but then he gave in to the reasoning that one person isn't worth more than the planet itself, and his Father, Samuel Beardon the Second, might have stopped the Revolution happening. But this still didn't sit right with his other version of Bodhi in his mind that he was the Son of God. It also seemed queer that the person who revealed this truth was a criminal in the form of Brady Mahone.

Rhea watched the struggle play out in Samuel's face. She said, 'If you didn't agree with the plan, and you wanted to stop it, would anybody listen?'

'Bodhi has spoken. It will be done. With or without a mere NanoSprayer™ called Samuel. I would leave a daughter without her Father.'

'Traditional Cultures with their armies and weapons couldn't stop the GreenRevs. Have you found a way to defeat them - a chink in their NanoArmour™?'

'No. Of course not. I am a humble servant of God.'

'What would your God want you to do?'

Samuel smiled, 'Ah, my friend. Now you've got to the heart of my problem. I do not know His plan. I believe I have been chosen, but in believing this, I feel utterly selfish.'

She took his sermon from him and read it through. 'This is fine. Consider it authorised.' She added, cryptically, 'If your mind troubles you, then maybe your mind can't be trusted. I would suggest that when the time comes to choose a side, then I suggest you follow your heart instead.' She pulled out another ledger and returned to her work. 'I'll see you at the UltraViolet™ ceremony. You have a good night, Samuel Beardon the Third.'

Samuel traipsed back home worrying about having revealed his doubts to one of Bodhi Sattva's most trusted advisers but also, considered whether she had shared with him her own reservations. He pondered on how she would have reacted if he had proposed an alternative course of action.

When he entered his home, the place was quiet. All its residence, Shako and her family, and his daughter Alicia had gone to bed, ready to get their three hours sleep. He didn't want to disturb anybody, so he crept quietly up the stairs to his bedroom. He heard laughter coming from Tyrone's room. It didn't sound like the kind of laughter between an intimate couple. It sounded like something from long ago - it sounded like they were watching TV. He listened with his ear pressed against the door. He could make out muffled sounds and then something that sounded like an explosion. It wasn't noisy because the volume was low. Samuel knew that they would turn this off if he knocked on the door, so he took a deep breath and marched in.

He saw the two lovers sitting entwined in an embrace and the unmistakeable flashing images on the Sattva Systems™ computer screen. 'What is the meaning of this? How could you?' He sobbed, 'Why? After everything I have ever said.'

Tyrone said, 'You can't just barge into my room like this. I deserve some privacy.'

Raelynn said, 'We aren't doing anything wrong.'

Samuel looked at one of the scattered entertainment Files. He examined it, but was careful not to touch it. The snake was the first thing to catch his eye, as it was captured twisting through the capital yellow letters on the black background. The letters were BMEE. Samuel knew what this File was, but it took a moment to work out what they stood for, and then he remembered. *Brady Mahone Entertainment Enterprises*. He pointed at Raelynn, 'You did this. I should have banished you the moment you got your claws into my nephew.'

Raelynn said disbelievingly, 'Me! I didn't even like old Science Fiction TV shows until...'

Tyrone interrupted, 'They're mine. I've had them for years, and all my science friends love them. Brady offered, and I took him up on it. Xe has given me some great titles over the years - because xe is my best friend.' Samuel was sobbing like a baby. Tyrone continued, 'It's no big deal. There's no point behaving this hysterically over us watching a TV programme together.'

Samuel took a deep breath. 'You're right. There is no point - now.' He marched out and slammed the door behind him. Alicia came out of her room to see what was happening, and others popped their heads around the bedroom doors. 'What's happened, Daddy?'

'Tyrone has been dealing with Brady and buying his entertainment products from him.' He heard crying, and he saw Shako shaking her head with tears streaming down her lined Native American face.

Alicia was stunned. 'It's Bodhi's fault. He should never have made you stay so close to Brady.'

Samuel Beardon the Third held his daughter, 'No. It's my doing. I should have let the past die with the rest of the Trads. If I hadn't been so obsessed with the death of my Father, I would never have had any dealings with Brady Mahone.'

14: HAZY DAYS OF SUMMER

Whenever the ceremonies took place to launch a new instalment of a GreenSuit™, it became something akin to a superstitious ritual for Brady to base himself at the Mahone Ranch. There had been seven at various intervals in the last hundred years, and this year was supposed to be the eighth, and intriguingly, the final upgrade.

In the past, he had always detected the colour of the upgrade within the Shells™ surrounding the Green areas. But now everywhere was Green, the sky adopted the glow. The new colouring only lasted a few hours, and Brady sometimes thought he was the only one who could see it.

Intuitively, he believed the existence of the Trads was dissolved and buried in the ground, but the NanoShells™ were recycled into the atmosphere as if they were protecting the skies from intruders. This was the kind of conspiracy theory his Pops would have loved, but now it might have a grain of truth in it, especially as there was life on another planet now that Tia Cassandra and her pioneers had colonised Mars.

He recalled how strange it was on the last two ceremonies when the night sky turned a hazy blue and then to violet, respectively. It was as if day and night had been temporarily fused. He was curious to see the effect when they conducted their ceremonies for the UltraViolet™.

Brady had done his reconnaissance of McFarland, and although there were a few lucky ones who were to receive the UltraViolet™ early, he was surprised to learn that Lizzie, Siddha and Cain had been specially selected to receive theirs at a separate ceremony in Boulder Creek. Brady knew in his gut that this had meaning, and his criminal paranoia made him sure that they were plotting against him. Even when Siddha pretended to be his friend, he never fell for it, and Lizzie never hid her contempt for him. However, Cain had a persona that made him hard to dislike - it still didn't mean that he trusted him.

While walking around the grounds of the Mahone Ranch, seeking out the best viewing spot, he searched out his memories from a century ago to see if the ceremony was held in June that year. He remembered escaping Ridgecrest with his buddy, Lucian. He also recalled that it was a day or so before the GreenShell™ appeared in McFarland - the Shell™ which cut the town of McFarland in half, either side of Highway 99. It didn't matter now, but he deduced that this was when the Green townsfolk were at their most vulnerable. They were without their NanoShells™ for a couple of days, and they were without their RedSuits™ for six whole months. *No wonder they were so scared of me.* These recollections confirmed what he was thinking - that tonight was the first midsummer ceremony and that all the others took place on their New Green Year Day.

The barn caught his eye, and with the excitement of youth belying his one-hundred and forty-two years, he scrambled up on the sloping roof and lay back and gazed into the heavens. It was late, but the Sun hadn't long set. He checked his FusionWatch™ and its luminous green display lit up with the information that it was the 25 June 2184 and 23:45. He thought it was mildly amusing that it was 2345. Brady thought that it was good planning to make it a Saturday. He liked the idea that this was a weekend.

Tyrone always came into his mind when he looked at the night sky, and he had a few moments to kill before the McFarland ceremony commenced. Tyrone had been waxing lyrical on something called a triple conjunction, so he thought he would try and find it. He recalled him saying something about Saturn and its rings - Brady recalled this more from the mention of rings because of his old business of jewellery heists. The one he did remember clearly was the red glow of Mars as this was more interesting now that he knew that people were living on that tiny dot in space, the third one he couldn't remember, but Tyrone had said that it was like the Star of Bethlehem that the three kings followed to the birth of Jesus, and even Brady could recall that old Christmas Carol. After scanning the heavens, he found the three bright dots in the unpolluted night sky - he found them mildly interesting but nowhere near as spectacular a sight as Tyrone had made them out to be. He looked at his watch again, just as the display flicked over to 23:59. He cast his gaze to the skies above McFarland.

Nothing happened at first. He kept his gaze fixed. For the briefest moment, everything went black, and then the whole sky appeared transparent and clear. It was the most remarkable sight he had seen in years. The sky was as clear as day, but the moon, stars and the planets were still visible. It wasn't just over McFarland. The effect stretched to all horizons. As far as Brady was concerned, this may have lacked the pyrotechnics of a Fourth of July firework display from the old days, but it was nonetheless a fantastic show of power.

Brady watched the skies for about twenty minutes until the transparent effect began to fade, and streaks of the inky black skies started to seep back through. For a moment, he wondered when the Greens were going to get their sleep tonight - it was way past their bedtimes.

He clambered back off the roof, got in his FusionCar™ and headed off to the celebrations. Their ceremonies bored him just like church services used to do, but he was in the mood to party, and maybe, he could find out what was so special about these new UltraVioletSuits™.

McFarland wasn't the party palace he imagined when he got there. He wandered through the crowds, and yes, there was a lot of Greens commenting on the transparent skies - which confirmed that he wasn't unique in observing this phenomenon - but many were quietly grumbling about favouritism, nepotism, and cronyism. It struck him that there didn't seem to be any Security Protocols™ interfering with the discussion. He had learned over the years what he could get away with saying, but some of the remarks he picked up on were being left unchallenged. There were gripes about the older generation and their constant droning on about the Green Revolution and how apparently *bad* everything was before. The so-called Pure Greens - those born post-Revolution however, had never experienced living in the world of the Traditional Cultures, and they were grumbling about how that way of life sounded like a lot more fun than working every day in the fields.

Already Brady was struck by how nobody was paying any attention to him. It seemed that Brady Mahone and his entertainment products were way down on their lists of priorities. *I don't blame 'em. They wouldn't have been enough for me when I was younger. I woulda wanted to party, drink, have a good time and even do a bit of hellraising. I wasn't the kinda guy to stay stuck in my room watching a movie. What did Bodhi expect to happen? No wonder the kids are getting into sex and dabs - they are the nearest things that pass for living in this boring Green world.*

He listened in, discreetly to the raised voices of the younger Green generation. They questioned the idea of Heaven on Earth and how Bodhi's idea of heaven was for them to live forever in their place of work - it was still work, even if the bosses called it heaven. One of them shouted, challenging the Security Protocols™, 'I'd rather be free than to work my fingers to the bone for your fucking heaven, Bodhi fucking Sattva!' This drew gasps and laughter from his friends but frowns and mutterings of disgust from the older Greens.

One of the original GreenRevs came over to challenge him. 'There would be no Earth, never mind Heaven on Earth if it wasn't for the bravery and sacrifice of our fighters.'

He was cut down with a simple, 'Fuck off.'

As he walked away, Brady laughed at the altercation. He listened to other conversations, and not all were quite so negative, but there was still a palpable sense of distrust. Many were speculating on the meaning behind all this. He wondered if the lack of Cain, Siddha and Lizzie's presence had sparked the unrest, but then his thoughts turned closer to home, and this attitude wasn't as unusual as it appeared.

He thought of Debrock and his large gang of hangers-on, high on dabs, and they came from one of the most pious Green spaces on Earth, San Martin, with the Bear as its preacher - even Tyrone would rather spend all his time with Raelynn, who he had helped raise, than with Samuel and Alicia. For a moment he laughed at the thought of Bodhi's project unravelling, but this was quickly replaced with a feeling he hadn't had for precisely one hundred years to the day.

Brady vividly recalled the Modern Ridgecrest Supermax Penitentiary, the memories of the smells of sweat and defeat, and the moment everybody thought that Guard Askew had loosened his grip by allowing everybody into the Communal Area to have the gift - the little luxury - of watching TV. He replayed the carnage which followed and the piles of dead inmates. He had that same sense of overwhelming caution now as he did then.

Bodhi doesn't lose his grip; this is deliberate.

Brady needed information.

He searched the crowds for the most likely of the recipients of the UltraViolet™. Brady spotted Rowena, or was it Woodrow, Mrs

Wilson's Grand-whatever. Her YellowSuit™ had a female appearance, 'Hey, Rowena. Have you had the UltraViolet™?'

She looked at him suspiciously, 'Yes.'

'Does it do any new fancy tricks? Y'know like make you invisible or something like that...'

'I'm curious about your logic. What made you think of that?'

'It kinda made the sky disappear.'

She laughed, 'That actually makes sense - but no. The UltraViolet™ doesn't do tricks, as you quaintly put it.'

'It does something, though...' He wanted to see if she would give anything away without her realising, as it was evident that she was going to state precisely what the new qualities of the Suit™ were. 'Does it make you feel any different?'

Her hands slid down her body as if it was a pertinent question, 'No. I am the same as I was before.' She giggled at him as if she was teasing him.

'Nothing special then...'

'No. Same old me - same new me.' She added, 'I can't tell you more. Maybe, there's nothing to add. There's only one way to find out, and that's to try it yourself. But we both know that will never happen.' She strode away arrogantly. But as she did, Brady kept an eye on her, and she joined a group who Brady suspected were fellow recipients of the UltraViolet™ - they were the goody-two-shoes brigade of McFarland, and they all seemed like the cheerleaders and the jocks from his old high school days - and he despised those who thought they were so special - so Goddamned cool.

Beyond the self-selected special ones, he saw a familiar face dart away - he was obviously steering clear of him. Brady shouted, 'Hey, Vance!' *After all these years, you'd think the little creep would not be so fucking afraid of me. He's the one with all the fucking NanoArmour™*, he thought.

Vance pretended that he had only just seen Brady. 'Hey, Brady. Good to see you.' He lied.

'Can we talk somewhere quiet?'

'Sure thing.' He led Brady to a wooded area behind the New Green Town Hall, and the dry twigs crunched under Brady's boots. He made them both stop for a moment as he listened carefully for eavesdroppers. 'There's nobody here, Brady. Remember I've got enhanced hearing, I could hear someone breathing from fifty yards away - all I can pick up on are nocturnal mammals.'

'Have the Security Protocols™ stopped working?'

'No. But they've had their sensitivity settings widened. Now almost anything is allowed except murder or any kind of physical assault.'

'Why?'

Vance shrugged, 'Dunno, maybe a fault...'

'I don't believe that.' Vance looked away. His fingers were scratching on his thighs, and Brady knew he was hiding something. 'Look. I want information is all. Tell me what you know - or think you know. I'm not bothered if it makes me look bad...'

Vance sighed, 'There's been a lot of weird shit happening. It's kind of freaking everybody out.'

'When did it start?'

'I'd say from the beginning of this year.'

Brady shrugged, 'Probably just this hundred-year thing of Bodhi's...'

'It is.' Vance took a moment. He breathed in and out deeply a couple of times. 'Normally, we know years in advance what's happening with any Suit™ developments, but this year it's all been surrounded in secrecy. There's a sense that something bad will happen - some are even saying that we will be treated like the Trads.' Something in the way he said this relayed a sense of dread which he had never seen in a Green before.

'Welcome to my world.' Brady joked. He looked at Vance. 'Tell me.'

'I saw you watching the crowd of goys, which Rowena joined. They are the Devout of McFarland. Every Green town has them.'

'What makes them Devout?'

'They are the true believers in the Green Ideals of Sattva Systems™. They are the hardest workers...'

'Ok. Kinda makes sense to me. You've done well out of me when you've pulled in good sales figures. So, Bodhi looks after his high performers. Good for him.'

Vance flinched. 'There's something else they have in common, but it might just be a coincidence...'

'I don't believe in coincidences.'

'They are the only people who won't buy your entertainment products.'

Brady shrugged, 'No skin off my nose. Brady Mahone is doing well enough without 'em. It's their loss if you ask me.'

Vance said with false bravado. 'Too right, man. Fuck 'em. That's what I say.'

This didn't reassure Brady. Instead, it made him distrust Vance even more. 'What is everybody else saying about this? I heard them talking - they ain't happy.'

'It's who is happy which is freaking me out.'

'Who?'

'Siddha.'

'I don't get it. What's he got to do with this?'

'He's, my Disciple.'

'Yeah, whatever. So, what's making Siddha smile.'

'Your son, Bill.'

Brady was perplexed, 'You got me there. What's Bill got to do with this?'

'I don't want to speak out of turn, with Bill being...'

'For fucks sake, Vance, just tell me everything you know, then the quicker you can back to your geeky friends. If you annoy me, I'll tell you, ok?'

Vance said dejectedly. 'Bill came over, pushing us hard to shift your product. Siddha made a beeline to talk to him, but instead of dissuading him, he thought it was...funny. He encouraged him - that has never, ever happened before. He played Bill like a fiddle, and Bill was dancing to Siddha's tune...'

'I said to tell me - not to turn it into a fairy story. So, Siddha wanted more people to experience the superior products of the Brady Mahone Entertainment Enterprises.'

'Yes. Exactly. It felt like his goals were the same as yours. Which would be fine if it wasn't for the fact that you know, as well as I do, that he despises you.'

'What did Bill make of all this?'

'To tell you the truth, Brady, he was more concerned with the orgy his more grateful customers had laid on for him. He couldn't give a fuck about Siddha - but I know you do.'

'What else is there? What do your friends make of all this? I bet they've all got their conspiracy theories.'

'I'm sorry, Brady. I've spoken to the other Reps I know in the other areas, and they have similar ideas to me.'

'Go on.'

'I think there's something really fucking special about the UltraVioletSuits™, but there aren't enough to go around - that's why the Devout and the Disciples are being so secretive and smug about it. But worse than that is the theory about the selection process and what it means.' He shrugged, 'Do I have to spell it out, Brady?'

Brady nodded. 'Say it.'

'They've used you to select which ones are going to live longer and which ones are going to be left to die. By self-selecting to use the services of Brady Mahone Entertainment Enterprises, we have chosen to forego a life-extending or life-enhancing upgrade. We have given in to the temptation of nostalgia for the Traditional Cultures, we have allowed ourselves to be corrupted, and you are the Tempter, the Deceiver, and the Corrupter. I don't believe that, of course, it's just the word on the streets.' Vance added belatedly, 'I'm sorry, man.'

'It's ok. Don't worry. I can't get my head around the implications of what you've just told me. I'm gonna have to let it sink in.'

15: THIS IS YOUR CAPTAIN SPEAKING

A couple of days came and went at the Mahone Ranch as Brady considered his next move. He had been on an emotional roller-coaster, but now he was calm. He trawled his mind for the best people to approach to find out exactly what was being planned. He even considered asking Bodhi outright what his plan was, but he knew he would get half-truths and platitudes from him. If he could, he would have loved to have consulted with Rhea, but she was expert at evading him. He went through the list of all the people he was close to or had a decent working relationship with, and he selected a suitable candidate to start his investigations.

He tried to work out what the play was. Brady focused on what he had to lose - it seemed like the most logical place to start. He had his business and his Green credits - his first thought had been a heist, or maybe Sattva Systems™ would have a more generous word for it - like a corporate takeover. This made sense to Brady. Wouldn't it be a good ploy to ruin his reputation with his customer base, thereby making his business worthless, and then buying it up on the cheap, with the wonderful Bodhi declaring that Brady Mahone Business Enterprises was now in good hands now that the discredited Brady Mahone had been removed. He deduced that a name change for the business would quickly follow.

Having considered this carefully, he was still uneasy about the threats to the existence of the ordinary Greens - it seemed heavy-handed, and he was sure there were other ways of discrediting him without causing this amount of discontent within the Green ranks.

He knew the Greens were spoilt brats and that they would bitch and moan if they weren't getting their new toys before the other kids. *Why didn't Bodhi just give the Suits™ to everybody at the same time? They coulda all had it now, or they coulda all had it in the New Year. Surely, they've got enough of this Nano-stuff to go around.*

This was the key to unlocking his decision on who to approach. One friendly face in Boulder Creek might have the inside track on Sattva Systems™ plans...

Before setting down his FusionPlane™ at the Sattva Systems™ HQ, he circled the grounds until he caught a glimpse of his target. He was reassured that she was in one of the most heavily industrialised areas on the outskirts of the complex. He hadn't been here often in this part as it was full of heavy machinery and chemical plants. He usually headed to the transportation areas to see the big machines, unless he wanted to talk with Bodhi, in which case he went to the HQ, which was miles away from here.

He watched Fleet Captain Marjorie Hampton chatting to fellow colleagues, and she appeared to be issuing instructions. Then she sat down for a moment, and that was when Brady decided to land his FusionPlane™ in the nearest open space to her.

She was alarmed to see a FusionPlane™ in the Sattva Systems™ Chemical Zone, as this was a non-existent event. Usually, only FusionCars™ would be allowed to travel, slowly, through here. She watched Brady climb out, and she was concerned about why he was here. It was apparent he had sought her out.

'Hi, Brady. So, you've heard the news then. Have you come to say goodbye?'

'Are you leaving?'

'You could say that.' She laughed. 'I'm not on the list because I collaborated with you. Your friend Hunter gave me up.'

'Hey, I'm sorry to hear that. I didn't mean to cause you no trouble.'

'It's not your fault. It was my decision.'

'Where are you gonna go? You could stay at mine if you want? You could treat it as a vacation...'

'You really don't know. I'm on the penultimate mission to Mars. It was one way to get my UltraViolet™, and it will be a new challenge for me. I don't think spending my life doing a census on wildflowers was really going to do it for me.' He had a puzzled look on his face. 'What is it, Brady?'

'It's happened before, but this time it feels like the Greens want me out of the way for good.'

'What makes you say that?'

He decided to state it is as a fact and not a theory. He wanted to test her reaction. 'They've selected the people who won't receive the UltraViolet™ yet, by using my entertainment products as a kind of bad news lottery ticket.'

Marjorie said, 'That's correct. Bodhi would state that they were self-selected. However, you will be the one who tempted them to stray from the path set out before them. That will be your legacy as the Trad who survived.'

Brady pulled out his Sattva ring hanging from a chain around his neck. 'It's not just my products, is it? It's any gift. I tried to give this back to Bodhi - y'know, just trying to be nice, and he looked scared. He knew even then what he was planning to do.'

'When was this?'

'Near the end of the last century. I'm sure of it.' As he put away his ring, he muttered, 'Fucking Hunter was the same when I offered it to him.'

Marjorie was troubled. 'That doesn't fit with Bodhi's rhetoric. He's explaining the delay away as to do with his illness in '42, that and a shortage of Nanomaterials...'

'And they are calling me the Deceiver or whatever...' Brady laughed sarcastically. He looked at Marjorie, and he could tell that he had escalated the possibilities in her mind. 'You never used my stuff.'

She laughed, 'I helped to protect you - that was far worse.'

'What happens next?'

Marjorie looked around her to see if anybody was watching. Even with the enhanced senses of the VioletSuits™, it was unlikely they could hear within this industrial white-noise. 'Me - I get to escape by working for Tia Cassandra on her Martian Colony. As for you, I think they are planning for you to take the blame for the shortened life expectancy of close to nine-hundred million Greens. These will include your family and colleagues in your business.'

'I don't want to bleat about it - but does that seem fair to you?'

'No. It's not. It's like blaming a mailman for delivering bad news. However, have you heard of the saying about the victors writing the history?'

'Can't say I have.'

Marjorie shook her head. 'Never mind.' She looked around again. 'I'm going to introduce you to someone. She's Bodhi's biggest embarrassment. He keeps her well-hidden.'

'Sounds cool. Will she know more?'

'Undoubtedly. She happens to be the richest person on the planet.'

'Richer than me?'

'By a proverbial mile. Once you get used to her - you'll like her. She's more like you than a Green.' She added, 'You can't go to her. It's too dangerous - health and safety and all that. I'll bring her to you. I might be gone awhile - she'll take some persuading. Do you mind waiting here?'

'No. I've got a packed lunch in the FusionPlane™.'

Marjorie rushed off as Brady took his seat back in the cockpit.

He liked noise, but he was glad to have a rest from the din outside. He ate his lunch, drank his black coffee from his thermos, and waited patiently for about an hour before Marjorie turned up with a woman whose skin was a couple of shades of bronze darker than his own. He alighted his FusionPlane™ in his jeans, white T-shirt with his trusty Poacher's coat - he was always prepared for the worst when meeting new influential Greens. His heavy boots endowed him with a military bearing as he strode out to meet them.

Marjorie introduced her guest. 'Brady. This is Professor Pinar Dogan. Xe is the brains behind our Nanotechnological and Enzyme research. Without xyr, Bodhi couldn't have achieved anything.' She joked, 'Don't let xyr gruff demeanour fool you - if there's one genius left in this world, then you are looking at xyr.'

If Pinar was flattered by her introduction, she didn't show it. 'Hi, Brady. Pleased to meetcha. Heard a lot about you - none of it good.' She laughed so loudly it took Brady aback.

'You're not from around here.'

'I'm from everywhere. I've got hundreds of the finest properties in the world. Wherever there was a Trad dictator or monarchy, I've brought their homes.' She laughed, 'But to answer your question, my family were Turkish - my emphasis on *were* - they are long dead, but I was raised in England. I went to Cambridge and then to Stanford.'

Brady was intimidated by her intellect. He said cautiously, 'I once knew a professor from Stanford University. He was a real nice dude.'

She looked at him inquisitively as she had never been informed of this connection. 'Who was that?'

'Professor Yuan Chu. He lived in East McFarland. He told me he worked on Nanotechnology to help families have kids.'

'NanoIVF™?'

'Yeah, something like that.'

'I think I remember him. Yes, I do, a long time ago. He left...'

'...That's right. He had his funding taken away; I think.'

'Yes. Yes, I do recall. You're right, nice guy. Where is he, now?'

'Long dead. He was a Trad.'

'I'm sorry to hear that - genuinely.' She changed the subject; she had no use for melancholy. 'As an undoubted genius, shall I share with you my four words that govern all of my dealings with the esteemed Bodhi Sattva?'

Brady dreaded a technical answer but seeing as it was only four words. 'Sure. Shoot.'

'Fuck you - pay me.'

Brady roared with laughter, utterly unconcerned if anybody was spying on them, and Pinar seemed to love it that someone finally got her humour. She looked Brady up and down in a predatory way. He had become hardened to the potential attraction of the female-looking Greens. He didn't like the thought of what was lurking underneath their NanoSuits™. There was a time when she might have been his type. This was the same time when anybody could have been Brady Mahone's type. She was slender and wearing skin-tight black leather trousers with knee-high matching boots, and her hair made her look more Japanese than Turkish.

'What do you wanna know, Brady?' She stroked his cheek with her black nails. 'Ask me something difficult - I don't want it to be too easy. I like a challenge.'

He knew this was an opening play in a seductive game, but he wasn't enamoured about her taking control. Thinking of Mrs Wilson's distorted and mummified body in her grave dampened his ardour. 'I saw this weird sight once - at a funeral. Yes, Mrs Wilson. It was running late, and there was this thing that looked like a NanoSuit™ of the dead woman, except the NanoSuit™ looked like it was kind of alive, and it was trying to find a place to go. What was the deal with that?'

Pinar said, 'Every effort is made to recycle everything manufactured at Sattva Systems™. Xe had no further use for the Suit™ so, it returned here to Boulder Creek.'

'Nah, I don't believe that.'

'I wouldn't give you incorrect information. It's not in my make-up.'

'She was heading in the wrong direction.'

'When was this?'

'Way back. Maybe '42 - the time when Bodhi got sick.'

'You should have said. Mrs Wilson's Suit™ would have been disorientated.'

Brady scratched the black stubble, streaked with grey on his head. 'What's that got to do with Bodhi?'

She laughed, 'These are interesting questions. Go, Brady. I thought you'd be asking me how you could blow this place up.'

'Would you tell me if I asked?'

'I'd tell you the truth. It can't be done. You really don't know me if you'd think I'd leave a chink for a grubby Trad terrorist to exploit. Fact is, even I couldn't destroy it. Everything is protected by high-grade DiamonoidShells™ and within the treated ceramic structures are impenetrable layers which even Nanoparticles fired at incredible speeds couldn't penetrate.'

'I've seen your vehicles being destroyed. Seen it with my own eyes at Cima.'

'The HeavyLoaders™ were exceptionally close to a *fission* nuclear blast, and the LeviathanLifter™ survived.' She paused, 'Yes, that was the only time in a hundred years - you're right - well spotted. However, there aren't any fission reactors left, so that threat has gone...'

'You're the genius. I bet you could build one.' Brady joked.

'Me, Tia and Dagny Cassandra could. But that's not going to happen.'

They strolled through the industrial grounds until they reached a quieter spot that overlooked the hills and forests. Brady said, 'So, that's it then. This will still be here thousands of years from now.'

'There were plans to dismantle it - in the early days, but there is more to do. The work never stops when Bodhi's gotta world to save.'

'Save from what?'

'Extra-terrestrial life, the red-giant Sun, comets, meteors, black holes...'

'I heard of the other spacey things from my friend Tyrone, but what's a black hole. All holes are black, ain't they?'

Pinar laughed. She never expected to be explaining black holes to somebody like Brady. 'I'll keep it simple. It's a place where everything is pulled into a tiny space, and it builds up a massive amount of energy. Imagine squeezing the size of the Earth into a penny.'

'No point. That's impossible.'

She shook her head. 'Think of something you could squeeze and let go which could return to its original shape.'

'You mean, like a sponge ball.'

'Yes. That will do. Tell me what is happening to the ball in your hand.'

Brady imagined picking up a yellow sponge ball and squeezing it in his fist. 'I'm tightening my grip, and the ball is screwed up to next to nothing.'

'And when you open your hand?'

'It springs right back to normal.'

'Imagine the Earth is a sponge ball squeezed by a God into a penny, and then he lets the penny spring back to the size of the whole planet. I know you'll say this can't be done, but it can, because the Earth is mainly empty space, and atoms are incredibly tiny.'

Brady couldn't figure this out. Rocks were big and not empty space. 'Are they smaller than your Nano things?'

At this, Pinar knew not to open the discussion on quantum electrodynamics. She didn't want to witness Brady's head exploding. She laughed at this image. 'You could say that.'

Brady continued to scratch his head. He wondered whether it might have been simpler to make a pass at her, but he thought of Marjorie, and she had guided him to Pinar for a reason. 'I kinda get it. I just don't know why people bother with that stuff. I can't even remember how we got on this subject...'

'...You were asking about what happened to an old lady...'

'Yes. Mrs Wilson.'

'She was trying to return to Bodhi as part of the recycling of her NanoSuits™.'

'Bodhi and not Boulder Creek? What's Mrs Wilson got to do with Bodhi?'

'Nothing. Nothing at all.'

'You lost me.'

'It's a classic case of quantity over quality.' Pinar said. 'She was supposed to find the magnetic position of Bodhi's homing beacon.'

'Like a homing pigeon.'

'Yes. Homing in on Bodhi's genetic code - and becoming another layer of Bodhi, where her memories would be accessible to him. The only problem for your poor Mrs Wilson was that Bodhi was in a Nano Sensory Deprivation Chamber - which is impenetrable to Nano-particles and repels magnetic fields.'

Brady laughed, 'I said she'd end up dancing around the North Pole.'

Pinar corrected, 'Magnetic North. She had quite the detour.'

'How many of these dead layers has Bodhi had?' Brady muttered, 'It all seems a bit creepy if you ask me.'

'A few thousand to date.'

'Don't they get heavy to wear - all those extra Suits™?'

'They are made of Nanoparticles; they are virtually weightless. After a few minutes, they become assimilated into Bodhi's body structure.' Pinar added, 'It's still too many...'

'Why?'

'Would you want to carry around with you the thoughts of thousands of Mrs Wilsons? I, for one, couldn't think of anything more boring. All the Greens are so dull...'

'Amen to that.'

'If I were to have the choice, I'd rather choose somebody with complimentary or even superior skills to my own, like Tia Cassandra - she's brilliant with comms technology. Like I said - quantity over quality - but he won't listen to me.'

'I'm listening.' Brady wasn't sure if he was learning.

She looked at him as if he was a puzzle to solve. 'He can be stopped, but not by force.'

'Go on.'

'He can be ousted as leader. Thirteen commandments, with thirteen representatives, mostly based in the Californian home of Sattva Systems™. A majority vote could ensure that every Green would receive the UltraViolet™.' Pinar said this in a way that suggested to Brady that he would have to do something to make this happen. 'There is no shortage of UltraViolet™. Bodhi doesn't want to threaten the world with the future over-population of humans. He'd rather let the population dwindle...'

'Like he did with the Trads.'

'*We* did. We voted twelve to zero to save the planet - but this is different.'

'Because it's Greens...'

'Because the planet is already saved. How much would you pay out of your fortune to give your sons a further thousand years - maybe thousands more?'

Brady had an incentive he could use as motivation, 'What would I have to do?'

'Persuade six of the thirteen to vote against Bodhi and for the distribution of the UltraViolet™ to all Greens.'

'Who's on this list? Presumably. I know them?'

'Most of them. I'll tell you the ones you won't be able to turn. They include Bodhi, obviously. Precious in South Africa - she's not enamoured with you. And Hunter - you've burned your bridges there, I'm afraid.' She added, 'Oh, and Bridgett Tarnita in Sweden, she would never go against Brady.'

'I'm not into politicking and votes and all that shit. It's not me.'

'Just hear me out. You have two votes in the bag already. This means you only have to turn four more people.'

'Who have I got?' Brady said insolently.

Pinar laughed, 'You got me. I'm a cross in the box.' She added before she could be insulted by Brady's rejection, 'And you've got Rhea.'

'Rhea? How? Why?'

'You've got to be very careful with this information. You could put her at risk. Marjorie has already been uncovered and replaced...'

'Ok, I get it.'

'Rhea is a Trad in Green clothing - you might say. She has been investigating Sattva Systems™ since before the Revolution. She has followed your progress with interest throughout. She had your back covered...and she likes you.' Pinar shrugged.

Brady said, 'So, you think me, and Rhea might...'

'Maybe, who knows, stranger things have happened.' She smiled knowingly.

'Who are the others?'

'Glenarvon Cole, Genesis Garcia. They will be difficult, but Sissy's kid Century is not on the UltraViolet™ list. Then you've got the McFarland trio of Cain, Lizzie and Siddha.'

'Fuck. They ain't gonna listen to me.'

'Cain is not wholly behind Bodhi on this.' She winked. 'And then there's Samuel Beardon the Third.'

'Ok. I make that twelve. Where's the casting vote.'

Her shoulders slumped, 'It's you. But you have to take the Green...'

That's how they get ya, son. Brady was as paranoid as his Pops about agreeing to wear their NanoSuits™. He was proud of being a Trad, even more so of being the last Trad on Earth. He wore that title like a badge of honour or like a medal worn with pride as a great war survivor. He felt like he had worn the Green for a moment, and he didn't like that slimy sensation coming back to him as if he had experienced it only yesterday.

It was the talk of Mrs Wilson which had triggered this feeling; when her ghostly apparition had tried to envelop him in her own NanoSuit™, it felt like he was being raped at a spiritual level. It was a feeling he never wanted to experience again. Brady would rather die. However, he had a duty to prolong the life of his sons, and if that meant going against his principles or going through some personal hell, then he would do it. There was always Rhea at the end of it, maybe waiting for him after all. Brady assessed the situation cautiously. There was no harm in agreeing here. It would buy him time to consider other options. 'Ok. I hear ya. I can't have long left in this world. I've had a good innings as a Trad, and maybe going Green is the way forward for Brady Mahone. You got yourself a deal. I'll get on it.'

She stuck out her hand, and Brady shook it, but he childishly kept his other hand behind his back with his fingers crossed in a ludicrous attempt to nix the deal.

Brady walked away back to his FusionPlane™, and Professor Pinar Dogan strode back toward her laboratory. After a few hundred yards, a figure emerged from the shadows in an old-fashioned hoody. He said, 'Is it done?'

Pinar waited until Brady's FusionPlane™ had disappeared over the huge cream-coloured chemical vats with their giant Sattva Systems™ moss green logos. She barked, 'Fuck you, pay me.'

'All in good time. When the job is completed. What did you say to him?'

Pinar looked around suspecting a trap, 'That he has to contact the twelve people on your list and persuade them to vote against you. If he fails, then his sons' life-spans will be considerably shorter.'

'And what will you say to the others?'

'That the traitor Marjorie Hampton tricked me into meeting Brady Mahone, and he wanted to find out how to destroy Sattva Systems™. He was seeking vengeance for the Trads, and he wanted to ruin our Centenary Celebrations. I played along and showed him some explosive devices and where to plant them. I took him to the FusionPower™ distribution network.'

Bodhi stepped out, and his face was revealed from under his hoody, 'And what possible hold over you did he have to persuade you to help him?'

'He offered me five-hundred million Green Credits, as he had heard I'd been complaining about my work being under-valued.'

'And what now?'

'Everybody is to report back developments to you and not take matters into their own hands. If they feel more comfortable in humouring Brady as opposed to confronting him, then you will understand.'

Bodhi moved in and hugged Pinar, 'Thank you, my friend.'

16: FAMILY BUSINESS

Even before his FusionPlane™ had completed its vertical lift-off manoeuvre, Brady had decided to enlist help in this election process. He knew the Greens didn't rate his intellectual prowess. They always made him feel like a dumb animal, a beast of burden, to who they would throw a treat if he let them pat him. *Something doesn't smell right with that Pinar chick. It reeks of an undercover op. I ain't too old to remember how they go down. Acting all friendly, trying to imitate your jive. I smell a rat.*

After setting his SattNav™ to head back to Malibu, he took out his Satt™ and stretched his legs and rested them with his boots on the cockpit dashboard. He called each of his sons who had scattered in the wind to all parts of the globe. He told each of them to come home urgently as he needed their help. Brady didn't do small talk on the phone, and he ran roughshod over all requests and excuses. He reminded them of his generosity and the fact that he never asked much from them in return.

A couple of days elapsed before his boys had all returned from their faraway places of business, leisure, and pleasure. After breakfast, Brady instructed them to pay attention. 'I'm going to tell you a lot of stuff - personal stuff. You are going to need this to understand what's at stake.' He growled, 'I'm fully aware that I might be being played, but for the time being, I want you to do as I tells ya. Do you follow me?'

Bill usually took up the role of answering for the group. 'Yes, Pops. What's happening?'

'You've all heard of this UltraViolet™, and presumably, by now, you've been told about the link between our products and the selection criteria to receive or not receive it.'

Bill looked around his brothers, they had all talked about it, but he wanted their approval to speak freely. 'We've all taken a lot of flak for it. Especially from the late converts who, probably fairly, feel aggrieved to have missed out on the first batch of UltraViolet™ upgrades. Still, it's only a few months to wait.'

Brady said, 'I'm hearing it's never. They are going to let you die out naturally.'

Troy interrupted, 'Like they did with the Trads?' The others gasped at the possibility.

'Most of the Trads didn't make it past fifty. You've got until you are a hundred, I believe - that's still a lifetime in my book. But still...' Brady was relieved that none of his sons panicked. He was proud that they were taking the news like men.

Wilder was the numbers man. He said, 'With the maximum life expectancy driven down to one hundred coupled with the massively escalating costs of raising your own children, then within about three hundred years there will be hardly any Pure Greens left. If the UltraViolet™ leads to a minimum one-thousand-year life span, then they will be the only ones left. The nine-hundred-million population today becomes just twenty-six-million by the year 2500.'

Brady added to Wilder's math, 'One human for every one square mile of hospitable land, a friend of mine said that - something like that.'

Rocky said, 'Wow, Pops - where on Earth did you pick up a detail like that?'

'I can't remember exactly. I think it was when I was in Florida with Glenarvon Cole, back in the 40s.'

'That's an eternity ago.'

'Yeah, a hundred years in the making.'

Wilder had been distracted by his own theories, 'I bet it's 2500, it's a nice round number, I can see those smug UltraViolet™ bastards' New Year celebrations, now. Can't you?'

Troy thumped the table, and the boys spat out their curses.

Bill said, 'You've never been afraid of death. Have you Pops?'

'Life's too short.' Brady joked, and it diffused the tension.

Hawk spoke up, he usually stayed quiet as the youngest, but he picked up on the worried frown on the brow of his Pops. 'That's not all that's troubling you, is it Pops?'

'No, son. It's not. I think they got something real special planned for me. You see, they always play this game where they spin things to make 'em look good - real nice and friendly like. What they don't do - is take responsibility for all the bad shit that goes down.'

He looked around and saw the puzzled looks on his boys' faces. This was why he had to tell them everything. They were a jumble of labels to him, Green, Pure Green, indoctrinated Green, and he had to shake them out of their Green dreams. 'Some stuff you've heard before from me, and some stuff you ain't, but it's gonna add context-like, you get me.'

Bill said, 'Sure, Pops.'

Brady wasn't keen on Bill's patronising tone, but he pressed on regardless. 'You all know that that I blame the Greens for the deaths of billions of Trads. They say that the Trads chose or self-selected themselves for their lives outside the GreenShells™, but I think they kinda neglected them to death.' He was aware that he sounded like his own Pops when he grandstanded about his latest conspiracy theories. 'Anyways, this means they have form in my book. They've done it before, and they are doing it again - only difference this time is they are doing it to their own kind.'

Rocky said, 'This means it's a Green-on-Green assault. This has nothing to do with you Pops because your Trad...' He added to reassure his Pops, 'and proud.'

'Except, they are going to make it all about me. That's what it means to be a Trad - I am here to take the blame. I'm sure they've kept me alive for this reason. There's no way I should still be alive and this healthy - I mean, look at me. In a fair fight without your NanoSuits™, I could still whoop your asses.' The boys laughed and joshed with him with mock bravado. 'They are going to rig this so that by using my entertainment products, they broke their rules, their commandments, and the only person left to blame - after they have absolved themselves of any responsibility - is me, for all time.'

He looked around the table. Bill said, 'We've sold them the stuff. They'll blame us. I don't mind being accountable.'

'But it's my name on the product. It's my baby. When the Devout and the Disciples talk about the Pure Greens' loved ones, they lost in years to come. It will be followed with, "If only Brady Mahone, the filthy Trad, hadn't been around - if he had rotted in that prison where he belonged, then our friends and family would still be here today." I'm gonna have my say if they give me a half-a-chance.' He peered into each of his son's eyes, 'I don't care about what happens to me. I'll lay down my life in a heartbeat to protect my family. If it comes to that, then I'll do it and don't stand in my way.'

The boys didn't want to contemplate this scenario. Bill said, 'We've still got time, Pops. Let's not waste it on worst-case scenarios. What's the plan?'

'I'm gonna bring you up to speed with the family history. Follow me.' He led them through the many rooms of his Malibu home. He spotted Hunter lurking with the pretext of offering his services. Brady abruptly told him to take the day off and not to hang around on the grounds. Hunter nodded and left them alone. Brady paused before changing direction and going back on themselves. The boys looked at each other with furtive gestures, which questioned Brady's sanity. He took them to Libby Skye's old bedroom. He gazed at the poster of Libby Skye in the movie, *The Virgin*. She was in gossamer white and looked like an angel. The words praised her *magical performance*. 'This is your Grandmother.'

Wilder said, 'Not Edie Mahone.'

'No. She was my Foster Moms.'

'Wait a minute...'

'Your Grandfather was John Kane - Bodhi Sattva's Father, or Xavier Kane as he was known back then.'

Wilder said, 'Fuck me, Pops. There's a lot of implications here.'

'Yeah, there is. Bodhi is your uncle, as is Glenarvon Cole...' He raised his hand to stop the outbursts. If they were anything like him, Brady Mahone, ex-con, they would be already onto how they could exploit this. Brady needed to put a lid on this. 'I don't think they know, or if they do, then that's part of their plan. The point is that they don't know that I know. Therefore, I'm ordering you not to say anything. This is my ace up my sleeve, and it will become worthless if they know I have something to play. I'll tell you more, but first, give me your word - on my life, not yours - because that's what you'll be giving to Bodhi if you betray me...'

Bill shouted, 'It will never come to that, you have my word, and I will do anything to help.' The others agreed.

Brady looked at the poster of Libby Skye, 'Take a moment, boys, to get to know your Grandmother - my biological Moms. This is the poster that made John Kane obsessed with her. This is where it all started.'

After a minute of revered silence, Wilder said, 'I just thought all these pictures and photos were artworks from the previous owners. I never knew...'

'...Neither did I. Tia Cassandra mocked me with this revelation, but it kinda made some sense.'

'Why did they not raise you? They had plenty of resources.'

Brady wasn't going to share anything about Archie Mahone's disgrace. He'd hoped that Amie hadn't spoken of it. He felt that if he told the whole disgusting truth about John Kane, he could be tainted by association - it was a time to reveal family secrets, but not all of them. 'John Kane - your Grandfather was a cold-hearted scientist, industrialist and business bastard. He brutalised Libby to have Bodhi born on the stroke of the Millennium, and he indoctrinated Bodhi with all his knowledge and values. He had stolen Libby's eggs for some kinda social experiment shit. Bodhi was born on the Millennium, and twenty-one years, later he had Glenarvon Cole engineered and indoctrinated with socialism and radical environmentalism...'

'Why?'

'Because he could. He wanted to see how his perfect specimens would turn out if they were raised in different circumstances. I suppose at some level, my biological Pops saw me as a perfect specimen unless he was keeping me to harvest my organs or something...'

Hawk moved in and hugged his Pops awkwardly, and then stepped back. He knew he shouldn't show sentimentalism in front of his Pops, 'What did that bastard do to you, Pops?' He'd sworn to consistently demonstrate his masculinity.

Brady glanced away and took a deep breath and then blurted out what he hadn't told another living soul. 'Tia Cassandra told me that John Kane paid a junkie to give birth to me but with some strings...' He was angry and ashamed and knew this would make him sound like a victim. 'He had all kinds of criminal lowlife talking to me while I was still in my surrogate Mom's womb about every kinda lying, cheating and crimes...they even had fucking scripts...' He held up his hand to put a halt to interruptions. He wanted to share - a feeling he rarely had. 'Even after I was born, this went on for years, until my surrogate Moms died of an overdose. He placed me as a four-year-old with Archie and Edie Mahone. Now, I don't want to speak ill of them, but even that was deliberate, Edie was an alcoholic who had given up on life and never really liked me, and Archie, my Foster Daddy, was a crook...' Brady half-lied, 'dabbling in all kinda illegal shit. Then things didn't go quite to plan...'

Hawk urged Brady to continue, 'It's ok, Pops.'

'Archie changed because of me. He loved me and treated me like I was his own. I musta been hell to raise, I was always in trouble, but he was always on my side, no matter what I did. Don't get me wrong, boys, he was a real bad character, but he was the only one who coulda handled me. That's why when John Kane came to reclaim me a few years later when I was eight...Archie murdered him...to keep me safe.' Brady let out a huge breath as if he had given testimony in his own defence with his sons as the jury. 'I am not a good guy. I've robbed and murdered all my life - not in self-defence but out of pure self-interest. That's who your Pops is...'

'You've always been good to us, Pops.' Bill said.

Brady paused. He felt the urge to say to his boys something he could never have countenanced before. However, he had told them about the impact on his life from his biological father's manipulations, and he realised he might have been committing the same crime. Brady's embarrassment was evident to his sons as he looked away before returning his gaze upon his beloved sons. 'I've done you wrong. I shouldn't have tried to make you live your lives in my image. It's your life. You live it how you want to be. You don't have to be...y'know...'

Troy could see his Pops struggle, 'Cisgender male. You are giving us permission to choose who we want to be.'

Brady uttered, 'Yes. That's what I mean.' Brady wanted to feel relief, but instead, he wanted to flee before any of his boys said something emotional or sentimental. All he needed was an excuse.

Wilder said, 'You don't think you're Green, do you, Pops? I mean, I bet John Kane did other stuff to you while you were still in the test tube. It makes sense, y'know, perfect specimens, a bit a gene-splicing, altered sequencing, InfraRedPrimers™, it would explain...'

'I'm a fucking Trad.' Brady yelled. 'I don't care if I am fucking being ignorant. I know they call me; I hear them laughing...Alpha-Male Trad or Trad Alpha-Male...whatever...they say I'm a fucking Silverback gorilla in human form. I'm not a Green, and I will never take their Green goo. Pops was right. He always said they would get me in the end, lure me in with promises, make out that I was some kinda hero. I don't want that Green shit in me. I am Trad. End of.' He looked around at his sons, he couldn't give a damn if they were Green, and he had hurt their feelings. 'Follow me, and I'll show you. I can prove I'm Trad and it ain't the word of some fucking deceitful human. God knows I can't trust anybody. Everybody's got it in for that old fool, Brady Mahone.'

After a moment's shock at their Pop's outburst, Brady stormed away, and the boys quickly caught up with him. Bill punched Wilder in the arm. Wilder said, 'What? What did I say? It was only a question of logic...'

'Well, think before you use it on Pops in future. Got it.'

Brady dug out his old sketchbooks. He quickly located the one with Bodhi's teeth marks in its leathery hide. He opened the page to reveal his drawings of the two man-eating lions. 'These are Msoro Monty and Bwana Devil. While the fucking Greens left the Trads in South Africa to their own devices, these two maneaters feasted on hundreds of Trads over many years. They never attacked Greens because the NanoSuits™ they were wearing emitted no living scent, this meant the lions, or any other predators didn't view them as animals or food.' He put it a different way to ensure they understood the significance of this information. 'The NanoSuits™ gave off no scent, and they would no more try and eat a Green as they would a vehicle. The Greens were like robots to them, but not me - oh no - they followed Brady Mahone for days before they attacked. I was Trad meat to them. No politics or ideals at play, I was meat, and this is what they looked like just as they attacked me.'

Bill traced his fingers over the teeth and claws. 'How did you escape, Pops?'

'They were doused in Film from the Security Protocols™. I asked for them to be left in situ while I sketched them. After I had finished and was led to a place of safety, they released them. Of course, they cared for the lions' welfare, but they were unconcerned if there were any more Trads to feed on out there. Still, it's interesting to think that the Greens were protecting me. I was clearly wanted more alive than dead.' He turned sharply to Wilder, 'What do you think now, boy? Is that enough evidence for ya?'

No matter what Wilder actually believed, he gave the answer which Brady craved. 'You're a Trad. Absolutely, Pops.'

Brady gathered his boys close around him as if he feared that somebody might be listening. 'They tried to make me believe that I can sway some kinda vote at the end of the year. Personally, I think it's bullshit, but I'll play along. You know my version of events but keep it to yourself. Instead, I want you to make it look like they got old Brady Mahone fooled.'

Rocky said, 'What do you need?'

'First of all, forget the business for a few weeks.'

'Not difficult. We are hardly welcome now.'

Brady stroked his stubble on his head. 'That could be a way in. There are influential Greens I'm supposed to win over. Go and throw yourself on their mercy and beg for help to get the business up and running again. They won't help. It don't matter, none. Just be seen talking to them, and make it look to others like you're being all secretive.'

'Ok. Why?'

'To buy me time. I'll do the same with a couple on the list who they would think I could influence.'

'Who are they, Pops?' Bill asked.

'There's Bodhi. I'll take him.' Brady laughed, 'Not to ask him to vote against himself, of course. I'll ask for marketing ideas, and this will draw Genesis Garcia in.' He added, 'Professor Pinar Dogan is the one who's playing me. She's the top broad of Sattva Systems™ manufacturing plant. The other one I'll take is Samuel Beardon the Third, seeing as he's my oldest *friend*.'

He looked around his sons. He was working this out on the fly. 'Troy?'

'Yes, Pops?'

'Do you know Bridgett Tarnita? She's from Sweden.'

Troy laughed. 'Yeah, there isn't a person in the whole world who hates you as much as she does.' The others joined in the laughter.

Brady smiled, 'Very funny. Just do your best to have some kinda meeting with her. Act like we're beaten if you have to.'

'And Wilder?'

'Yes, Pops?'

Brady gave his sketchbook containing his man-eating lions to him. 'Precious is a bigwig Green in South Africa. Use this as a way-in if you have to.' Wilder nodded vigorously, trying to win back his Pops trust.

He looked at Bill. 'I want you to take the old McFarland trio.' Brady laughed at the recall of an old nursery rhyme that sounded like this. 'Lizzie and Siddha will be unfriendly, but Cain will be oh-so-nice. Don't be fooled. I mighta taken them myself, but they know me too well.'

'As for you, Rocky, I'm giving you the hardest ones to track down.'

'I can do it, Pops. Just name them.'

'I want you to locate Glenarvon Cole and Rhea Laidlaw. She might, just might be on our side, but still don't reveal our hand. It might be useful if she looks surprised if we find an opportunity to make a decisive mood.'

'Why might she be on your side?'

'She and Fleet Captain Marjorie Hampton have made it their mission to keep me alive. I'll leave it at that.'

Hawk said, 'Is that who I've got to find? She's the only one left by my reckoning.'

Brady laughed, 'Not unless you follow her to Mars.' He said, 'She's been exposed as a traitor, I believe - for helping me. No, the person I want you to get close to doesn't need to be found, but he is probably Bodhi's closest confidant, and he works here. He is very slippery. Maybe use Debrock and his buddies to spread a little disinformation.'

'I'm lost, Pops. Who are we talking about?'

'Hunter.'

17: VEGETABLE MAN

Ahighly unusual sight greeted Brady as he drove his FusionCar™ on Highway 99 to San Martin. He had already felt a tinge of nostalgia for the old days, as he elected to take the FusionCar™ and not the FusionPlane™ for his journey. He had been chilled about the traffic - it took him back to a time before the Greens. However, it was a shame that all the vehicles were identical, with their ceramic appearance and cream-coloured livery all featuring the moss green Sattva Systems™ logos.

There were banners along the side of the Highway and even crudely built billboards. *We refuse to be treated as second-class citizens. UltraViolet™ is a right, not a gift. No man can play God, not even Bodhi Sattva. No UltraViolet™ - No Work!* The fact that they were written in gaudy colours and not the standard Sattva Systems™ moss green seemed rebellious.

Brady turned off the Highway and soon found the demonstrations blocking his way. The crowds of the younger Greens - if you could call under sixties young - chanted: *What do we want? UltraViolet™ - When do we want it? Now!*

He braced himself for trouble, but they cheered as he went past. *Hey, Brady! Stick it to Bodhi...He don't care about us...Make him change his mind, man...We know he wants us to blame you, we're not stupid...He's not my God...Not in my name...It's so fucking unfair...*

Brady occasionally shouted back an encouraging reply. *I'm sure we can sort it out...He's trying to frame me...I ain't gonna stand for it...He's gonna regret messing with Brady Mahone...Can I count on your support?*

Hell, Yes!

The crowd slowly parted to let Brady through. He drove through the centre of San Martin when he saw Samuel Beardon the Third being pelted with produce. Of course, they couldn't harm him within his NanoSuits™ - the flying fruits and vegetables bounced off him harmlessly, but Brady knew this would psychologically damage his old friend.

Brady judged the direction of flight of these squishy projectiles and alighted his FusionCar™ and stayed out of harm's way. He called to the crowd with mock authority, 'It's ok. I'll deal with him.' The demonstrators did not seem appeased. 'I'll persuade him to talk to the big man, and I'm sure we can get you the UltraViolet™.'

His hundreds of onlookers muttered among themselves. 'You know I'm a Trad, and I'm not interested in NanoSuits™, but I have five sons who have missed out - just like you. I'm gonna get justice for my boys, and I'm gonna get justice for you all!' He bellowed, and the crowd cheered.

'Get in the car, man.' He said softly to the Bear. Samuel jumped in the passenger side while Brady moved the car slowly away. 'What's going on? Where are the Security Protocols™ when you need 'em?'

The Bear - this indestructible big man in Brady's eyes, crumbled before him. Tears gushed from him, and he sobbed like a baby. Brady said, 'It's ok, man. I'm here. You know I'll try and help my oldest friend.' The Bear seemed to struggle to catch his breath. He spluttered, 'It's all gone wrong, and it's all my fault.'

Brady drove on, letting the Bear calm down, and he pulled up to the Beardon home. As they entered, he asked, 'What's happened? I can't believe it's just the demonstrators.'

He took a lung full of air and let it out slowly. 'I should blame you.'

'Blame me for what?'

'Tyrone. If he hadn't used your entertainment products, he would have been ok. He would have received the UltraViolet™ like Alicia and I.'

'Hey, man. I got broad shoulders. I can carry the weight. But I have to say in my defence that I never got Tyrone started on my products. He always talked about his scientist friends in Boulder Creek and San Diego and how they were really into Science Fiction films. They got him started. After that, when he used to ask me for rare stuff, I gave it to him, freely, as a friend. I never made the first move. Ask Alicia. She will tell you that Brady Mahone never tried to sell her anything.'

The Bear slumped on the chair. Brady made a tactical retreat to allow his explanation to sink in. He went to the kitchen and made them both coffees. The home was quiet, and he guessed that the others were working. None of the other residents had shown any interest in his product, and he assumed they had all received UltraViolet™.

He handed his friend a coffee. The Bear said as if he was in a dream, 'Forgive me, God. I know not what I have done. I shouldn't have interfered with your plan.' Brady gulped his coffee and let the Bear continue his rambling speech. 'I have sinned. I have let the pride of ownership distract me. I should never have let the feeling of being the chosen one - allow me to take the UltraViolet™ ahead of my flock...'

'I gather this UltraViolet™ can give you another thousand years of life at least.' Brady said, interrupting his old friend's self-pitying monologue in Brady's opinion. 'I've had to give it some thought because of my boys, but truthfully, if they get a hundred years, then they've done well - we both would have sold our souls for a hundred years of life and in good health - don't you think?' Brady smiled broadly, but the Bear wasn't taking the bait. Brady continued,

'Though I understand the greed for life, it's only natural, and if I can secure it for my sons, then I'll move heaven and Earth to get it. However, I think another thousand years in your boring Green world sounds more like hell to me.' He teased the Bear, 'Don't you think, old man?'

Samuel Beardon the Third slumped in his chair and looked petulantly out of the window like a sulking schoolboy.

'Hey, man. Yell at me if it makes you feel better.' Brady said. 'It helps to get it out of your system, y'know, get all the bad stuff out in the open...'

'It's my fault. I interfered. If I'd have let him make his own decisions as a man, and not the boy I treated him as, then he would already have the UltraViolet™, but I had to meddle like an old fool, and I have cost him his life.'

'You're gonna have to tell me more, man.'

'Tyrone had applied to join the space mission to Mars...'

'No surprise there. He loves all that space stuff.'

The Bear shook his head. 'If only I had taken it as simply as that. What would you have said if it was one of your boys?'

'I would have been proud. Maybe, they coulda turned out like that Commander Rocky Fitzpatrick - he's a real all-American hero. I coulda lived with that.'

'Wouldn't you have missed them?'

'Sure. I woulda had to change my plans to accommodate them, like. But they would be forging their own path in life - that's a good thing in Brady Mahone's book.'

The Bear shook his head, 'Well, I pulled in a favour from Genesis Garcia, and she delivered. She pulled Tyrone from the list of applicants and used an underlying health issue as justification for Dagny Cassandra.' He banged his fist on the coffee table. 'What's maddening is that her child, Century Brady Garcia, made the same mistake as Tyrone, and she put him on the ticket reserved for Tyrone.'

Brady grimaced, 'Ouch, man. Who'd have thought that politicians would be corrupt, eh?'

'I think she knew long before I asked her. I think she and Bodhi are in cahoots in all this. I don't trust them anymore.'

'You've lost your faith in your so-called Son of God?'

The Bear declined to answer.

'What's the deal with the whole colonising Mars thing?' Brady leaned in and smiled, trying to encourage his friend to talk.

'They've been sending FusionSpaceShuttles™ to and from Mars every few days for decades. The deal was that the mission from Earth has to close a month before the New Year.'

'Boy. They musta have a lot of people and equipment up there by now.'

'Tyrone told me they had nearly twenty-thousand people on Mars.'

'I suppose they've had forty years or so to do it.'

'That's not all. This will interest you.'

Even if it didn't, Brady had decided to feign interest as the topic seemed to be unlocking Samuel's defences. 'Go on. Rock my world.' He laughed.

'Tia Cassandra has fifty Trads with her. They call themselves the Originals, not Trads.'

'Whoa! You mean I'm not the only one left. Wow! Now that is a mind fuck. Brady Mahone, a true Original. Hey, it's got a nice ring to it. How come?'

The Bear shook his head and chuckled. Brady's humour made it easier for him to continue his explanation. 'Her experiment in the desert was to see if they could build a human colony on Mars. Some of the original volunteers wanted to keep the experiment pure. The older ones died out, but not before they had Trad children of their own. They were proud of their roots and refused the Green when it was offered on the LeviathanLifter™ when they escaped the Ruin of Cima.'

'But the rest of them are Green, aren't they?'

'Yes. Even Tia and Dagny. Tia wasn't going to pass up the opportunity to exploit the scientific breakthroughs. All the others are UltraViolet™, but they have pledged to keep the Trads, the Originals, alive.'

Brady said sourly, 'More than the Greens did down here.'

'Yes. I concede the truth in what you say, brother.' He added, 'Tia Cassandra, with the help of the exodus of Sattva Systems™ technicians, have developed a NanoSpaceSuit™ for the Martian Trads. This gives them the Green benefits, but it can be removed when they have recovered or been repaired from injury. Tia's reasoning is that it is a logical development of their technological journey, and therefore the Trads can be at ease in using it.' He added, 'Would you use such a Suit™?'

That's how they get ya, son. Brady thought deeply about this fundamental question. 'I've never regretted refusing the Green. I can't see me changing my mind, now.'

'You see me as tempting you...'

Brady roared with laughter, 'I get accused of that all the fucking time. Welcome to my world, brother.'

18: THE LAST MISSION TO MARS

Rhea had completed her regular catch-up meeting with Bodhi. She had shared and acquired secrets to Bodhi's satisfaction. As she left the main entrance, she headed to the transport area to meet Fleet Captain Marjorie Hampton on her final day in that role. She joined the party onboard a parked FusionPassengerJet™. This was a commonplace occurrence over the years, wishing a fond farewell to workers and technicians at Sattva Systems™, as more and more of them joined the brain drain to Mars.

They used Bodhi's own words and the keeping of his promises to justify his actions. From the outset, he had proclaimed his disgust for this industrial monster and pledged that Sattva Systems™ was to be returned to nature once the one-hundred-year plan was completed.

The exodus of talent alarmed Genesis Garcia, who tried to beg and bribe people to change their minds, but with the recent debacle over the allocation of the UltraViolet™ - they didn't trust her. And Bodhi had remained silent on the subject. Thus, Marjorie was not unhappy about being effectively fired and labelled a traitor by the inner sanctum of the Sattva Systems™ hierarchy. The closer this final day came, the more she was delighted to be leaving Bodhi, Genesis and even Glenarvon Cole more than thirty million miles behind.

Bodhi had always claimed to have loved and respected all his considerable workforce, but although they happily received every development of the GreenSuits™, from InfraRed™ to Violet™, they were industrialists, chemical engineers, and factory workers. They took pride in their work, but they still felt more Trad than their more fragile-at-heart Devout Greens. They assessed their positions and potential upcoming redundancies, the quality of life - or lack of it on Mars, and then threw into consideration of the guaranteed UltraViolet™ and the potential of a further thousand years of life - courtesy of the deal Tia Cassandra agreed with Bodhi, and they aligned their future to hers.

Rhea boarded the FusionPassengerJet™, and she was greeted warmly by the partygoers. They would be leaving as part of the wrap-up crew just before the New Year celebrations, which were only a couple of months away. They would be mothballing the launchpad and taking the final industrial components with them, but today was the last mission for taking civilians to Mars.

Marjorie threw her arms around her comrade and acted as if she was drunk on one of the technician's concoctions, but this was an act. She needed to be sharp. She whispered for Rhea to go to the cockpit with her, where they could talk more discreetly. 'I managed to persuade Sissy to let me use the rental FusionPassengerJet™ to travel to Cape Cassandra as a kind of goodwill leaving present. I told her I wanted to fly myself and a few friends down there to see me off. But obviously, I'm planning to leave alone.'

'I've wrapped up the details from my end. That's all I'm going to say.'

'Understood. I'll meet you there.'

Marjorie watched Rhea walk away from the party and head to her own rental FusionPlane™, and she was almost superstitious about not making her next move until she had watched Rhea take-off and fly away, unhindered.

She headed back to the party, which was petering out on the FusionPassengerJet™. She thought she would bring it to an end by utilising a small closing speech. 'My friends, and colleagues for more than one-hundred-years in some cases. I just want to thank you all, so much, for being here and giving me all your best wishes. The Green ride was brilliant while it lasted, but I think we can all sense that the wheels are falling off the FusionCars™...'

They laughed politely at her joke.

'I know I'll see some of you again on Mars at the end of the year. But for those of you that are remaining to be a part of Bodhi's project, for I truly believe it is now all about him, and not us, I would like to make one small request. I would like you to please try and stop him from destroying the launch and landing pads. I know we are supposed to be gone forever, but I'm sure that one day, myself and your other good friends up there would like to know we would be welcome to come and visit you one day...in the distant or not-so-distant future. Thank you.'

Her colleagues and friends gave her warm applause. They came up one by one to give her goodbye hugs and slowly drifted back to their work duties.

Marjorie headed back to the cockpit. She was alone in the vehicle but still felt the need to be in the cocoon of the cockpit while she sobbed gently. She then sent the FusionPassengerJet™ into a vertical lift-off and flew from the Sattva Systems™ Parking Lot for the last time.

She headed to the outskirts of San Martin. She landed her vehicle on open ground a couple of miles away from the nearest building. She waited until darkness fell. She turned on her VioletSuit™, as the increased sensory perception was disorientating if used over long periods. To Marjorie's technical reasoning, it would have the same issues as if her windscreens were made from magnifying glass. She heard the nocturnal creatures busily searching for food. She was surprised at how many rabbits appeared in the quiet stillness of the open ground. At about 1:30am, she saw her guests approaching upon Green Rental Bikes. They pulled up about fifty yards away from her and then placed the Green Bikes carefully on the damp grass. The rabbits scurried back into hiding.

They approached Marjorie cautiously, looking all around them with their heightened senses as if they were paranoid about being watched or followed. They also tried to breathe as slowly and calmly as possible in case it attracted the Security Protocols™ to them. Marjorie put a finger to her lips and gestured for them to follow her on board. She placed them in their seats, headed back to the cockpit and set the autopilot to Cape Cassandra.

It was 1:55am before she dared to speak to them. She crept out of the cockpit and sat close to her passengers. She whispered, 'Hi. Is there anything that I should worry about?'

Tyrone answered, 'We did everything you said. Every night for the last two weeks, we have refused to go to bed at the normal Greens' time of 11:00pm. And we always took our rebellious Green Bike ride at 1am.'

Raelynn joked quietly, 'They thought we were acting like naughty children in refusing to go to sleep at bedtime.' She placed her hand on Tyrone's arm.

Marjorie looked at them and considered there was a time in the old days when a lanky, bespectacled, black man would look seriously out of place with a ghostly white Goth, but in these times, they could adopt any look they wanted, and many just found a look that suited how they felt and stuck with it like a comfort blanket. She asked, 'What did you do with regards to Samuel?'

Tyrone answered, 'I left him a note in his Bible because he looks at it every morning when he wakes up. I informed him that we had gone to Brady's home in Malibu, and that he must head down there, alone, as this would be the only way he could see us for the last time. I added that our lives were at stake if he told anybody about this, even Alicia.' He looked through the window and at the stars as if this was one part of the plan he disagreed with.

Marjorie looked at her watch. 'This was the safest time to help you escape. I want you to use your sleep period now, as it will guarantee your vital signs will remain normal.'

Tyrone and Raelynn used their chosen sleep phrases in their minds which triggered their sleep as surely as any anaesthetic.

19: SURPRISE GUESTS

B rady woke up, showered, and shaved just as he would have done on any other autumnal day. He had nothing planned. Despising Hunter took too much effort, so he became comfortable with just instructing him with his wishes. Today, he fancied a vegan cooked breakfast. He would have liked a traditional cooked breakfast, but there hadn't been any meat products since he had eaten his way through Archie Mahone's apocalypse supplies in his bunker decades ago. Still, he had to admit that some of it didn't taste too bad at all.

He put on his swimming trunks as he fancied a dip in one of the many swimming pools later. He pulled a white dressing gown around him and slipped his feet into comfy white slippers and meandered down to a massive balcony with an infinity pool merging into the Pacific Ocean in the distance.

Hunter had laid out his breakfast table, and a steaming cup of black coffee was already poured. Shortly afterwards, his breakfast arrived, and he ate it hungrily. He listened to the waves crashing on the shore, and as thoughts of problems in the Green world emerged, he dismissed them, as today he wanted to rest and enjoy his peace and the trappings of his success. He let his breakfast meal go down for about half an hour before he climbed into the pool. He swam the short lengths repeatedly and leisurely for a while until he rested his elbows on the edge of the infinity pool and gazed into the blue sky streaked with white clouds.

After an hour in the pool, he spied a FusionPlane™ coming into land in his Vehicle Lot. He wasn't expecting visitors, and more to the point, he wasn't in the mood for them. He called Hunter. 'If it's nobody I'm friends with, then I'm not at home. I'm not expecting any visitors today.'

'Yes, sir.' Hunter headed off to the Vehicle Lot to intercept Brady's uninvited guest.

The rogue visitor was Samuel Beardon the Third. Since his first visit here - at the reading of Brady's will, he had been made aware that Hunter was a Disciple and that as part of his role was to spy and report back on Brady's activities. Samuel wasn't sure whose side he was on here. He thought of Tyrone's secrecy and decided to throw his lot in with Bardy Mahone on this issue.

Samuel Beardon the Third prepared himself for battle. He pushed his shoulders up and stood straight and strong and marched away from his rental FusionPlane™. Within a few minutes, Hunter blocked his path. 'I'm sorry, but Brady Mahone is not at home. If you'd care to leave a message...'

'I want to speak to him in person.'

'Then if you'd care to make an appointment.'

'I need to see him, now.'

'I don't know where he is. Now, please leave.'

'But...'

Hunter commanded as a Disciple to a Devout. 'You will leave.'

Samuel marched disconsolately back to his rental FusionPlane™ and considered his options. As he boarded the vehicle, he noticed Hunter talking to the Vehicle Technicians, and he was sure that he would be instructing them not to let Samuel go near the house.

He pulled out his Satt™ and dialled up Brady's number. He let it ring and ring, but there was no answer.

Hawk had been chatting with Debrock and his friends inside the house but needed to use the bathroom. A rare occurrence with

GreenSuits™, but one of the dabs side effects was that it sometimes made users want to urinate, even if they didn't. He heard a Satt™ ringing for ages. It was coming from his Pops' bedroom. He was about to check it out, but it stopped. He went to his room down the hall and made his futile attempt to pee in the toilet in his en-suite bathroom. He couldn't go.

He staggered lazily back to Debrock's room when he heard the Satt™ ringing again. This time he wondered whether one of his brothers was trying to reach Pops. He picked it up, 'Hello...'

'Brady. Is that you?'

'No. It's Hawk. Pops is in the pool.'

'Could you get him for me?'

'I don't think so. He's all wet, y'know.' There was a short silence.

'Ok.' The Bear added as calmly as he could. 'Is there any way you could take this Satt™ to him? It could be a matter of life and death.'

'Err. I suppose so. Who is this?'

'Samuel Beardon the Third.' When he received no confirmation of recognition, he added, 'I was at your party. When your Daddy left you his share of the business.' The Bear let out a huge sigh. He knew he had to resort to the lowest common denominator, 'I was the big black guy who talked a lot about the Bible.'

'Ah. Yes. I remember you, man. Why didn't you say?'

'Could you do me one more thing?'

'Sure. Shoot.'

'I'm kinda hiding from Hunter, so as a favour to me, could you not let him see you give your Daddy this Satt™ - or any of his staff for that matter.'

'Definitely. Pops doesn't trust Hunter as far as he could throw him. You leave it to Hawk.'

The line was quiet apart from the padding of Hawk's feet on the shiny hard floors. After a while, Samuel Beardon the Third picked up the sound of water and the more distant sounds of the Pacific. But then the sound went muffled. He heard Hawk shout. 'Hey, Hunter. You can fuck off for the day and take the staff with you. I'll look after Pops - we'll have us one of those Father and Sons' days. Do you dig?'

'Yes. Certainly, sir.'

There was a further period of silence, and then the muffled sound turned back into the sound of swimming pools and distant waves. 'Hey, Pops. You gotta call. It sounds real important, and he says that Hunter mustn't know about it. Now, I know you gotta a beef with him, so...' There was the sound of splashing water on tiles, and Samuel guessed that Brady had got out of the pool.

'Who is it?'

Hawk had forgotten the name, 'The black dude from the party with all the church stuff.'

There was the sound of the Satt™ being passed over. 'Good boy, son. You've done well.'

'Cheers, Pops.'

Samuel heard Hawk padding away, and he knew the silence was part of Brady's cautious approach to being caught unawares. Brady spoke first, 'Hey, brother. You use the Satt™ about as often as I do, which is barely ever. It must be important.'

'I got a note that I had to visit you.'

'I didn't send you a note...'

'It was from Tyrone. He left it for me to find in my Bible.'

'I'm real confused, man. I've got no idea what you're talking about.'

'It said I had to come and see you here in Malibu, in person. That it was the last chance, I'd ever get to see Tyrone and Raelynn...'

'What's Raelynn gotta do with this?'

'I wasn't even allowed to tell Alicia.'

'I don't know, man. This sounds fishy to me. Are you setting me up? I know how this goes down. We used to compare notes in prison, y'know. The authorities would always pull this scheme where they'd panic ya and make you rush out without thinking...'

'I'm sitting in a rental FusionPlane™, and Hunter has told your technicians that I'm not allowed to leave the vehicle. They are watching me now, waiting until I take off. I'm not going to do that until I know what's happening with Tyrone and Raelynn.'

There was silence for a few seconds. 'Ok. I'll come to you, but if this is a trap, I swear...'

'It's not a trap. I swear by Almighty God.'

It wasn't Almighty God who troubled Brady. It was Bodhi Sattva. 'I'm not coming down in my dressing gown. I want to be prepared. Give me a few minutes while I get changed. I'll come to you.' He cut the Satt™ off to ensure that the Bear understood that his decision was final.

Brady got changed into all his *Trouble Man* gear as he had come to christen it. He had his NanoRepaired™ jeans, boots and white T-shirt, and his trusty Poacher's coat. He even made sure he had his favourite shades on. He made his way to the Vehicle Lot the long way around. He chose to avoid any lingering staff and technicians, and after about thirty minutes, he crept up to the rear of the Vehicle Lot. He decided not to order the technicians away, as he didn't want any gossip reported back to Hunter. He patiently waited until there was a gap in the informal patrols, and he threw some dirt at the windscreen of the Bear's rental FusionPlane™. The NanoShell™ would protect the FusionPlane™, but he hoped the Bear would look where the flying dirt came from. After a couple more attempts, Brady got the the Bear's attention, and he signalled with walking fingers to let him sneak onto the FusionPlane™.

The Bear left the cockpit and crept to the back of the vehicle, where there weren't any windows. He had his Bible with him. He handed Brady the note from inside the Bible as if this somehow gave it more credibility. Brady read it and handed it back to his friend.

Brady said, 'It's definitely Tyrone's handwriting. I'd recognise it a mile off.'

'But you don't know any more about this?'

'No.'

The Bear scratched his head, and he had the look of utter bewilderment. 'Why would he want me to travel all the way down here to meet you and then not tell you about it?'

Brady considered the possibilities, 'He clearly felt the need to keep it secret - even from Alicia. He intended for me to know about it, but he couldn't get the message through. Sounds like he's in trouble if you ask me.' Brady took off his sunglasses and hung them off the neck of his T-shirt. 'Where would he go if he felt the need to hide? Where would he feel safe?'

The Bear wanted to reassure Brady that this wasn't the old Trad world and that all Greens were safe, but the secrecy of Tyrone's actions made a lie of this assumption. He discounted anywhere in San Martin. He then traced a route from San Martin to Malibu in his mind and extended it southwards. 'He has friends in San Diego. They are astronomers at the Palomar Observatory.'

'Yeah. I've heard him mention that. It's one of the few places that your Green friends didn't dissolve with your goo.'

'We have Green reasons for studying astronomy.' The Bear said, trying not to sound too defensive.

'What are we waiting for? Let's go - seems like as good a place as any to make a start.'

The Bear crept forward and looked out of his cockpit window and waved goodbye, sarcastically, to the watching technician. The technician didn't know that Brady was on board, and the Bear wanted him to think that he'd given up on seeing him. He set the coordinates to the Palomar Observatory, and he put the FusionPlane™ on autopilot and auto-landing. He guessed there would be plenty of places to land in an old scientific research centre, but he was still wary of trusting himself to fly and land in the mountains.

This was the Bear's rental FusionPlane™, and the autopilot settings flew the vehicle about as slowly as he did. Brady used the autopilot when he was tired or busy, but usually, he liked to fly as fast as he could. He sighed and tried not to get frustrated at the slow pace.

The journey to the Palomar Observatory was a relative hop, skip, and a jump from Malibu, and they were at the old National Park inside half an hour. Brady had his face glued to the window as he reeled off the types of trees he spotted. As a Green, the Bear was embarrassed to lack in the knowledge and appreciation of the vegetation that Brady demonstrated.

Brady reeled off names and an occasional whistle as he spotted a particularly impressive species. 'Oh wow...you gotta see this...look at the size of that baby...I'm sure that's a Bigcone...been here for more than five-hundred years...Incense Cedar...Douglas Fir...Ponderosa Pine...' They soon reached the scrublands high up in the mountains which were traversed with the grey, NanoProtected™ roads.

When they left the FusionPlane™, Brady took in huge gulps of the fresh mountain air. Samuel Beardon the Third hid his frustration with Brady, as he seemed to be treating the situation as no more than a day trip.

Brady strode on ahead and went into the vast entrance hall of the observatory. It amused and troubled him to see that the signs advertising guided tours and an events calendar from 2084 still were on show - as if these had become museum pieces in the intervening hundred years. He yelled, and his voice echoed in this immaculately clean hallway. 'Hey! Service!' He laughed. 'Has anybody seen my friend Tyrone Beardon?'

He thought he heard echoing footsteps, so he stood still and went quiet. The footsteps were heading this way, and then a young man appeared, and Brady thought he looked like his old buddy Lucian in his younger days. He assumed he was probably one hundred years plus - going on twenty-five. Brady said, 'Hey, buddy. I'm looking for a good friend of mine. He seems to have gone missing. His name is Tyrone Beardon. He usually appears as a black, skinny...tall kid, kinda geeky, wears these tortoiseshell glasses...'

'I know you. You're Brady Mahone. Have you got any rare Science Fiction product?'

Brady dug around in one of his big pockets in his Poacher's coat. He always had sample products on him. He pulled out a big handful of Files. 'I ain't sorted them out into categories, but if there's anything here that takes your fancy...' He asked, 'What's yer name, kid?'

'Destin. My male form is Dustin, and my female is Destiny.' He rooted around in Brady's big hands, and he took about half a dozen rare samples. He seemed absorbed in one of them.

Brady said, 'Are you the only one here?'

'Yes. I'm the day shift.'

'Funny, I thought there'd be lots of workers, y'know, scientists and shit.'

'They've taken up other positions on the Mars colony. They're building observatories up there.'

'That's cool. Anyhows, have you seen my good buddy, Tyrone?'

Destin looked suspiciously at the Bear. 'Who's this?'

The Bear said, 'I'm his uncle, Samuel Beardon the Third.'

'Ah. Yes. Of course, you are.' Destin looked around and then back into the face of the Bear. 'Tyrone was right. You have a real problem with letting go, don't you, old man?'

'I don't know what you mean. What has Tyrone been saying? I've loved him like a son...'

'...But he's not your son, is he?'

'Look. Destin. I just want to find out where he is. I think he's in danger.'

Destin laughed, 'The only danger Tyrone is in is from you interfering with his life. This is why we are so pissed off with the Old Greens. You won your Revolution and built the life that you want, but you don't listen to what we want. In fact, we reject your way of life. What possessed you to think that all we would ever want to do is work in fields and document the local wildlife for the whole of our lives. At least Brady here was bringing us Entertainment Files to fire our imaginations and show us that there are more exciting ways of leading our lives, but what do we get? I'll tell you what you Green Fossils did next. You punished us by depriving us of the UltraViolet™ - God forbid if we want to enjoy ourselves, and then, you try and pin the blame on Brady Mahone. Well, fuck you, we are not so easily fooled.'

Brady said, 'What was Tyrone's beef with Samuel? I've known him a long old time, and he never had a bad word to say about his uncle...'

'Your friend here used his influence with his cronies in Boulder Creek, maybe even with the man, fucking Bodhi Sattva, to pull favours to stop Tyrone's application to go to Mars. It's what Tyrone wanted to do, he had dreamed of something like this for all his life, but this old Green fucker decided for him. Like I said, the Old Greens want us to live their lives - they don't want us to live out our own.'

Brady turned to the Bear, 'Is this true? Did you ask Bodhi to block his application?'

The Bear sighed. 'Yes. I asked Genesis Garcia to arrange it. She put her own son in his place. The one she named after you...'

'I know the one. Real good customer...'

The Bear said to Destin, 'It's true. I did it in his best interests...' Destin shrugged and shook his head at this confirmation that

Tyrone's possessive uncle still hadn't got the message. 'But Tyrone left me this note.' He took out the note from inside his Bible, and he passed it to Destin.

Destin read the note and looked up at the two huge men towering over him. 'It looks convincing, but I just need to check with a sample of his handwriting. I'll be back in a minute.'

He marched off with Tyrone's note in his hand and went to the elevators. Brady and the Bear watched the elevator numbers light up as the carriage reached each new level. Then there was a minute's pause followed by the sound of the elevator being shut down.

Brady and the Bear looked at each other. Then Destin's voice came over the Tannoy system. 'Tyrone is my best friend, and I will never betray him. You'll never find me - I know this complex. Fuck Bodhi. Fuck Sattva Systems™ and fuck you!'

20: HUNGER IN A TIME OF PLENTY

Of all the times Rhea didn't want to be called in for a meeting with Bodhi Sattva, it was now. This would throw her timings out, and she cut a frustrated figure as she marched down the corridors toward Bodhi Sattva's spartan office. An image flashed in her mind how this office was like something the Stasi of the old East German Republic would have looked. She smiled at the realisation that she still had a keen sense of the history of the old trad days.

She looked at her watch. Rhea worked out that she had already lost an hour by diverting to Boulder Creek. She hoped Bodhi wouldn't keep her for too long. She knocked on his office door three times and decisively marched in.

Bodhi smiled beatifically, 'My dear Rhea. Thank you for seeing me at such short notice.'

Rhea wasn't sure if the use of the term *dear* was appropriate, but she couldn't care less about trivialities at this point. 'No problem. What did you want to see me about?'

'I'm keen to understand what Brady Mahone has been up to.'

'Why now?'

'He hasn't been in to collect his Green Credits from his business for quite some time. This is almost unheard of for him. Brady likes his money, and he doesn't usually like to leave it in our care for a moment longer than necessary.'

She resisted the urge to defend Brady, as she knew that there had been numerous times before when he had left his money in Bodhi's trust, especially when he was busy touring the world, establishing new markets. She assumed he was testing her, so she determined that the strategy to adopt was to give him the answers he wanted. 'Brady has scattered his sons to the four corners of the globe to meet up with key Disciples.'

'For what purpose?'

'To influence or plot against you, I assume.'

Bodhi stroked his chin. 'And you know this for a fact?'

'No. But maybe you could check it out - if I gave you the names of the Disciples and the Devout, they have been seeking out...' Bodhi slid a blank piece of paper across his desktop screen which covered his desk, and he selected a pen from an office tidy made from recyclable materials. Without delay, Rhea wrote down the names:

Troy - Bridgett Tarnita
Wilder - Precious
Bill - Cain, Lizzie, and Siddha
Rocky - Glenarvon and Rhea
Hawk - Hunter
Brady - Samuel Beardon the Third, Professor Pinar Dogan, Genesis Garcia, and Bodhi Sattva.

She passed the note nonchalantly over to Bodhi. As he perused the names, he smiled and then laughed as he came to the last name. He quickly returned to a more concerned demeanour. 'The protests emanating from our younger Green communities are troubling. What are your thoughts?'

'They didn't have to put their lives on the line and make the sacrifices that you and the GreenRevs did.'

'But not you?'

'No. I worked for Free News, the Greens' TV Station, but I came to the party late - you could say. I wasn't a GreenRev.'

'What do you think I should do?'

Rhea said without hesitation. 'Give your word that the UltraViolet™ will be given to all at the New Green Year festivities.'

'Is it so wrong of me, that I want them to feel that they have won it, rather than that I just gave it to them - like I have with everything before?'

Rhea shrugged, 'If they win this - what's to say what they will try and win next?'

Bodhi left the question unanswered, he paused for a moment as if it had been considered, but then he changed the subject subtly. 'What do the Disciples and the Devout feel about these protestors?'

'They consider them to be lacking in moral fortitude and generally ungrateful. The Disciples and the Devout have followed every rule to further repair the thousands of years of damage caused by the Trad industries. They were not going to put their reputations at risk by falling to the temptation of the Trad ways - and they certainly weren't going to partake in anything that an old Trad like Brady Mahone was offering them.'

'Have you used any of his entertainment products?'

She thought she detected within his question that he was already confident that he knew the answer. 'No. Never.'

He tapped the paper with the list of names. 'Is there any possibility that anybody here could fall under Brady's spell?'

'None whatsoever.' Rhea knew from her interrogation training to answer decisively.

Bodhi brushed his bald head as if he was sweeping back some imaginary hair. 'I want you to stay out of Rocky Mahone's orbit. I'm sending you to Sweden to contact Bridgett. Ensure she's aware of Troy Mahone's mission.'

Fuck! Please, not now. She thought. 'Sure. When would you like me to go?'

'Sometime in the next couple of days. That will be fine.'

Thank God for that. 'Consider it done. I'll report back on Troy's movements while I'm at it.'

As Rhea left the room, she checked her watch. She knew she was probably already too late. She hurried along the corridors but not so quickly as to attract unnecessary attention. She raced past the Main Entrance - glancing briefly at the one-hundred-year-old banner with the thirteen promises written with Glenarvon Cole's scrawl. She was stressed as it seemed to take forever to pass all the cream-coloured buildings and giant vats to reach the Vehicle Lot.

She located a spare rental FusionPlane™ and was further frustrated when she had to await clearance before she could leave at the back of a queue headed by the other Disciple's privately owned vehicles. As she lifted off, she rapidly headed toward Malibu, hoping she could catch them in time.

She checked the tracking of Brady Mahone's FusionPlane™, FusionPassengerJet™ and his FusionCar™. She breathed a sigh of relief as they were all still in Brady's Parking Lot.

When she touched down at Brady's Malibu home, she was greeted by a technician. 'Hello. How can I help you?'

'I've come to visit, Brady Mahone.'

'Is he expecting you?'

'No. But he will want to see me.'

The technician sneered. 'I'm sure he would, normally. But I'm afraid, Mr Mahone is not currently in residence.'

'Can you call the house? Maybe you could get Hunter to see me?'

'Hunter's services have been dispensed with for the day. He won't be reporting back for duty until tomorrow.'

'Ok. Who is in charge?'

'That would be Hawk.'

'Well, call him, then.'

'Who shall I say is calling?'

Rhea worked in the shadows of the Green hierarchy. Many knew her as a Disciple close to Bodhi, but this person obviously didn't recognise her. She knew that somebody, probably Hunter, had informed Sattva Systems™ of Marjorie's impromptu visit, so she felt she should adopt a fake identity. She considered which names to choose from, where it could gain Hawk's attention but not raise suspicions among Brady's staff.

'Angela Skye.'

'Of course.' He marched away, presumably to discuss this visitor out of earshot.

After a couple of minutes, he returned. 'Hawk will receive you in the main lounge. I'm sure you know the way?'

She didn't, but she wasn't going to let him know that. 'Yes. Thank you.'

Rhea followed the trail to the house, and she came across Debrock on the grounds. He said, stoned, as usual, 'Hey, Rhea. Am I dreaming this? It is you, isn't it?'

'Hello, Debrock. Don't worry. I'm not here to take you home to San Martin. I'm looking for the main lounge. I'm here to see Hawk. You couldn't do me a favour and take me there - could you?'

'Sure thing. You follow me.'

Rhea was conscious of wasting precious time, but stoned Debrock only had one pace - and that was dead slow. They seemed to meander meaninglessly for long minutes until they finally reached the main hall. Hawk didn't say anything as he looked at his uninvited guest. His Pops' paranoia was ingrained in him. He said to Debrock, 'Thanks, man. Hey, I tell you what. Why don't you and your friends use the hot tubs? Pops is away on business, and I'm the only son left, so you have my permission.'

Debrock cheered lazily, 'Yay! That'd be sweet.' He zigzagged away as if he was dancing to an imaginary song.

Hawk said, 'I presume you are the Angela Skye I was waiting for. Funny, I did think that Pops had never mentioned any relatives of Libby.'

'I'm Rhea Laidlaw. Disciple of San Martin...'

'...Close friend of Bodhi and his cronies.'

She had to be careful not to blow her cover or do anything that could arouse suspicions with Bodhi back in Boulder Creek. She already knew she could locate Brady with the tracking device in his coat. 'I really wanted to see Brady. I suppose I should have made an appointment.'

'Pops isn't here. I don't know where he is. I'm sorry.'

'When did he leave?'

'About an hour or so ago?'

'And he's not due back anytime soon?'

'I honestly don't know. I'm sorry you've had a wasted journey and all...'

'It's no problem. It's not that important. I was just asked while I was in the neighbourhood to drop in and let Brady know that he has a lot of Green Credits to pick up in Boulder Creek, but I'm sure he's aware of that already. Anyway, I better be going. I've got a lot of other errands to complete. Would you be so kind as to walk me back to my FusionPlane™? I don't want to get lost. I wouldn't want you thinking the worst of me if I ended up being somewhere I shouldn't.'

'Yeah. No problem.'

As they walked, Rhea was conscious that she needed to find out more, but she had to take it slowly, as she knew Brady's sons were fiercely loyal to him. 'Hawk...you're the youngest, aren't you?'

'Yeah, that's right.'

'And was your Moppa Amie or Helgarth?'

'Amie is my Maddy.'

'Does she ever talk about the days when she was a Trad living at the same ranch as Brady?'

'Sometimes. But she tries not to in front of Helgarth - xe really loves xyr.'

The Parking Lot came into view, 'Brady loves his fleet. I'm surprised he didn't use one of his own private vehicles.'

Hawk carried out the inventory of his Pops' fleet in his mind. She was right. They were all still here. 'Yeah...He musta gone off in that black dude's FusionPlane™.'

Rhea knew that there was a time before the Yellow™ that any remotely racist utterings would have been challenged by the Security Protocols™, but now that anybody could choose any identity, it ceased to become an issue, and the Security Protocols™ sensitivity settings were so broad that it wasn't clear whether this remark could trigger them. All of which was beside the point to Rhea as she had her information.

21: OUT OF TIME

B rady banged his fist on the elevator door a few times. He couldn't bring forth much more in the way of anger and frustration as deep down, it was futile. The Palomar Observatory complex was massive, and Destin would know the place intimately. There was no point in searching for him as they would just be wasting time.

He turned to the Bear, 'Any more ideas? I don't know where he hangs out.'

The Bear went over to the gift shop, which now looked like the tackiest museum in the world, with plastic telescopes, mugs decorated with planets, and Palomar Observatory T-shirts wrapped in plastic. The Bear picked up a map from the bookshop which covered the South-western states. He opened it out and examined it.

Brady was distracted by the T-shirts, and he decided to buy one as a souvenir. He didn't care that it now cost a lot of Green Credits as it was technically an antique. Shortage of Green Credits was not an issue for Brady, so he took out his Distor™ and placed it in the Green Self-Service Receptacle and gave his two-hundred and fifty Green Credits freely.

Welcome to NanoPay™ at the Green Palomar Observatory. NanoPay™ is part of Sattva Systems™ Green Finance Initiative. All proceeds will go to saving Mother Earth. Your custom is important to us. Have a nice Green Day.

Brady had spent the equivalent of two weeks wages of the average Green worker for his T-shirt. He sniffed around his armpit. It was ok, he had showered and bathed this morning, but he was looking for an excuse to put his new T-shirt on. He looked around - out of ancient habits when undressing in a gift shop would be considered bad form. He realised there was only the Bear here, and he didn't count. So, he took off his Poacher's coat and stripped off his trusty white T-shirt and put on his black *I've been to the Palomar Observatory...* on the front, and on the rear of the T-shirt with stars and galaxies pictured within the black cotton it stated for all to see *...and it was out of this world, man!* He looked at himself admiringly in the mirror. He held in his belly and flexed his biceps, and he was pleased with his appearance and physique. He liked this new addition to his wardrobe. Brady stuffed his old T-shirt in one of his Poacher's coat pockets and fingered the other goods on display in the gift shop. He hadn't had a hit of retail therapy lately.

The Bear looked up from his map and was frustrated at Brady's lack of urgency. 'If you've done shopping - we've still got to find Tyrone...'

'Yeah, man. Sure.' He sauntered over and checked out the map the Bear was hunched over. 'Watcha thinking?'

'He was heading south, that's for certain. Otherwise, he'd have never sent me to you. He wanted me to be this neck of the woods.'

'Yeah. Makes sense.'

The Bear circled an area of the map with his chunky forefinger. 'He's got to be south of Malibu.'

Brady moved in closer, 'I've obviously had dealings in all these parts.'

'Any places in particular which mean anything to you and Tyrone?'

'Well, yeah. But I ain't going there?'

'Where?'

'Encinitas. Y'know, where the International Space Station crashed at the turn of the century.'

The Bear was excited. He knew that Brady was onto something. 'Yes. Yes. That's it.'

'It might be, but I can't go there.'

'Why not?'

'Maybe you'd be alright, what with your UltraVioletSuit™ and all. But that place might still be contaminated with all that radiation shit. I ain't taking a risk like that on one of your wild goose chases.'

'I hear you, brother. Can we just check it out by air? It's not far from here. We could do a quick flyover...there's nothing else there...he should be easy to spot...a FusionPlane™ or FusionCar™ should stick out like a sore thumb...'

Brady nodded, 'Ok. I know we are in your rental but promise me you won't land. I mean it...'

'I promise. You have my word.'

They walked back to the FusionPlane™. Brady dumped his Poacher's coat on the rear seat. He put his shades back on while the Bear set the autopilot to fly to Encinitas. Brady quipped, 'Hey, man. I thought we are in a hurry. You do know you can fly faster...'

'Better to be late in this world than early in the next...'

'Yeah, yeah. But I still hate being late.'

They were both quiet as the FusionPlane™ reached the airspace above Encinitas as they scanned the ground from their windows. If there had ever been a nuclear explosion around here, then Mother Nature had done an excellent job of hiding it. They were travelling in Level Two, the lowest level to the ground and usually used by the slowest rental FusionPlane™ pilots. Brady only ever flew at the higher and faster levels, those being Level Four for the quickest FusionPlanes™ or occasionally in Level Five if he took his FusionPassengerJet™ for a spin. They circled slowly over the remnants of Encinitas without spotting anything like another vehicle and certainly nothing resembling Tyrone and Raelynn.

Brady spotted another FusionPlane™ coming in rapidly, two Levels above them. It flew past them. He watched it as it descended, decelerated, and then crept up behind them. 'Hey, man. We're being followed.'

'Who by?'

'I can't see. I don't know.' He was more alarmed when the trailing FusionPlane™ was manoeuvring to overtake them. 'I thought you guys didn't have cops anymore?'

'We don't. The Security Protocols™ replaced them.'

'Well, this sure feels like a cop stop to me.'

The trailing FusionPlane™ pulled up alongside, and they were both shocked to see Rhea frantically waving to grab their attention. The Bear said, 'She's attached to us in convoy mode.'

Rhea disappeared from the cockpit for a moment and then returned, and she held up cards to the window:

Follow me quickly.

Very little time.

I'm taking you to Tyrone and Raelynn.

Hurry.

Brady shouted, 'Move over, old man. We ain't got time for Granny driving.' He could see Rhea racing away, and he was up for the chase.

The Bear wanted to object, but Brady had already started to slide over from the passenger side. He struggled to move his considerable bulk around the driver's seat. Brady wasted no time taking over the controls and showed little concerns for the Bear's feelings on the matter, 'I'll demonstrate that this baby is built for speed, not comfort, old buddy.' He laughed heartily as he switched to manual flight mode and upped the FusionPlane™ rapidly to Level Four and pushed the vehicle to its' speed limits to try and catch up with Rhea, who was already in the distance.

He struggled but finally squeezed himself around Brady and eventually settled into the passenger seat. 'Why didn't she call me? I've got my Satt™.'

'Same reason Tyrone left you cryptic notes. She doesn't want to be traced or overheard.'

'Where are we heading?'

'East. I don't know much else. You keep an eye on the ground and the display screens. I'm concentrating on keeping up with her. I think we may have to do some nifty driving when we fly over any major Green areas.'

'Why do you say that?' The Bear struggled to disguise his concern.

'I know you Greens aren't supposed to be nostalgic, but it sure ain't no coincidence to me that every time it's the Holidays, every Level gets packed.' He added to emphasise his point, 'I don't think it's only the Brady Mahone entertainment products they keep secret from the powers that be - is all I'm saying.'

The Bear couldn't answer. The speed terrified him, and he gripped the sides of his seat as if his life depended on it.

Brady joked, 'Hey, you're the guy with the protective Suits™ on. It's me that should be worried if we crash. Stop being such a pussy.' He added, not too reassuringly, 'If we did crash. Do you really think holding onto the chair would do much good? Y'know, in the circumstances?'

'I know. I never did like flying. If God had meant us to be in the skies, he would have given us wings.'

Brady ignored the platitudes. 'Where are we now?' I'm catching Rhea, but she's changing her flightpath slightly...'

'New Green Tucson.'

'Ok. This will be fun.' Brady could see the traffic building ahead, but he also saw that Rhea was dodging and weaving through it without slowing down. 'Jeez, she's one helluva racy lady.' He swooped past any vehicle that wasn't flying at maximum speed, which was every other vehicle on Level Four. The one thing that Brady was grateful for was the innate politeness of the Greens on the road. The Trads in his day would have given him hell and every type of derogatory gesture known to mankind by now. He moved as close as he could to keep on the straightest route, trusting the shield around every Green vehicle to prevent collisions - not just with other travellers but also the flying insects and birds. The traffic eventually thinned out again as they headed over more open land.

The speed of travel didn't stop, but now Brady had Rhea closer to him. The lack of nearby vehicles as reference points made it feel to the Bear as if they had slowed a little. Brady said, 'If we pass over El Paso and then head in the direction of Houston, then I think I can make a pretty good guess on where she's heading for. However, it's gonna be a long flight.'

'The Bear looked away and then at Brady, 'Where?'

'Florida. Cape Cassandra. I think they've got a one-way ticket to Mars.' Brady said, 'Do ya think she's trying to stop them?'

'No. I think she wants us both to have the opportunity to wave them goodbye.'

'Oh. Ok. You mean, Raelynn...'

'Yes. Both of them.'

Samuel Beardon the Third and Brady were both quiet as they considered their options and potential next moves. The likely destination hurt Samuel as he realised, he was losing Tyrone forever, but he also was grateful to Rhea for this second chance to make it right with him. He asked his God to give him the strength he needed to tell him goodbye and to do it with good grace.

Brady, too, was more emotional about losing Raelynn than he ever would admit to another man. He never wanted daughters, but he liked Helgarth's baby girl a lot. He liked her otherworldliness. *Well, she sure is going to be otherworldly now. I ain't gonna blub. I'll have to use some man-up spray as this is gonna be tough for old Brady Mahone.* He was grateful for the distraction of the excuse of rapid flying and overtaking over Green El Paso, but he was also saddened at another piece of evidence confirming his theory. Rhea began to stretch her lead over him in her FusionPlane™, and Brady put it down to his concentration being negatively affected.

The Bear stared disconsolately out of the window and replied to Brady's questions and cajoling with grunts and curt phrases until Brady knew to leave him be. He occasionally heard the Bear praying for strength and forgiveness in hushed tones.

They came upon a massive amount of air traffic over Houston. Brady cursed and gestured angrily. 'Fucking Greens! If I had my own FusionPlane™ and not your rental piece of shit, I coulda headed to Cape Cassandra like the crow flies. But no - life's never that fucking simple. You have to restrict the air traffic within imaginary columns above the road network. Fucking dickwads. If we fucking miss them because of these bastard cheating Greens going home for the Holidays...' He gestured angrily and shouted uselessly as he slowly passed a woman pilot with a kid next to her. 'Hey, lady. Only Trads are allowed to celebrate the Holidays, and you murdered the fucking lot of them. Yeah, so go back home.' She looked across at Brady, and this only encouraged him, 'I wish you fucking Greens had died and not the fucking Trads. You hypocritical fuckers make me sick...yeah, I'm talking to you, bitch.'

She turned her head away, and Brady could tell she had instructed the kid to look the other way. He turned to see the Bear glaring at him. Brady let out a deep breath and shrugged, 'I told ya, didn't I? This is Holiday traffic...ok, ok, I shouldn't have let it get me so mad...'

He felt his FusionPlane™ tug, and a warning came on his screen: *Hand over controls to Disciple remote capture. Y/N?*

He didn't feel he had a choice. The traffic on all Levels from One to Four had come to a standstill. He said, 'Yes.'

The FusionPlane™ seemed to move of its' own accord out to the edge of the traffic and over an imaginary hard shoulder. It then moved so close to Rhea's FusionPlane™ that it felt like it was attempting to dock with it. And then both vehicles sped away - not at maximum speed but at least at a rate quick enough to let Brady's blood pressure fall to a more natural rate.

Once through the traffic jams of Houston, the FusionPlanes™ undocked, and they raced at maximum speed and Brady knew what was happening; they could only fly at half-speed in convoy. Therefore, he knew that if they couldn't bypass the traffic quickly, then Rhea would use this tactic again. They travelled with little difficulty over Green Beaumont and New Green Lafayette but docked once more over the congested New Green Orleans. They had no problems with Green Pensacola and New Green Tallahassee, but they needed the convoy mode to make their way through the final major obstacle of Green Orlando, and then they finally arrived in the vicinity of Cape Cassandra.

22: ROCKETS AND DREAMS

The rental FusionPlanes™ docked again as they glided slowly over the Green Port of St John and onto Green Merritt Island. Brady trusted Rhea to know what to do next. He relinquished his controls to let both FusionPlanes™ land together.

Brady alighted the FusionPlane™ looking like a tourist, with his black T-shirt and shades on. The Bear followed him out, muttering complaints under his breath. Rhea said, 'Hi. You two.'

The Bear growled to Brady, 'You drive like a mad man, and you should show more respect to your fellow travellers...'

'Hey, wait a minute. They shouldn't be travelling today, not in those numbers, and you know it. You're just taking their side...'

Rhea laughed, 'You remind me of my old mum and dad, with your bickering. They were always the same, every holiday, no matter how much my mum would promise not to lecture dad on his driving, or how he would promise to take it easy on the gas...'

Brady and Samuel both looked at the ground and made some uncommunicated agreement to drop the argument on the grounds that it was making them look bad. Brady said, 'Long time, no see. Good to see you again, Rhea. I keep meaning to bump into you, but you're a hard lady to track down.'

'Good to see you too, Brady.' She kissed him lightly on the cheek. 'You wouldn't believe how much work I have to do. I think some people think that being a Disciple is a stroll in the park. Anyway, there's very little time - you'll have to follow me.'

The Bear said, 'Will I get to meet Tyrone before he goes?'

'No. I'm sorry. We are too late for that. I knew it would be a struggle with the traffic. That's why I flew at maximum speed. However, if we are lucky, we might be able to see them pass by as they board the FusionSpaceShuttle™. Come on.'

She marched away, and Brady and the Bear encouraged their stiff legs to run after her. She was waved through checkpoints as if the guards were already aware of her arrangements, and Brady knew that every minute she saved them was precious if they were to make it on time.

At the final checkpoint, Brady could hear Rhea confirming her position as Disciple of San Martin and confirming that she had escorted the close relatives of the astronauts to see them off on their journey to Mars. He watched the guards eye him suspiciously, and Brady wondered whether it would matter whether they recognised him or not. He recalled the feeling of trying to sneak on a ride that he was too small for when he was a kid. The checkpoint guard stood to one side, and Rhea waved them through. She gestured for them to join her on an escalator with no sides which rose more than a hundred feet into the air.

The Bear was less freaked out than Brady about travelling on this. Rhea said, 'It has a NanoShell™ over it for uninterrupted vision. You cannot fall or jump for that matter.' She joked. 'This Shell™ is impenetrable. It's the same when you reach the viewing platform at the top. It's protected from the sub-sonic booms of the blast-off.' She wagged her finger at them, 'So, no Sonic Boom Surfing for you boys.'

Brady found it hard to relax. He had entered their impenetrable Shells™ before when it should have been impossible for him to do so. What if the reverse could happen here? What if he could fall through it? He had a sense of vertigo, which wasn't helped by the thought that a sub-sonic boom could blow him off the platform if the structure was geared for Greens and not Trads. He was on a stairway to heaven with no means of getting off.

When the escalator let him off at the end, Brady was greeted by a bridge with no sides and far above the ground. His legs felt heavy. He wouldn't have minded revealing his fear to the Bear, but he desperately wanted to keep his masculinity intact for Rhea. He took one leaden step after another until Rhea selected the spot for them to observe from. Brady stood straight, but his body wanted to sway into the void. He reached out tentatively, and he touched the NanoShell™. He wanted to feel something, he expected it to feel squishy and filmy, but instead, it felt tough like reinforced glass or Perspex. He sighed and caught a glimpse of Rhea smiling at him.

'Hey, you Greens are used to this. Us mere Trads can still be killed easy like, y'know.'

'As if I would let anything bad happen to you, the great Brady Mahone, the Trad King of the World.' If she was playing him then it worked, as Brady stood straight and tall as if watching over an empire. It eased his mind as other Greens came up to him and greeted him as if he was a movie star being among them. These were brief encounters for the Greens on the viewing platform, as their attention was pulled back to the walkway that briefly ran parallel to their own, the walkway that would lead to the FusionSpaceShuttle™ mission to colonise Mars - a mission that used to take months had been whittled down to weeks with the advent of Sattva Systems™ FusionPower™.

And then the cheers rang out amid spontaneous clapping and the shouting of the names of loved ones. He loved the look of pride on Rhea's face. It was the look of a woman who had achieved her mission against all odds. She caught him looking at her, and she gestured him to put his eyes forward in case he missed it.

There were dozens in the procession. The astronauts didn't need space suits like he remembered from times long since passed. They had their UltraVioletSuits™, and Brady thought he could make out a misty green bubble around them. He recalled the bubbles his Pops described when he first brought him up to speed with how Sattva Systems™ had made their money in the early days. They rescued the aviation industry with their use of NanoBubbles™ for each passenger in the wake of the three pandemics of the 2020s and 2030s. He wondered if this was an extension of that to help them survive the spaceflight and thrive on Mars.

'There he is. I can see him. Tyrone. Tyrone!' The Bear jumped up and down as he desperately waved, hoping for Tyrone to see him among the crowd.

Brady bellowed across the void, 'Hey, Tyrone...Raelynn!' He saw Raelynn look over, and then she nudged Tyrone, and then he saw Brady Mahone and his Uncle Sam waving vigorously. They shouted uselessly back and forth, but their words were lost like all the others in the din. But just like all the other astronauts and the crowds which had come to see them off, the smiles and the tears were evident for all to see. Brady found it difficult to contain his emotions and was grateful for the chance to release them by playing the fool. Tyrone pointed at him. He pointed at him again and laughed and then mockingly bowed. He said something to Raelynn, which she obviously thought was hilarious, and then she looked at Brady as if she was touched by his loving gesture. It was then that he remembered the black T-shirt he was wearing proclaiming proudly: *I've been to the Palomar Observatory.* He laughed loudly enough to force back the tears. He pointed to the front of his T-shirt to leave no doubt that he got the joke. He then turned to show them the punchline: *...and it was out of this world, man!* As he turned, Rhea grabbed his hands and kissed him as if somebody had just announced that the war between the Trads and the Greens was over. She pulled away and smiled, and then she promptly turned him around before he could lose the last vital seconds of waving his loved ones away, forever.

He was giddy as he felt as if his legs would buckle under the sheer joy and sadness he felt in that moment. He watched Tyrone, and Raelynn put all their effort into one last wave goodbye, and then they slowly disappeared from view. The Bear was sobbing pools of tears, and he grabbed Brady and hugged him, and buried his head in his shoulders to hide the fact that he was crying. He felt the heat and dampness from the tears soak into his new T-shirt. He felt awkward hugging his friend. He saw many others in the viewing crowd doing precisely the same with no shame or embarrassment. He slapped the Bear on the back and then hugged his fellow giant of a friend to give the Bear and himself the comfort they needed.

After a minute, they unwound from each other awkwardly. It was then that Brady realised that Rhea had gone.

23: WITHOUT YOU

B rady let the Bear fly the FusionPlane™ back to Malibu. If he wanted to fly like a granny on weed, then that was fine by him. He looked out at the passenger window wistfully, trying to land his emotions without crashing.

He was grateful that the lift-off had gone without a hitch - and that he had been entirely safe on the viewing platform as it had been completely insulated from the sub-sonic booms. He knew it was useless, but it still didn't stop him from checking out every crowd for a glimpse of Rhea.

The FusionPlane™ made quiet if painfully slow progress westwards across the Green States of America - its given name from the New Year onwards in 2185. There were other changes planned, which Brady had no intention of adopting. It had recently been announced that the Green citizens would be adopting GreenMetricTime™ or GMT™, something which had caused consternation among the Greens, young and old alike. Sattva Systems™ believed it would simplify their calculations and computational power as they worked on the next big project - that of saving the Earth from a future cataclysmic event, with the advent of the Sun turning into a super-red giant star over the next few billions of years. They would be adopting measures of one thousand days, which meant three imperial years would become one GreenMetricYear™, which would then be split into one-hundred Green Intervals, each comprising of ten Green Days.

There were already protests about the haves and have-nots of the UltraVioletSuits™, and to many Greens, this felt like a deliberate act of provocation from Sattva Systems™. All old mechanisms of marking time were scheduled to be replaced in the New Green Year, and the Security Protocols™ were rumoured to be set to challenge anybody using Traditional or Trad-Time, as it became more colloquially known.

Brady knew he didn't have a strong suit for math, and he couldn't get his head around one hundred Green hours, with ten Green minutes each comprising of a thousand Green seconds. He wondered if it would be easier for him to resort to the phases of the Moon if they found some way to stop his watches and clocks. He knew they would win in the end. The powers that be always did. When the metric system came in, most of the world caved into it, but America held out for as long as it could. He always used the imperial measurements, but slowly but surely, the scientists and the engineers turned to metric measurements. He knew that the Satts™ were already programmed to switch to the New Green Time on New Year's Day, and that would force people to become accustomed to it. This new development seemed to be the last straw for Brady's willingness to play in this New Green World. Maybe he was getting too long in the tooth to be a player anymore.

The blue sky gave him the impression that they were barely moving at all, and he was dismayed when he looked down to see they were passing a busy Green area and then checking the display screen to see that they had only travelled as far as Green Pensacola. Brady sighed, and the Bear barely acknowledged him.

'What do you think is going on?' Brady said, trying to break the ice.

'What do you mean, brother?'

'I dunno. The long-term plan which Bodhi is working on. Do you think he will let everybody have the UltraViolet™?'

'I think he will, eventually. If I were Bodhi, I would want the younger Pure Greens to be more grateful for what we had to go through to save the planet. They have become accustomed to the easy life.'

'What's it like, y'know, the UltraViolet™? Does it make you feel any different? I don't want to get deep and heavy, but today has kinda got to me.'

'I feel you, brother. It has had a profound effect on my soul. I thought I'd experienced all there was in life, but life has a habit of giving you something new to consider.'

'So, are you going to tell me what it's like to wear the UltraViolet™?'

The Bear fiddled nervously with the flight controls and then double-checked that he had correctly put it into autopilot. 'You know I can't divulge...'

'Ok. I get it. But surely you can talk about vague stuff, maybe even spiritual differences...' Brady felt as if he had made a mistake, in the same way as if he had asked a question about the night sky to Tyrone. He half hoped that the Bear would refuse to answer. He watched the Bear's facial movements and concluded that he wasn't going to be able to get out of this now.

'I am the same man, deep inside, that I ever was.'

'Just go along with me here. I'm not questioning your faith...' Brady bargained. 'But let's say you are 80% Nanoparticles and 20% human; does that mean that only 20% of you worships God?'

The Bear laughed, 'That was almost spoken as a man of science, my friend. When I die, I will be 0% human, but my soul will be 100% spirit, and God will welcome me to Heaven if I am well judged by him. Heaven is 0% Earth, and yet my spirit will reside there for eternity.' He was pleased that Brady didn't retort immediately. Brady put his hand on his chin and then pushed his fingers through his stubbly grey-black hair on his head and stared out of the window.

Minutes passed before Brady said, 'I think I had one of those near-death experiences, y'know.'

'You mean you nearly died? When was this, brother?'

'Not me. No, I was thinking about a time, more than forty years ago, when I attended Mrs Wilson's funeral.'

'Mrs Wilson?'

'Oh, sorry. You wouldn't know her. She was an old woman I knew in West McFarland, I mean, Green McFarland as it's known now.'

'It doesn't matter. What happened with this Mrs Wilson?' the Bear asked gently, as he assumed his role in San Martin as a preacher and spiritual guide.

Brady was uncomfortable with the memory. He took a deep breath as he prepared to revisit the horror of that day. 'It was like she was two different people living inside the same body.' He paused to gather his thoughts. He wasn't sure if he understood the depths; he was about to travel. 'If I put this wrong, then I'm not trying to offend anybody - least of all you...'

'I understand. Go on.' He smiled.

'At first, I thought I saw a ghost, her ghost, everybody did, even the Greens were screaming, but it was her NanoSuit™ rising out of the grave. Not Mrs Wilson...it wasn't her...it was just her NanoSuit™ leaving the grave like it had a mind of its own.'

'That must have been very scary - even for you. I've never seen this phenomenon, but I know about the recycling. What happened next?'

'It was disorientated. It was the time when Bodhi was ill, do you remember that?'

'Absolutely. Many of my faith equated that with Jesus's walking into the wilderness.'

Brady was concerned about being side-tracked from his story and being led into one of the Bear's Bible tales. 'Bodhi was safely tucked away in a Sensory Deprivation Chamber and wheeled away to a storage room with dozens more of them. It was like a morgue. Anyway, Bodhi wasn't in the wilderness. He was in a stockroom in Boulder Creek...'

'Of course. You were saying?'

'Yeah. It was weird. Mrs Wilson kept turning slowly and then stopping at intervals as if she was tuning into something. And then she found me. I'm not explaining this very well. Of course, Mrs Wilson didn't find me - her NanoSuit™ did. It tried to jump me, like a drunk broad in a nightclub. It was fucking horrible.' He grimaced as he vividly recalled the slimy substance trying to envelop him. 'I forced it off me, man. It was horrible. I was glad to see the back of it.'

'Is that what troubles you. I assure you that if you took the Green, the feeling of wearing the NanoSuits™ is joyous. You felt the effects of a second-hand and old Suit™, not a new one.'

'It's not that. I wondered if she was giving me her soul.'

The Bear was astonished at this thought. 'No. It was a recycled NanoSuit™. The soul cannot physically manifest itself...'

'Not even with the smallest of particles and the technology of the greatest minds that ever lived?'

'No. What you saw, and what you experienced on that dreadful day, was the recycling of Nanoparticles. Nothing more.'

Brady nodded, 'I don't want to argue with you. After all, you're the expert.' He paused, 'And it makes me feel better to tell you the truth.'

The Bear laughed warmly, 'Glad to be of service, brother.'

It wasn't the end of the matter for Brady, though. The FusionPlane™ glided serenely along, but Brady knew he had only reached third base. His mind was a whirl of recollections from the past. He thought of his Pops and the Mahone Ranch and the Los Banos files in his bunker. He thought wistfully of his times with Lucian, Mary-Lou, and Amie, and he considered his unlikely friendship with Professor Yuan Chu and Judge Audre Jefferson. He wanted to reread her two-hundred-page summary. Brady now appreciated the trouble she had taken to make it palatable for him to digest. He also recalled his *Crime of the Century* in blackmailing Bodhi into making him the richest man in the world. He still had those incriminating files as an insurance policy. Maybe they could be wheeled out again and used as leverage? However, he hated it when even criminals went back on their word. But still...He dwelled on this pact he had with Bodhi. Bodhi had never mentioned it again. But why would he?

'Hey, man. Instead of going to Malibu, could you drop me off at my ranch in McFarland?'

The Bear fiddled with the controls and checked it three times until he was reassured that he had correctly entered the details. 'Consider it done, friend.'

While Brady was thinking about Bodhi, he said almost absent-mindedly, 'Do you think Bodhi believes he has saved their souls?'

Samuel Beardon the Third took a moment to jump back on-board Brady's train of thought, 'I'm sorry. What?'

'He's recreated parts of your bodies with his Nanoparticles. I mean - you could be 80% Nano...'

'...You are the one that put a figure on it. I have no idea.' He was conscious not to have given away too much information on the UltraViolet™.

'Ok. But you've got to admit that if his scientists and engineers have made this much progress...'

'I'm sorry, Brady. But as much as I'd love to believe that Bodhi is dedicated to Christianity, he is ultimately a scientist and engineer.'

'I'd have said businessman.' Brady corrected. 'Just go with me here. Would he experiment with the idea if it didn't cost anything? I mean, it's not just the Nanoparticles he is recycling. Mrs Wilson still had the essence of Mrs Wilson, I know, I felt it.' He involuntarily squirmed. 'Bodhi wanted her to go to him. He was her light at the end of death's tunnel. And it isn't just Mrs Wilson, is it? It's every dead Green. He's collecting their discarded NanoSuits™ and their memories and feelings.' He looked into the eyes of the Bear, 'If it isn't collecting souls, then it's the next best thing.'

For the first time in his life, the Bear tried to retreat from discussing the Bible and its teachings. 'I agree with it feeling unethical, but not from a religious point of view but from Green perspective. This feels more akin to the data mining from the twenty-first century Trad tech companies. If Bodhi is at fault, and I'm not saying he is, but if he is, then he could be accused of a borderline Trad crime.' He said resolutely. 'I will question Bodhi on the ethics of this.'

Brady laughed. 'Ok. Cool. I'm on a roll now. You don't mind, do you? It's just that you seem a little aggravated, old man.'

The Bear shook his head and laughed, 'You certainly know how to make this flight go quicker. What's next from the pulpit of Brady Mahone?'

'Ok. Get this. Bodhi is always one step ahead of the rest of the world when it comes to NanoSuits™, am I right? When you were all Red™, he was Orange™ and so on?'

'This is correct, but he also stated that one day we would all be equal, and that day has come for those who now are UltraViolet™.'

'I'm not buying that. I think he is always going to stay one step ahead of you.'

The Bear chuckled. 'Bodhi has never been a cult of personality type. He lives and works simply, humbly. His whole life has been dedicated to fulfilling our wishes, not the other way around. It was the Greens who gave him the commandments, not God handing the tablets to Moses. You have him all wrong, my friend. He is a good man, and he helped bring peace and stability to the human race.' He added before Brady could retort, 'I know there are some who desire more out of life, and who are stirring up trouble, but even this, I see as Bodhi's plan, and just because I don't understand it, doesn't mean it won't turn out alright in the end. I trust him. Whenever I have doubted him, he has always come through on the big issues. My personal problems are trivial when they stand beside the goal of saving Mother Earth.'

If he thought that his summary was the last word on the subject, then Brady was about to disappoint him. 'I don't know much about this Moses dude, but I know criminals. I think he's like your Godfather of the Green Mafia...'

'Bodhi shows no desire for accumulating money.'

'Some of the gangland bosses had so much money that I doubt if they could count it. They had other motivations. It was about power and respect. They used to bang on about family, but it was more about ego. They were self-important...'

'I'm unconvinced. Bodhi can be challenged without fear of reprisals...'

Brady chewed this over and then spat out, 'I think he's handing out reprisals right now.' He asked, 'Do you think Bodhi would ever just retire? Y'know, step back and let someone else take over. I dunno, Sissy or Glen?'

'Those are questions that are above my pay grade. I wouldn't want to see that happen. Bodhi Sattva is wiser and more knowledgeable than any other candidate.'

'Ok. Yeah. Bodhi's into accumulating knowledge, wisdom...'

'Nothing wrong with that, brother.'

'I wish Professor Chu or Judge Jefferson was here. A clever Trad would help a brother out here.' Brady muttered.

He looked out of the window and was glad he had suggested going to McFarland instead of Malibu, if only because it was a change of route on this long flight home. He looked at a significant Green blot on the landscape, and his display screen indicated that they were now flying over Green Albuquerque. They were heading into the latter stages of their return journey. Brady kept his thoughts to himself for a while. Apart from when he chuckled when the screen informed them that below was the Petrified Forest. He wondered how a forest could be scared.

Brady berated himself for being grumpy company, 'Hey. Do you think Tyrone and Raelynn will be ok?'

'I can't lie. I'm really gonna miss Tyrone. Rhea helped me rectify the biggest mistake in trying to stop him from leaving.'

'If it helps, then I know that Raelynn loves him. I know it ain't been long, but it must have been a massive decision to leave behind the luxury of Malibu to go with him to another world.'

The Bear said softly, 'You didn't upset me with your questions earlier. It's good to challenge entrenched positions. Take Raelynn, for instance. It's like you were saying, the younger generation are getting bored of Green way of life, I'm not stupid, I see it. I just took it personally that Tyrone could feel like that, and as for Raelynn, I guess there's no challenge in having it all from the moment you were born. It's always been true that familiarity breeds contempt. I didn't mean...'

'I know. You aren't the sort to go scoring points off people. You've never tried to break my balls. I've always liked that about you.' He added, 'It's kinda capturing the old American pioneering spirit - heading off to a new frontier on Mars. Don'cha think?'

'Yes. I suppose it is, like the Mayflower heading to the New World.'

Brady didn't know what the Mayflower was but guessed he agreed with him. 'I know that Glenarvon Cole disagrees with this business of colonising Mars. He told me so. He thinks they are betraying this world and that Mother Earth should be restored with the resources we have, and not wasting them on messing with other pristine worlds.'

'I can empathise. Glenarvon Cole has a pure heart.'

'Yeah. He's ok. I like the guy. I know he doesn't trust me - me being a Trad and all, but I never sense that he wants to give me grief about it.' Brady recalled Glen clambering up the old, abandoned rocket in Cape Canaveral, and it made him smile. It was his sense of doing it for the fun of it and not because there was a specific reason. 'You know when we were talking about souls, and you were kinda saying that humans - or even part-humans as I was playfully accusing you UltraViolet™ Greens - you indicated that we have souls made from a kinda spirit material?'

The Bear wasn't keen on returning to this topic, but evidently, Brady was still striving to ease his mind. He wondered whether Brady was preparing for his own death. He had seen countless conversions to Christianity in the latter stages of life, especially in the pre-Revolution days. He reminded himself to view Brady Mahone as a very old man under his still youthful exterior. He took a deep breath, and reset his tone to one of a preacher, and not as a buddy to this mere mortal. 'It's a close enough analogy for the purpose of our discussion. I would have said not close enough for scientists, but they don't believe in souls.'

Brady said, 'Are all these Nanoparticles you have in your Suits™ the same size?'

'Now that is quite a question, and not one I'm really qualified in answering.' He laughed. 'However, I did receive training in my old job as a NanoSprayer, and we were told that our sprays consisted of a mixture of Nano and Microstructures. These Microstructures were far more dense and larger than the Nanoparticles, by powers of ten.'

'I don't know what that is. But basically, you say they weigh something?'

'Yes. The RedSuits™ had a tiny but barely noticeable weight, as they were made of Microstructures with an interactive NanoCoating™. The same with the Yellow™ as these had to imitate textile materials. However, the Orange™ was pure Nano as these operate within the human body. So, the short answer to your question is that our NanoSuits™ have a trace amount of weight but a high amount of density.'

Brady didn't want to ask for an explanation of density, but he thought it was interesting that the Greens wore the NanoSuits™, well, some of the Suits™, others were a part of their inner bodies. It explained how he felt as if he was being smothered by Mrs Wilson. It also made sense that the Greens called them Suits™ like they were dressed in something, even if it was lightweight. The Bear watched Brady working it all out as if he could picture the cogs in his mind turning. 'Have you ever changed weight? Y'know, the last time I weighed myself, I was about two-hundred and fifty pounds. If I had all these Suits™ of yours, would I still weigh the same?'

'You are in a strange mood, my friend.' He laughed. 'After all this time, don't tell me you would have become a Green to lose a few pounds in weight. I don't think going Green was ever sold as a new dieting fad.' They both laughed, and it broke the tension for a moment. 'The answer to your question is that we did lose a little weight. But that was mostly due to the reduction in water usage and retention due to the GreenSuits™. I think most of the other repairable parts of our bodies were replaced cell by cell.' The Bear laughed softly. 'Where are you going with this, friend? I thought you knew all of this already.'

'I've never been into the science stuff. I kinda understood at some level.' Brady laughed, 'Usually when I was having intimate relations with a Green. I knew they were solid and felt the same as the Trads I'd slept with. Sorry, man - too much information, I know, but I knew the Greens I slept with were neither more solid nor hollow than the Trads. They were the same as they ever were.' Brady added, 'I was just wondering if say the UltraViolet™ Greens weighed the same with say, 80% Nanoparticles, then would Bodhi still weigh the same if he was 100% Pure Nano. I bet that's what he'd call it, Pure Nano, just like the Greens born after the Revolution were called Pure Greens.' He muttered, 'He'd like that - Pure Nano.'

'What makes you think he's Pure Nano, as you say?'

'I figured out what drives him. Once you've done that, then it kinda makes sense where he would go next - that's if he hasn't already done it.'

'Go on.'

'It's not money, power or respect he craves. It's progress. The rest is easy.'

The Bear scratched his head. 'I don't see that...'

Brady said, 'He let all the Trads die because he had no use for them. He needed the Greens to do all the work to save the planet. But I think he's replacing you from within. You've gone through all your colours from InfraRed™ to UltraViolet™, and if it was 10% at a time, then maybe you are 90%, not 80%, Pure Nano already. There's only 10% left of you, my friend.'

24: STRIKE

The FusionPlane™ came into to land at the Mahone Ranch. After such a long journey, Brady insisted that The Bear should stay for dinner. The Bear was still deeply troubled with Brady's theories, but he didn't want to discuss it further with him. The implications were massive. Humanity was either being set up for extinction or, more benignly, it was on the verge of evolving into a new race of Pure Nano beings. He searched his teachings in the Bible and wondered if they applied to non-humans if indeed that's what they might become. He began to doubt whether he had chosen the wrong path but couldn't reconcile this with the counterargument that an ex-con without a religious bone in his body had chosen correctly.

Samuel Beardon the Third had barely ever visited the town of McFarland in his long life, and this was his first visit to the Mahone Ranch. Brady was keen to move the subject on. He had made his connections in his mind but hadn't found the philosophical crisis which his friend had. Brady had always thought the Greens, or more specifically, Bodhi Sattva was up to something. He'd thought he had busted his criminal plans and nothing much more serious than that. He was more concerned about how Brady Mahone was being used in the heist.

After they had eaten, Brady gave the Bear the tour of the property. He showed him where Amie lived and slept before she ended up in the Bear's care in San Martin. Brady talked proudly about the barn and his Green Bike, which was instrumental in the start of his business. Brady chuckled as he recalled taking the trailer by force from the bad-mouthed neighbour of Small Hand Don. He stressed to the Bear how he started without a Green Credit to his name and how he had forged his own international business. Brady even showed Samuel Beardon the Third his bunker and his collection of Los Banos police reports, all securely wrapped up in plastic. Temptingly, the two-hundred-page summary laid untouched in its plastic outer on Archie Mahone's old bench.

This overwhelming wave of nostalgia made Brady insist on retracing his movements with the Bear of that very first day after the Green Revolution back in 2084. He suggested they walk to West McFarland - now Green McFarland. The Bear agreed, and he wanted to know how the first days of the Revolution felt from Brady's point of view.

They walked for about twenty minutes, and Brady talked excitedly about protecting Mrs Wilson from the Hodgson Boys and how he fell through the GreenShell™ for the first time. As they strolled into Green McFarland, they were both taken aback by the sight that greeted them on the edge of McFarland Park. There was an open-air encampment of about a dozen young but emaciated Greens.

He saw Lizzie pleading with her pupils and ex-students. 'You must eat. You will die, and it will all be for nothing.'

A Green of indeterminate gender acted as the spokesperson for the group, 'We no longer accept the validity of your teachings. We are second-class citizens, and we are not free.'

'I'm sure Bodhi will give everybody the UltraViolet™...' Lizzie implored.

'It's no longer just about the UltraViolet™. We no longer want to work forever as slaves to Her.' He emphasised *Mother* Nature to suggest that she was a binary sexist and traitor. His cutting remark slashed at Lizzie's pleadings. 'We want to live our lives as free citizens

- or not at all.' The starving Greens cheered feebly, and Brady could sense that they hadn't long to live.

Brady cheered sarcastically. 'I've been saying that along. You Greens should get out more.'

Lizzie snapped, 'You're not helping, Brady.'

'Why should I? It's your mess. I'm just surprised it took so long.' He looked over at the Bear. 'Sorry, man. I think we'll have to postpone. This situation has kinda taken the edge off.'

Lizzie said, 'Brady has never had any manners. I'm Lizzie, the Green McFarland Educator.' She shook the Bear's hand.

'I'm Samuel Beardon the Third. I'm the preacher for San Martin. You've probably gathered that I'm an old friend of Brady's.'

'Oh, you're a Green Educator, now. You used to be a teacher...' Brady quipped.

'Please. Ignore him. I think that should be a Green rule, personally.' Lizzie looked at the Bear, 'Are you one of the Devout?'

'Yes. I'm UltraViolet™.'

'We are having a gathering of the Disciples and the Devout at our Green Town Hall. We have an important update from Bodhi. You probably have the File waiting for you back home, but I thought you might like to join us?'

The Bear looked across at Brady, who said, 'I'm whacked. You do what ya gotta do, man. Ain't no skin off my nose.'

'I would like to see his latest message. It might have something which could alleviate the tensions and offer a message of hope to our young protesters.' The Bear nodded in the direction of the Green hunger strikers.

'No problem, man.' He glanced at Lizzie, 'I'm sure you don't mind dropping him off at my place to pick up his rental FusionPlane™.'

'I can do that.'

'Good. I won't wait up.' He said to the Bear. 'I'll catch up with you the next time I'm in San Martin. I won't forget today. I had a blast.' He turned and marched away before the Bear could reply.

Lizzie and Samuel ambled over to the New Green Hall. Siddha was on stage with a projector set up, ready for the viewing. He was issuing orders and micromanaging the event. Lizzie guided Samuel to a couple of free chairs at the back. About twenty people were in attendance, and many of these were the original GreenRevs, known for their bravery, devotion, and fanaticism for the Green cause. One or two others were her ex-pupils, and she was proud that they had turned their backs on temptation. She pointed discreetly toward the stage. 'That's Siddha. He's the Green McFarland Disciple. We share the same home. Have you met him before?'

'I've seen him several times at the Sattva Systems™ HQ, but I've never spoken to him at length.'

'What do you do in Boulder Creek?'

'I'm a long-time friend of Bodhi...'

'Really. Then we have an honoured guest among us.'

Siddha called for silence. He then led them in reciting the Green prayer:

Our Mother.
Who art Heaven on Earth.
For what we are about to receive
May we be truly grateful
And lead us not into temptation.
Show us the way.

Siddha signalled to one of the old GreenRevs to play the movie, as Vance was not one of the Devout, and therefore his services were dispensed with for the evening. As Siddha left the stage to take up his seat at the front and centre of the audience, the short movie began. The title credits rolled, followed by a screen with the Sattva Systems™ logo in moss green against a cream background. And then the head and shoulders of Bodhi appeared, and it was apparent that the movie was shot in his sparse office in Boulder Creek.

The audience cheered their leader's emergence on screen. Bodhi spoke softly, not in the manner of a Trad Leader of old, who may have spoken pompously in reverence at their own self-importance at addressing a global audience of more than twenty-six million Disciples and the Devout and the owners of the UltraViolet™. Bodhi's words were as quiet as if he was talking to everyone as a trusted confidant.

'My dearest friends, the bravest of the GreenRevs, my most trusted Disciples and the purest Green citizens of the Devout. I have important updates I want to share with you, and I will attempt to answer frankly some of the topics which are causing you the most concern.'

The New Green Hall was utterly silent.

'Firstly, to put today's issues into context, I want you to visualise where we came from, to illustrate just how much we have achieved.'

Movie footage shone out for fifteen minutes, with the horrors of what humanity had inflicted upon the Earth in the time of the Trads. Along with visions of toxic waste plants, dying animals, birds and plant life, there were sequences of violent storms intermingled with the laughing decadence of the wealthy elite.

Bodhi reappeared, 'You, my Green friends, have ensured, through your hard work and dedication, that Mother Earth will never suffer harm, such as you have witnessed, ever again. You should take pride in your accomplishments, and I thank you with all my heart for your sacrifices.'

There was a short pause as if he had deliberately intended to leave time for reflection.

'I now want to discuss some of our trickier issues, and I need your help.' Bodhi's bald head glittered under the harsh lighting of his office. His apparent lack of make-up endeared him to his audience, as it was the Trads who were so obsessed with their self-image. 'Many of you are wondering why we have left the Security Protocols™ on a broader tolerance setting.'

There were murmurs in the audience, indicating that he was tackling the controversial subjects.

'The research, development and investment in the UltraViolet™ program is massive. However, if I believed it would lead to a population of productive workers who were wholly committed to serving Mother Earth, I would authorise the issuing of the UltraViolet™ to all nine-hundred-million Greens on the planet, without a moment's hesitation. However, this would be a thousand-year commitment for all of us, and I wanted to be certain that I wouldn't waste Her resources. The Disciples, The Devout and my beloved GreenRevs have nothing to prove to Sattva Systems™, which is why we gave you the UltraViolet™ freely.'

The GreenRevs cheered loudly.

'I am saddened to say that early indications are that the young Pure Greens and those who have given into the temptation of the Trads have demonstrated by their actions that they think the old world had something to offer them. Remember the destruction of those days...'

He looked away from the screen in disbelief.

'The indications are that they would not work to make the world a better place, and they would rather indulge their selfish needs at the expense of others. But...' He paused for dramatic effect. 'I will give them as much time as they need. I will not force them to alter their attitude. Instead, I will leave it to you to teach, instruct, and help them to return to our Green ways. Even if it is just one person at a time, then each born again Green will be a victory. Mother Earth needs all the help she can get. I needn't remind you of the potential depletion of Her resources which would be required to keep nine-hundred-million people alive for a thousand years if they weren't going to give anything back. That is what's at stake here, and that is why they are going to have to contribute toward their thousand years of life the UltraViolet™ will offer them.'

Siddha clapped loudly, which encouraged the others in the audience to follow. Lizzie applauded enthusiastically while the Bear clapped gently, as he was troubled by this harsh approach. He was a man who helped sinners. He didn't punish or deprive them. Samuel Beardon the Third forgave them their sins and reinforced the message that God loved all his children.

Bodhi continued his Boulder Creek sermon. 'And to a matter which has troubled many of you. Some may be hearing this for the first time. If it is, and this message alarms you, please, do not worry because it is a matter that we have in hand. I am drawing your attention to a terrorist plot to disrupt our New Green Year celebrations - our Centenary of the Green Revolution...'

The Bear didn't understand this, but the raised fists of the GreenRevs at the front made it apparent that they knew.

'Brady Mahone, the self-proclaimed avenger for the Trads, has been trying to mastermind this terror plot. Let me make myself plain. I do not want to see him harmed in any way. We do not harm any living creature, even those who would do harm to us. Please let him go about his business unchallenged and unhindered.' He paused before emphasising, 'I mean it. Let him be.'

The Bear was utterly bewildered.

'Our own Head of Engineering and Nanosciences - Professor Pinar Dogan, was approached by Brady Mahone, in person, with questions about whether explosive devices in our chemical plants or, indeed, our power supply facilities could cause a catastrophic event.'

The members of this elite Green audience who didn't know of this plot against them gasped.

'He has sent his sons out across the world to ingratiate themselves with some of the most influential and knowledgeable members of our Green organisation with the express desire to gather information on our perceived weaknesses.'

He added a footnote to this, 'And Brady Mahone has been asking anybody he encounters about the weaknesses in the Sattva Systems™ working practices - he even asks about how he could destroy me. If you have had dealings with this man, then think about his questions in this context - I beg you.'

As the movie ended, Bodhi said reassuringly. 'Our facilities are safe. There is no threat to our power supplies. We have increased the sensitivity of the Security Protocols™ on Brady Mahone and his close family. You are safe, rest assured. Go to your fellow Greens and bring them back into our family. Let's look forward to our New Green Year celebrations and let us continue with our quest to make the world a better place to live. Thank you.'

The screen went blank at the end of the recording. Many of the Greens in the audience flocked around Siddha to solicit more information. Lizzie excitedly dug Samuel in the ribs. 'Fancy a walk. We could trade stories about Brady, and I'm sure Siddha would love to meet you - when he's finished up here.'

'Sure. Why not.'

They strolled back to Lizzie's home, and she spent most of the time recalling the first day when Brady Mahone appeared in West McFarland. She didn't divulge that she had slept with him. She still had an old-fashioned twinge that a preacher might disapprove of. She revelled in pulling apart Brady's business reputation by describing in detail Brady's pathetic attempts at shoplifting. She laughed as she juxtaposed this with tonight's revelation that he was being elevated to a terrorist mastermind.

Once at home, she offered Samuel a selection of fruit juices, and he chose a glass of fresh, locally produced, Californian oranges. 'So, you are unconcerned about the threat posed by Brady?' He said, between gulps of sweet, refreshing juice.

'He's a dumb Trad who got lucky in business.' Lizzie added, 'I'm reassured that Bodhi has increased the sensitivity of the Security Protocols™ on him, though.' She slumped back in an armchair, which encouraged Samuel to relax. 'How did you meet Brady?'

'I was a NanoSprayer™ in Los Banos back in 2099 when I first met him.' He wasn't going to share his reasons why he engineered this meeting. 'We got along, and my nephew took a shine to him, although Lord knows why.'

'And where's your nephew, now?'

'He had stayed with me his whole life. But now he has made a new life for himself and his partner on Mars.' He added, 'I'm going to miss him.'

'Who's his partner?'

'Raelynn. Xe's not Brady's progeny, but xe's part of Brady's extended family.'

'You and Brady have a lot of bonds. Did you know he was plotting an attack on our Green society?'

'No. It's come as quite a shock. In fact, I'm struggling to believe it. It doesn't feel like the Brady I know at all.'

She put a leg up over the arm of her comfy chair. 'So, you believe that Bodhi is mistaken? Maybe he's a little bit delusional, paranoid even...'

'Of course not. Bodhi is the epitome of reason. He's not angry. He's calm and appealing for restraint. The doubts are entirely my own. I thought I understood Brady Mahone, but I have blinkered myself to the truth. I think you could say I'm still processing...'

'Don't torture yourself. I'm an educator and believed myself to be intellectually superior to Brady, but there have been occasions when he outplayed me. I think it's the cunning of the criminal within him. You can't take your eyes off him for a second.'

Siddha came in and sat next to Lizzie. He looked at Samuel and said, 'You were a stranger at our meeting. I wondered where you had gone.'

Lizzie said, 'I thought you'd like to meet him. He's almost family with Brady Mahone and has been close to him for eighty-five years. Siddha, this is Samuel Beardon the Third, and Samuel, this is Siddha, the Disciple for Green McFarland.'

The two men shook hands. Siddha said, 'It can't be a coincidence, but I knew of a man called Samuel Beardon the Second?'

'Yes. He began the creation of the Green Communities long before the Revolution.'

'Wow. We are graced by the presence of Green royalty.'

Samuel laughed, 'I am a preacher, and before that, a mere NanoSprayer™ - but I am proud of my Father's and Grandfather's achievements.'

Lizzie intervened, 'Siddha. Samuel is a close confidant of Bodhi Sattva.'

'It's the family connection. My parents worked closely with John Kane.' Samuel smiled.

'So, you are uniquely positioned between Bodhi and Brady. Was it you that informed Bodhi of Brady Mahone's plot?'

'Not at all. This evening was the first I had heard of it.'

'I'm going to come straight out and say it - I hate Brady Mahone. He's a nasty piece of work, and I wish he could be disposed of. He's been nothing but trouble since the first day he set foot in Green McFarland. Think of all those people who are missing out on the UltraViolet™ because he tempted them into his criminal enterprise. Personally, I think Bodhi has gone soft on him...'

'I'm hoping that he is trying to forgive him. Maybe that's the preacher in me talking.'

'I do apologise. Discussions about Brady Mahone tend to bring the worst out in me. Thank heavens the Security Protocols™ have been set too broad for me. Otherwise, I'd be asking you to release me from the Security Film™ by now.'

They all laughed. Samuel asked, 'Do you mind if I asked how you came to be a Disciple?'

'I worked with Genesis Garcia and Bodhi in the years running up to the Green Revolution. Although, it was many years after the Revolution before I got to meet Bodhi in person.'

'I don't understand.'

'In the old world, I couldn't be seen with Bodhi because of my job. It had implications...'

'What implications?'

'I oversaw corporate finance and governance at the Treasury. It might have raised questions about my proprietary if we had been seen together.'

Samuel was puzzled at first but then remembered that Sattva Systems™ was an industrial conglomerate, albeit in a high-tech field. 'So, you corresponded with him?'

'No. I dealt with Genesis Garcia's people and rubber-stamped the trillions of dollars of loans. You must understand that I hated my work at the Treasury. I went into it, all starry-eyed until the debauchery and the decadence was utterly shocking. Then there was the cronyism and the utter disregard for the natural world. By the time I was approached by Lizzie via Cain, I was delighted to do anything I could to bring down the capitalist world.'

Lizzie said, 'I was an Ecology teacher, and I flat-shared with Cain in my student days. Cain went on to be the International Head of Deep Mind. Cain was appalled at the respect his company was receiving while using enormous amounts of the Earth's resources to mine the Earth of precious metals and consume vast amounts of energy in powering the Cloud and the Grid. I was far enough removed from anybody's contacts lists to liaise with others in the group unhindered. We set up in McFarland because it was off the radar to the other Big Tech firms but still close enough to Los Angeles to the south and Silicon Valley to the north.'

Samuel pondered this information, 'So, the Revolution began with the few and not the many.'

'The catastrophic failure of the climate summit in 2050 gave us a whole army of recruits from the highest echelons of thinkers. These people joined us secretly while leaving their political masters to entertain the doomed Trad crowds. All the hard work began from there.' Lizzie answered. 'The rest is Green history.'

'Yes. It is written. The questions remain about the future. Does it not worry you about the young ones, the hunger strikers?'

'Of course. But the Green kids don't realise the sacrifices we made when we were young. They are choosing, self-selecting to learn the hard way. We cannot be distracted by relative trivialities so close to the completion of the hundred-year plan.'

Siddha said, 'I can tell you what comes next. It will still mean we have to work. Sorry, Lizzie...' He teased. 'Would you like to know?'

Samuel nodded eagerly.

'Glenarvon Cole has completed the selection and authorisation for the twenty-six million Green Disciples and the Devout. This number was hammered out after heated discussions in Boulder Creek...' He said salaciously. Siddha enjoyed his moments of rapt attention from an audience. 'It represents one square mile of hospitable land to be monitored daily.' He sat up excitedly. 'It's no longer a secret, but I have to deliver my address at McFarland's New Year Celebrations. I will have responsibility for the central square mile of McFarland, and all other UltraViolets™ will have a square mile allocated at random - as we don't want to be accused of favouritism. Of course, there will be logistical issues to be ironed out, but globally every square mile of hospitable land will have a person to watch over it. Now there are some discussions about titles. At first, Guardian was considered, but I believe we will choose Caretakers with the emphasis on *care*.'

Lizzie said, 'This is the first I've heard of it.'

'I know.' Siddha said triumphantly. 'I imagine that most of the time, there will be little to do. Hop in a FusionPlane™, check everything's ok and then back home. If there is a problem, then we can call on others to help.'

'What problems?'

'Plagues, fires, floods - anything where humankind can give Mother Nature a helping hand.'

Samuel said, 'How did Glenarvon Cole have the time to recruit all those people?'

'It wasn't difficult. It was passed down the pyramid, so to speak. Cain had his allocation, which he parcelled up and handed over mine. I put forward seventy-five McFarland citizens, of which sixty-eight were approved.'

'Who was not approved - the other seven?'

'They were late converts to the products of Brady Mahone Entertainment Enterprises when his son Bill Mahone came selling his wares like a snake-oil salesman.' He folded his arms. 'More evidence, if it was needed, of the misery which Brady Mahone has inflicted on the Greens with his corruption, temptation and lies.'

'Lies?'

'Yes. He was telling every Green he met that the UltraViolet™ wasn't worth waiting for - that it was no more than an outer coating for the NanoSuits™. Only a cynical mind could conjure up that ruse. They have learned the hard way that they paid a thousand years of life to satisfy their lust for second-rate Trad entertainment.'

Samuel said, 'These hunger strikers and the other Green rebels - do you think they will come around? It doesn't look like a phase they are going through to me.'

'I'm deeply concerned about them.' Lizzie said. 'It's heartbreaking to see my old students succumbing to this nihilistic rhetoric. I hope Bodhi does something about it soon. It's going to be such a shame to see the Centenary celebrations tarnished by their misery.'

Siddha stroked his chin as if he was deciding whether he could share his inside information. 'You haven't heard this from me, but I have it on good authority that Bodhi will offer everybody the UltraViolet™ in the last days of December.'

'But that still might be too late for some...'

'Maybe you could spread some rumours of your own. I don't want to be a Disciple with my own dead citizens on my watch. Personally, I think we've been given this information to use it in this manner. I'm not the only one who knows, and the word is spreading.'

'What should I say?'

'That Sattva Systems™ have taken on their concerns, and they will receive the UltraViolet™ with no strings other than they give up their hunger strike.'

'That might placate them.'

'Being told you've won has that effect.' Siddha added, 'On a more positive note, I know they want everybody to use the Yellow™ to its most outlandish uses on the New Green Year Party. Genesis Garcia has been tasked with putting plans together on the themes of the colours of the rainbow to mark the completion of the distribution phase of the NanoSuits™.'

Samuel laughed, 'I can't be the only one who dislikes being forced to dress up. I am just fine as I am.'

'I think most of the older Greens feel the same. It's comforting staying as one outward persona. However, the younger Greens like showing off, and if it brings back a sense of peace and Green harmony, then one night of dressing up is a small price to pay.

25: THE BOYS ARE BACK IN TOWN

Thanksgiving had become a guilty pleasure in the Green States of America. It was conducted furtively in the homes of the Greens, who celebrated it. The main difference from the Trad times was it was a wholly Vegan affair. There was nothing furtive about the celebrations in the Mahone residence, even if Brady or his sons had little idea about the details of its origins and traditions. All that concerned Brady was that it was a big deal in the Trad days, and he did it as one-in-the-eye to the Greens.

His sons all returned in time for the feasting and Debrock's fresh supply of dabs, and it was time to eat, talk and get high.

Brady made a point of seeking out Helgarth. 'Hey, Raelynn will be ok, y'know. Tyrone is a good guy. I've known him for years, he's kind, and he's crazy about her.' He added, 'For what it's worth, she loves him.'

'I know. But I'm going to miss xyr.'

'Come here.' She fell into his arms, and he squeezed her tightly. He held her until she had finished sobbing. 'If it's all too much for you, and you want to leave the table, I'll understand...'

'No. No, I'll be fine. It will be good to have the family back. Don't worry about me.' She kissed him on the cheek, smiled, and made her excuses for being needed in the kitchen. Brady knew she had never cooked a meal in all the years she had lived in his Malibu home - that's what the Green staff were for, but he didn't challenge her.

At the Thanksgiving meal, the whole family was together. His five sons had returned from their fact-finding missions across the globe, and they excitedly interrupted one and other with confirmations or contradictions to the other's reports. Amie, Helgarth and Lucy-Ian seemed subdued, but occasionally Brady could see them quietly discussing what he assumed was the Tyrone and Raelynn situation.

Bill attempted to summarise the discussions to date, as the elder and therefore the unelected spokesman for the boys. 'We've compared notes to try and find out what the Greens are up to, and there are one or two things which we all agree on.'

'Let's hear it.'

'We all managed to find everybody except Rhea Laidlaw and Glenarvon Cole.'

'I'm sorry, Pops.' Rocky said, 'they are always on the move, and I'm not even sure if Bodhi even knows where they are half the time.'

'No problem, son. I know you tried.' Brady wasn't going to embarrass the boy in front of his peers and say that he had recently spent the day with Rhea. Thinking of her stirred strange emotions of the loss of Tyrone and Raelynn, his friendship with the Bear and whatever it was with Rhea. He didn't like using the word *love,* even in his inner monologue. It felt like the kind of word a weaker man would use. However, it seemed hard to deny when he remembered that kiss.

Bill continued, 'The ones we did find, all let us talk to them. And that was the funny thing about it - there seemed to be a kind of pattern to our meetings.'

'Go on.'

'It was as if they knew we were coming, and they had a playbook. We found them real easy. They greeted us and ensured we were seen to be meeting them. There were lots of people around, but they spoke to us in private.'

'What did they talk to you about?'

'Absolutely nothing, really. They pretended not to know anything about voting. All they talked about was how great the New Green Year's party was going to be.'

Brady Mahone's sons nodded, and even Amie, Helgarth and Lucy-Ian had suspended their own separate conversations to listen into these updates.

'There was something else. In the last couple of days, the atmosphere around us changed. Nobody said or did anything - you know what the Greens are like when they get angry - they kinda shun you - quietly.'

'Spoken like a true Trad, boy.' Brady laughed.

'It wasn't just the Disciples and the Devout. When we first arrived, we saw a lot of protests and even hunger strikes...'

'Yeah. I've seen those too. The young Greens were skinny to begin with, but now - well, let's just say they didn't look like they had too long to live.'

'I know Pops. I've never seen anything like it before. None of us had. Anyway, when we first got there, they couldn't wait to tell us what they thought of Bodhi - none of it good. They were making all kinda plans to protest about the New Green Year Party.'

'That's interesting.' Brady rubbed his head. 'And what do these protests look like?'

'One thing Rocky did succeed in doing, was finding out from someone on the inside,' Bill looked at Rocky and smiled, 'that the New Green Year Party is going to be a Festival of Colour, based on the symbol of the rainbow.'

Rocky added, 'It's all about using the YellowSuits™ to the max - they think it will appeal to the younger Greens.'

'Yeah, I was there at the launch of the YellowSuits™, it was fucking weird if you ask me, and fucking unmanly.' Brady said this in a tone which stated he would be disappointed if his boys took part in this fey activity.

'Anyway, when we first got there, the Green rebels were talking about wearing sackcloth and ashes at the Centenary celebrations.' Bill said. 'They had this grand protest all worked out. They were going to march across the globe dressed in black. And to top it all, they were planning to commemorate all the dead, *including* the Trads who died as their sacrifice and contribution to saving the planet.'

'Fuck me. I would have loved to have seen Bodhi's reaction to that when he was first informed.' Brady laughed heartily.

Amie said, 'Hey, Brady. Don'cha think Lucian and Mary-Lou would have loved to have witnessed a parade like that.'

'Yeah. And Pops.'

'It ain't happening.' Bill said. 'That was the weird thing. The Hunger strikers caved, and the protests were called off. It was like somebody had flicked a switch, and it was like nothing had ever happened.'

Hawk said, 'I was waiting for Hunter to disappear for a moment, but it was the same here. He wanted everybody to know that I was talking to him, but only when we were in the Vehicle Lot. He said nothing of any importance, but he made it look like we had some kinda top-secret conversation. I don't get it.'

'He wants it to look like you are up to no good, even if you're not.' Amie said, 'Oldest trick in the book. It's a set-up.'

'You're right. They are trying to fit Brady Mahone up for a crime he didn't commit. Well done, Amie. You're right. I know it.'

'There is no vote. There is no meeting of the so-called thirteen.' She said quietly but authoritatively. 'They are destroying your business by character assassination. I bet the Green rebels are being told that this was all some kinda misunderstanding, and they were being played by you. It doesn't matter if it's the truth. I'm wondering what your crime is going to be.'

'Gonna be something big - to go to all this trouble.'

Bill said, 'Unless they just used you and us, to manipulate the Greens. They've done it before. Bodhi is the great listener, the man of his word, but you are always the outsider who shouldn't be trusted. I think he has killed off the business. After this, who's going to buy from us? The Greens who forked out a few Green Credits at a time, hell, some of them even got our products for free - well, they just learned that it nearly cost them a thousand years. I wouldn't take that risk again, would you?'

Brady nodded, 'I would rather go into rehab than lose a thousand years, and that's saying something.'

The gathering around the table laughed. Troy said, 'Do you think we'll get the UltraViolet™ now?'

'Yes. Precious didn't mention any exceptions.' Wilder intervened. 'She didn't say what was happening, but she kinda prophesied that everything would be ok and that I shouldn't concern myself. I didn't understand, but it makes sense now.'

'Well, at least we get to keep the money. There's plenty to last a thousand years, that's for sure,' Troy said.

Brady was still uneasy, but he didn't want to trouble his family any further. He thought, *I'll mull it over later when I've had a chance to let this information sink in.* 'Cheers, everyone. You've done well for the old man, and it's very much appreciated. Happy Thanksgiving.' He raised his glass of old moonshine made with his Pops' secret recipe and drained his glass. 'I think that's enough business talk for today. Let's start our month of partying, we've got all your birthdays to plan for, and I know you like your New Green Year celebrations. Let me declare here, and now, I don't want you boys to get your hopes up. I'm not giving away any FusionPassengerJets™ this time. I think we may have run our last sales competition. However, let this be a time for new beginnings.'

26: A MEETING OF MINDS

Brady spent the next few weeks in a dabaholic haze. He occasionally got so confused in his highs that he thought he was back in Cupertino with El Duque and his Brady Bombs. He had moments of clarity when he returned to the words of Amie about him being set-up, and he always decided to do something about it - tomorrow. But tomorrow showed no sign of turning up any time soon.

He was so stoned that he handed over the organisation of his sons' and Lucy-Ian's birthday party to Hunter. He even left the gift-giving for Hunter to organise. His brain seemed to be thinking that he no longer had an unlimited amount of cash to spend, so he may as well get his money's worth out of Hunter and his staff.

The thought of being, maybe, one-hundred and forty-three years old on January 1st, 2185, made him laugh hysterically. He had never known how old he was, he never knew his birthdate, he couldn't tell for sure if he had been born in 2041 or 2042. He tried to work it out using his fingers, but soon gave up. *It doesn't really matter*, he thought. *Who cares if I got it wrong? It don't mean a goddamn thing to me.* He laughed uncontrollably in his altered state of mind when he wondered whether he even had his hundredth birthday party in the wrong year. He didn't notice the hours passing on this circular inner monologue.

In the Mahone household, this was the final party of the season. There were the family birthdays on the 30th, the New Green Year's

Eve on the 31st, and then to welcome in the New Year, it was time to give thanks to the head of the household and the family business - the great Brady Mahone - the self-proclaimed King of the Trads, the Last Man Standing.

Tomorrow arrived in the idea that he would have it out with Bodhi Sattva. It was the dabs talking, and if he were in his right mind, he would have cleaned himself up before flying up to Boulder Creek. But Brady wouldn't have recognised his right mind if it came up and shook hands with him. The only morsel of logic that prevailed was that he had to do it before the big parties. And that meant leaving today. He wondered whether tomorrow had been and gone in the blink of an eye because he was now in his FusionPlane™ and it seemed to be flying itself. He giggled like a schoolboy as he wondered whether Brady Mahone was flying himself.

He was utterly confused as the autopilot delivered him to the Sattva Systems™ HQ in Boulder Creek. He believed he should be in the Park in Cupertino. His vehicle was parked outside the Main Entrance, and there was a touring party leaving the cafeteria. He fell out of the FusionPlane™ and landed with a thud on the floor. He stood up woozily and examined the grazed skin on his left forearm. One of the Greens in the party turned away, as it had been years since anybody had seen blood.

Brady looked at her and then back at his arm, and he seemed fascinated by his wound. He then laughed, and then he staggered into the Main Entrance. His reputation preceded him, and everybody gave him a wide berth. He stood at the banner with the thirteen promises and swayed dreamily. Minutes elapsed, and Brady barely moved.

Sissy had been alerted and informed of his injuries, and it took her a few minutes to locate an old First Aid box which was a relic of a distant age. She approached Brady warily.

'Hi, Brady. You've injured yourself. Let me help you.' She examined his saucer eyes and deduced he was on old-fashioned psychedelics. She lifted the dead weight of his heavy arm and examined the deep grazes. She wiped away the blood tenderly, 'I want to apply some NanoHealing™ spray. Is that ok with you?'

'Huh.'

'Your wound. On your arm.'

He looked at it.

'I don't want it to become infected. Have I got your consent to apply NanoHealing™?'

There was a small but curious group of Greens watching this interplay with Genesis Garcia and Brady Mahone. He stared at them. 'I always did heal real quick.' He laughed hysterically and yelled, 'Do ya hear that! I always did heal real quick.' His startled audience backed away and headed for the exit as it dawned on them that this might be the predicted terrorist attack. They could easily have intervened, but Bodhi had ordered them to let him be.

Brady's laughter subsided as he watched his audience float away like dandelion seeds in the breeze.

Sissy repeated softly, 'I'm going to apply NanoHealing™ to the wound, and then I'll apply a dressing to it.'

'Yeah. I heals real quick. I want to see Bodhi.'

'Ok, Brady.'

'He's fitting me up, y'know.'

She said softly, 'Now, who told you that?'

'Amie. She's got more going on upstairs than you think.' He pointed in the general direction of his head.

She sprayed on the NanoHealing™ and bandaged his arm. 'There. That should do it. I'll take you to Bodhi. He's cancelled his meeting for you when he heard of your arrival. You mean that much to him.'

Brady accompanied Sissy to Bodhi's office. He moved with a mixture of stoned staggering and occasional attempts at dancing, complete with pirouettes. He spoke in a jumble of words that made little sense to Sissy.

Sissy didn't knock when she reached the office as she had a falling over Brady to contend with. Brady staggered over to Bodhi's desk and rested his palms upon the screen covering. He felt like it was hard work to lift his head. Sissy pulled up a chair to the back of Brady's legs and cajoled him into sitting down. She checked the responses of Brady's pupils, which were like pinholes, and said to Bodhi, 'I'm not convinced that Brady even knows he's here.'

Bodhi said, 'What has he ingested?'

'I believe it's most likely a particularly potent form of marijuana in the form of dabs. The younger and more rebellious greens call it Mother Nature's Seed.'

'I suppose the branding is on message,' Bodhi said, 'Hello, Brady.'

Brady looked at him, but he just giggled.

Sissy said, 'Do you want me to leave?'

'No. Not at all. This could be fascinating. I have nothing to hide. I'm not sure I could say the same about our friend here.'

Brady laughed and muttered, 'Hide and seek.'

Sissy pulled up a chair and sat at the end of the desk so that she could clearly see both their faces. She was curious to see Bodhi's reaction to his gate crasher. She edged back a little as she didn't want to engage in head tennis, and she tried to view their responses discreetly.

Bodhi snapped, 'You've got me. I'm all yours. If you can get your act together, I will answer anything you want. That is why you've come all this way to see me, isn't it?'

The sharp words seemed to penetrate Brady's haze, as intended, and he sat up in his chair. 'Whoa. Wow. This is crazy, man. It almost feels real.' He touched the desk and then examined his finger as if he couldn't believe he had the sensation of touching something in a dream.

'Something is troubling you.' His tone had softened to that of a concerned doctor dealing with a psychiatric patient.'

'Yes. Yes, there is. You don't treat me with respect.'

'I apologise. Do you accept my apology for the offence I have caused you?'

'Yeah.' Brady shook his head, 'I suppose so.'

'I know you've got a lot on your mind, and I want to ease your burden. I can't have an unhappy Brady Mahone spoiling the party now, can I? What is it that you would like to know to make you more comfortable with your predicament?'

'Are you going to steal my money?' Brady pointed at Bodhi as if he had worked out that Bodhi might give him a trick answer. 'Or my sons' money. I earned those Greenbacks.' Brady made a pathetic attempt to appear in control of both his mental and physical functions.

'Nobody is going to steal your money or your business. However, your profits will grind to a halt in the New Year, as our people now fear the cost of doing business with the Mahones. But on the plus side, you will still be exceedingly rich by Green standards.'

Brady wobbled in his chair, 'Cross your heart and hope to die - and no crossing your fingers.' He wagged his index finger at him.

'Cross my heart and hope to die. I will not involve myself in your business affairs.'

Brady chuckled. His mind groped for more questions, but he couldn't find a coherent string of words. He was frustrated but also thought it was funny. He couldn't remember being this stoned. 'This is some strong shit.' He muttered. 'Whoa.' He rubbed at his face, 'Are you trying to make Green souls?'

Sissy looked at Bodhi in bewilderment.

'What an interesting question. Brady, you surprise me.' Bodhi sat up straight. 'You are going to have to develop this line of questioning further. You have my complete and undivided attention.'

Brady smiled, 'There was this ghost, except she wasn't a ghost, and she was looking for you, but she couldn't find you, and she tried to grope me...ugh...fucking slimy...' He laughed, 'She wasn't my type.' He giggled at his joke. 'She was more your type.' He laughed uncontrollably. Sissy was dismissive of Brady's ramblings, but she could tell that Bodhi was taking it seriously. Brady recovered, 'You've got her, haven't you? She's been recycled. I know it's true, you think I'm dumb...'

'I've never thought you were dumb, my friend. I have always had the highest regard for your cunning. You are talking about Mrs Wilson, aren't you?'

Brady stabbed the air, 'Yes. That's right.' This affirmation energised him.

'Were you tempted to try on her NanoSuit™?'

Brady shuddered at the thought. 'Would it have worked? Y'know, been all indestructible...'

'It was an incredibly rare event, with me being temporarily unavailable - that and the delay to her funeral - but yes, it would have been possible to use her recycled Suit™ until I returned. Her Suit™ would seek out the nearest match to me, I'm guessing. Which raises questions. Some would be obvious...' He looked closely over Brady. 'My Father had a vasectomy after my birth, and I have the proof, and I know my Mother didn't have any other children, of that I'm certain. However, I'm wondering what trickery Professor Chu got up to...'

Brady was surprised to hear Bodhi dredge up Professor Chu's name from the past. He hadn't been obviously connected to Bodhi. 'He was a kind and considerate man - unlike John Kane - and he was a Trad.' Brady stated this as if this was all the proof he needed. 'If he had been a Green, you would have searched his soul. You would have crept around inside him like a sneak thief, stealing his knowledge.'

'It is common knowledge that we recycle the old NanoSuits™...' Bodhi waved his hand dismissively at the suggestion.

Brady slammed his fist on the screen, which covered Bodhi's desk. 'But is that what they really are? Or are they Green souls? You've got the soul of Mrs Wilson in you.'

'There is no such thing as a soul. It is a scientific fact. I have the life history of every dead Green within me, to access their reasoning and observations. It is a waste of a life and resources to let all this just rot in the ground.' He said to Sissy, 'I'm sure our friend here is emerging from his drug-induced haze quicker than possible for a Trad.'

Sissy replied, 'I applied NanoHealing™ to his arm. He grazed it badly when he fell out of his FusionPlane™.'

'Where on Earth did you find that? We haven't needed NanoHealing™ since before the Green Revolution.'

Sissy laughed, 'In an old First Aid box - it was almost a museum exhibit. It was the only thing I could think of to tend to an injured Trad - well, that and a dressing, of course.'

Bodhi rubbed his chin, 'It's been so long, I can't recall if it would have additional healing qualities...'

'The early versions had additional healing qualities. Remember the NanoBubbles™ for the holidaymakers?'

'Ah yes. You're right. Thank you for reminding...'

Brady felt like he had been forgotten about while Bodhi and Sissy tripped happily together down Memory Lane. He wanted answers, and he'd got Bodhi talking. 'Did she take a long time to find you? She was ok, y'know. Mrs Wilson, in case it had slipped your mind.'

Bodhi didn't appreciate having the functionality of his faculties questioned. 'Yes, I had a number of dead to accommodate when I emerged from the Sensory Deprivation Chamber. It was a challenging time. She liked you, and I was fascinated to have the full details of her first encounter with Brady Mahone, an ex-con, on the run...'

'I didn't just fall through the NanoShell™, did I?'

'No. You were genetically engineered. Your DNA sequence was modified at birth as part of the NanoIVF™ studies at Stanford University by Professor Yuan Chu under the patronage of my Father, John Kane. Unfortunately, they had a falling out, and my Father had him removed. My Father was a perfectionist, and he wasn't happy with his work.'

'John Kane...' Brady's wobbling hand touched the side of his nose knowingly. 'Didn't want the Trads to have any more babies. That's why he got rid of him.' Sissy kept her eyes on Bodhi when she didn't understand the signal which Brady had given Bodhi. Brady continued. 'I don't know what it means when you say I was genet.. whatever, engineered. I'm still a Trad, right?' Brady's mind wandered as he considered Professor Yuan Chu and whether he was related to him in any way. After all, he had contributed to Brady's development before he was even born. He would never know, but he wondered whether John Kane had sabotaged Project Brady to punish the Professor.

'Yes. You are still a Trad. Your genes were edited to remove inherited diseases and purified. Therefore, you have led an extraordinarily long life.' He added, almost as a note to himself, 'He may have seized the opportunity...' He stopped himself from going any further with this line of thought, for now. However, Sissy was considering the possibilities.

Brady rubbed his eyes. He knew why he had these Green abilities; he just wanted to know if Bodhi had arranged it. Apparently, he hadn't been fully aware until now. Brady suggested his own ignorance by asking a redundant question. 'So, this is why I can go where the Greens go?'

'Maybe. It is the most likely explanation.'

'But I'm still a Trad. I'm still a human being, y'know, a straightforward guy.'

Bodhi smiled, 'Yes. Undoubtedly.'

'Cool. I can live with that.'

'Are you feeling better, now?' Bodhi asked with mock sympathy.

'Yeah. I'm still me.' He added, 'So, I keep my money, and I'm 100% Trad, and you've got no plans to take my sons' inheritance off them?'

'None at all. You have summarised it perfectly.'

Sissy intervened. 'Why did you use the term 100% Trad?'

'It's just a figure of speech. We know what he means.' Bodhi grimaced.

Brady shook his head and then his whole body to shake the fogginess from his mind. 'I've heard people talk like that.'

'I don't understand.'

'Shutting the conversations down. It's what the criminals do when they don't want you to find out what they're planning. I've done that when one of my gang was starting to brag about our next job, and they were blabber mouthing.'

'I'm not a criminal, Brady.' He shrugged.

'It's an inside job, and you're the inside man.'

Sissy said, 'In Trad terms, I was a corrupt politician, and Bodhi was defrauding the US Government out of trillions of dollars, and yes, in that world, we would be criminals. But we only did it to save the planet from destruction, and we are in the Green world now. We are not the lawbreakers here; we are the promise-keepers.'

'Ok. So now you don't want to know what Brady Mahone thinks. I don't blame you. Once you get in my mind, you might not find your way out.' He looked into her eyes.

'I do want to know. What did you mean by using a percentage term?'

'I'd have thought it was obvious. I think every new layer of NanoSuit™ you get, you lose more Trad. I suppose, that's the same as saying that if I'm 100% Trad then 100% human. I guess if you've got nine NanoSuits™, then I'd estimate that you were at least 90% Green by now, or to put it another way, you'd be 90%+ Nanoparticles. You're losing your humanity, baby.'

Sissy looked sharply at Bodhi and was about to challenge him; then Brady put his hand up and laughed at her. 'Well, I suppose that's still a trace element of humanity left, looking after number one, only thinking about what this means for you. You should be looking at him.' He pointed at Bodhi, who reclined in his chair, either relaxed about the topic or in a gesture of resignation. Brady stated, 'He's Pure Nano. He ain't human at all. That's my theory.'

Sissy said to Bodhi, 'These are the ravings of a lunatic. Tell me it's not true, and I'll believe you. We can't let him go around making accusations...'

Bodhi said, 'Do you feel the same? Are you still Genesis Garcia? Your children's Moppa? Do you still have all the same emotions of love and fear?'

'Yes. I am still the same person as I ever was.' Her mind raced to search for confirmation that her diagnosis was correct.

'Then you have the answer you need.'

Brady attempted to stand but slumped back down again. His mind may have recovered its clarity, but his central nervous system was still stoned. He said sarcastically, 'Sissy, baby. Way to do denial. Total masterclass.'

'Hey, Bodhi, man...' He chuckled, 'Never thought about it before, sounds like Bogey Man.' He giggled away for a while, but the solemn look on Sissy's face brought him back to reality. 'Admit it, you are Pure Nano.'

'I'm interested to know your reasoning.'

'No, you're not. You're stalling. You can't kid a kidder.'

Bodhi smiled and spoke as softly as ever. He remained on brand. 'I like your term, Pure Nano. Maybe Sissy would have labelled it in that way.' He looked at Sissy. 'You always had a better way with words than me.'

Brady interrupted, 'Hey, but don't worry, one day you'll die, and then he'll inherit your soul.' He stared at Sissy as if he was imploring her to come to her senses. Brady knew he was stoned, but to him, Sissy was the one who had lost her mind.

'I've never called it Pure Nano, but I'm assuming you took it as a logical extension of Pure Green.' Bodhi was keen to bring Brady's intensity back to him and off Sissy.

'Yeah, that's what I was thinking. What did you call it?'

'Project X.'

'That's a crappy name. No logic there - I recall Libby talking about John Kane having a Project X, Y and Z. Is that where it came from?'

'I've never heard of that. You've got me at a disadvantage. No, it is perfectly logical. After UltraViolet™ comes X-Ray™. I'm wearing the X-RaySuit™.'

'And you are not human?'

'I would disagree. I would argue that I am the next step of human evolution. I have human form and thoughts. The only difference is that every human cell has been imitated, replicated, and replaced. All the human susceptibilities to illness and death have been modified and improved. I could operate for millions of years.' He looked at Sissy, 'I don't do this out of self-importance. One day in the far-off future, Mother Earth will need saving from the threat of the expanding Sun. She will need beings like me to save her. She is unique within the universe.'

She said, 'But you made that choice. Did we?'

'It's your choice, now. You could be the next to take the X-Ray™. Trust me, you won't feel any different.'

27: PARTY TIME

Sissy had Brady wheeled out of Bodhi's office, and then she put Brady in his FusionPlane™ and waited until the autopilot was set for home. When she was convinced that he was ok, she watched him leave. The questions raised were almost too big to contemplate. Sissy wanted to take her mind off them for now, and she needed reassuring and an overwhelming desire to be with family. She had the unsettling sense of being duped, but she hoped her unconscious mind would work on the issues in the background tasks of her brain and come up with more palatable and digestible answers to these most fundamental questions about humanity. It was the same pragmatism that had held her in good stead as a politician. She had learned to trust her process.

She used her Satt™ to call her partner, Annabelle and asked her to arrange a dinner party for her three children who were still on Earth. She added that their own partners and grandchildren would be more than welcome. Annabelle suggested a Vegan barbecue as it was easier to arrange, and Sissy acquiesced. She thought of Century Brady Garcia, her youngest, starting his life on another world far away from Earth. She recalled that he had taken the UltraViolet™ before he left for Mars, and therefore, he hadn't escaped her predicament. She pondered whether it was more human to rebel than succumb to the wishes of Bodhi Sattva - the unelected leader of the Green World.

The young grandchildren lifted her spirits as they hugged her and talked excitedly about the trivial things in the world that brought them so much joy. They were thrilled to have the opportunity to play in the extensive gardens in the Californian winter sunshine. She watched them play their imaginary games for many minutes before attending to her own grown-up children. She had never felt guilty about having this home to herself and Annabelle. She had earned it, and Bodhi had sanctioned it. But she always knew that the other Greens wouldn't understand.

At least I'm not greedy like Pinar. God knows how many homes xe's got around the world.

Annabelle was delighted to host a party, and she doted on their children and grandchildren. Sissy mixed with her family, but she never entirely shed her political skin enough to eliminate the sense that she was canvassing them. It gave her an affectation of aloofness which made her appear colder than Annabelle. Therefore, most relationship issues reached Sissy through Annabelle's filter.

Sissy asked the same questions of each family member but in such roundabout terms so as not to make plain her anxieties. Her questions to the young children were about if humans were animals. And what animals would they like to be, but this delved into how the creatures behaved and what they might think.

With the adults, she explored philosophical themes of what it meant to be human and even covered the general discussions about the history of the Trads. As Brady was known to all, he couldn't fail but to have his name appear in the conversations.

By the time that her extended family had drifted away, she wondered whether this had been an exercise in futility, as if she and everybody she asked were mostly Nanomachines as Brady had suggested, then was she or anybody else suitably qualified to ruminate on what was or wasn't human. If she was a machine, she could only answer in the same way as a computer...and then she contemplated whether she was an android. It amazed her that she had never considered this possibility before.

As she wiped away the mist on the bathroom mirror after she had showered, she forced herself to remember that she was more than one-hundred and fifty years old. The fact that this was a commonplace occurrence had removed any sense of abnormality about this. She then remembered her old political analogy about the frog not noticing it was being boiled to death if you put it in cold water and increased the temperature so slowly it never knew when the temperature reached boiling point. They had taken the NanoSuits™ freely, one at a time, and sometimes with more than a decade between each new upgrade, and each one only replaced a fraction of their physical being.

She got into bed next to her exhausted partner after a days' entertaining, and she thought about the journey she had been on. She recalled the heady days as a successful politician with firebrand views on tackling climate change. The victory was intoxicating and life-changing, not just for her but for the world. The only focus on the RedSuits™ was that these additions to the outer layers of their skin had brought them victory. It was the OrangeSuits™ and the SecurityProtocols™ that troubled her most in this darkening hindsight. These two developments at a stroke removed the need for doctors and the police. This was the moment when any investigations into what was happening to humanity had ceased. She deduced that everything which came next just completed the takeover one Suit™ at a time.

Sissy slept fitfully, tossing and turning, kicking away the bedclothes, which weren't necessary with the Suits™ but were kept as human comfort. She flipped over her pillow for the umpteenth time before Annabelle finally woke up. Deep down, she wanted to wake her.

'What's with you tonight, Genny? Just go back to sleep.' Annabelle turned to look at the face of her partner and lover. Only Annabelle called Genesis Garcia, Genny.

'I can't.'

'Do you want to talk about it?'

Sissy smiled. 'Yes. I need a sounding board.'

'I've been called worse things - usually by you.' Annabelle laughed softly.

'I had a meeting today.' Sissy said, 'You know you're not to...'

'I think you've only told me a thousand times over the years.'

'Sorry. Anyway, Brady Mahone staggered into the HQ today to see Bodhi.'

'I've always thought that odd, that people can wait years for an audience with Bodhi, but he drops everything when Brady Mahone comes to town.'

'I think I've gotten so used to it that I barely give that a second thought anymore, like so many other things.'

Annabelle sighed, 'Look, little old Genny, honey, tell me all about it, you know I like a little bedtime story.'

'Brady raised a very big subject at today's meeting, one I dismissed as the ramblings of a stoned Trad at first, but as the day has gone on, it's troubling me more and more.'

'Ok.'

'You're going to have to promise not to laugh. It's going to sound quite ludicrous at first, but trust me, it's incredibly important, but I don't know why. It's life-changing in a way, but at the same time, it doesn't alter our everyday lives. It's a philosophical puzzle...'

'You're losing me. I did notice you were getting deep and heavy with the family today.'

Sissy winced, 'Do you think they noticed?'

'A little. But they know you've got a difficult job.'

'I'm sorry.' She hugged Annabelle and then lay back on her pillow. She let out a deep sigh, 'Brady questioned our humanity. He believes that the UltraViolet™ Greens are in excess of 90% Nanomaterials, and therefore we are no longer human.'

'Wow. That's some claim. Tell me again about this man who is qualified to pontificate over us. Humour me, what are the characteristics of the esteemed King of the Trads with his kingdom consisting of, let me count...oops...' She raised one finger, she laughed as it was her middle finger.

Sissy laughed and then recounted the stains upon Brady Mahone's personality, 'Let me see, he's an ex-convict, murderer, thief, drug addict, misogynist...'

'What about his bad points?'

They both laughed, 'I suppose I should try and be fair.' Sissy added. 'There are people that are fond of him. He has some Greens who have been friends with him for many years. By all accounts, his family love him. And over the years, he's won over the Pure Greens, but this is more out of their own misgivings about menial work they are required to do, rather than Brady actively wooing them.'

'Century had a more nuanced view. Remember, xe didn't see why expanding the mind through movies and music was borderline illegal. Xe wasn't lazy or entitled. You could argue that xe has opted for hardship on a hostile planet to be a part of something different.'

'I tried to explain that xe was exchanging the possibility of a shorter life here on Earth than a longer one on the hell of Mars. As it turned out, xe would have got the UltraViolet™.'

Annabelle turned over onto her side and brushed a stray hair away from Sissy's face. 'It wasn't about the UltraViolet™. Xe used to confide in me because xe knew you would disapprove. Xe was enthralled about Tia Cassandra reinstating the internet, streaming, smart devices and all the other Trad-cons. Tia had no use for Files in her brave new technological world. I think that upset xym more that xe had to leave xys precious collection of BMEE Files behind, but xe was promised more content than xe could ever watch on Mars. Apparently, Tia had her Server Banks rescued from under the Mojave near Cima and transported to Mars.' She watched Sissy's expressions as she didn't want to upset her, 'Century wanted to be a part of that culture, not working in fields, and examining landscapes every day for the rest of xys long life. Xe felt that Bodhi made the rules before xe was even born, which made xym feel disenfranchised.' Annabelle smiled as she pushed her fingers through Sissy's hair, 'Xe still loved you, y'know.'

Sissy said, 'I understood Bodhi's logic at the time, that nostalgia for the old days could be corrosive to our plans. After all, there was an immense amount of work to do with Operation Clean-Up. We had a planet to repair, but...'

'Maybe, it was a little over-the-top to ban entertainment...'

'But it was all so binary and full of racial stereotyping. I don't just mean American culture. The entertainment industry across the globe was wholly exclusive, whether in China, India, Russia...they all pushed their own dogma. To complete the thirteen promises, the old ways had to be outlawed.'

'No wonder you can't sleep.' Annabelle sighed as if trying to get Sissy to echo her calm manner. 'You should listen to yourself. It's all defensiveness and justification.'

'I know. You're right.' She said, 'Brady might be bad or let's be kind and say he's flawed, but there aren't any doubts that he qualifies as human.'

'I suppose so. I'll concede that.' Annabelle used the opportunity to bring up something that had always troubled her. 'Did you have an arrangement with Bodhi Sattva to plant xys seed in you in a physical manner?'

'No. Absolutely not. I promise. Century was conceived via NanoIVF™. You were there at the *freely* given and received ceremony.'

'But Genny, honey. These things can be faked.'

'You know something,' Sissy wasn't angry. She wanted to allay Annabelle's fears, 'With it being Bodhi, if xe had asked, I would have considered it.' She put a finger softly to Annabelle's lips before she could respond. 'But this was a Trad method, in xys mind, and I believe xe wouldn't consider it. Bodhi has never shown interest in anybody, sexually, in all the time that I have known xym. It's only in the light of what we've talked about tonight that it seems weird now.'

'Century doesn't know who his Father is. I've never disclosed it. I kept the official line that it was an anonymous donor. I often wondered if xe would have a primal instinct that it was Bodhi.' She laughed softly, 'It's funny, but the only person that had any kind of impression on xem, in that way, was Brady Mahone.'

'That'll be the name. Century *Brady* Garcia.'

'True. But still...' Annabelle smiled, 'Xe's happy, you know. Xe's made some friends on Mars. Century loves Tyrone and Raelynn.'

Sissy said, 'I think he felt bad about taking Tyrone's place. I'm glad that it worked out ok for Tyrone in the end. I just can't figure out how Samuel reversed the decision. I should have been aware of this change.'

'Family finds a way.' She added, 'He's proud that he lives in a world where the Greens and the Trads, or Originals, as they are called on Mars, all live together and share a common goal of building their new home together.'

'I'll have to call xem. I've left it too long. I've been busy with the end of year preparations...'

'Sssh. None of us is perfect.'

Sissy sighed, 'What about Bodhi Sattva?'

Annabelle laughed, 'Well, you're the one always complaining about xys decision making...'

'Yes. Agreed. Xe's not always right...in my opinion.' She paused before asking, 'What if I told you that xe is now Pure Nano, 100%

made up of Nanomaterials. Would xe qualify as human or would xe be something else, something new?'

'In theory?'

'No. Bodhi admitted to Brady that xe is now X-RaySuit™. Apparently, UltraViolet™ wasn't the last Suit™. Bodhi has remained one step ahead. Xe claims humanity has evolved with xym.' Before Annabelle could answer, Sissy added, 'And I could be next? All I have to do is ask.'

Annabelle said without thinking - and this made Sissy believe that the love of her life was speaking with her human heart and not her Nano brain. 'No. I couldn't bear that. I couldn't love and share my bed with another *species*. You have to refuse.'

28: CELEBRATION DAY

At the Malibu residence of Brady Mahone, the Green staff had been made to work harder than ever to make the birthday party for his sons and Lucy-Ian and Raelynn in absentia the best ever. Brady was acutely aware that he had given his staff a relatively easy ride over the years, but now the Green Credits were slowing to a trickle, and his fortune would have to last his boys for a thousand years or more, he was going to get his money's worth out of his, or more accurately, Bodhi's staff of spies.

The banners were everywhere in the massive dining room cum ballroom, celebrating the birthdays of everyone, individually, in the family. And Brady even had netting erected from the ceiling with hundreds of balloons from Libby's old storerooms blown up. He didn't tolerate excuses about holes and leaks in the old stock. Instead, he had them painstakingly repaired with NanoFixant™. He took particular pleasure in sending Hunter out to find more NanoFixant™ when the home stocks had run out.

Brady had started the day with a workout in the fully equipped gym with his boys. He believed that they worked out every day, whereas they now only did this when their Pops was in residence. Brady was wearing only sports shorts and a sleeveless T-shirt, which left his natural South Sea tattoos on show on his shoulders and biceps. He was still in great shape as Brady worked out most mornings before breakfast. Despite all the theories about his origins, he always believed that physical strength training was one of the best things he ever did to remain this healthy into old age.

He always went back to his prison days when he worked out. Jail wasn't a significant hardship for somebody of Brady's criminal stature, and the one thing he enjoyed inside was the time given over to exercise with the weights.

He noticed Wilder blowing hard. 'Come on, boy. Harder. Faster. You've got decades on me.'

Wilder was pushing his legs on the exercise bike but was out of practice, and his lack of pace and coordination was betraying him. 'Aw, come on, Pops. Why do we have to keep doing this? The point of the Yellow™ and BlueSuits™ is that we can look any way we choose.'

'You know why. I've seen the shrunken bodies inside those Suits™. You want to maintain your own muscle. Anyway, it won't do you any harm, will it?'

'I suppose.' Wilder huffed.

'Trouble with you boy is you do too much thinking and reading and not enough doing.'

He watched Wilder gamely try to pick up the pace, and he was more impressed with his other sons' efforts, especially his eldest, Bill, who was pumping iron with gusto.

Brady shouted encouragement. 'Come on, boys, push it. I want you in great shape for the party tonight. You might be Green and all, but Brady Mahone boys are still real men.'

Alcohol was a rarity in the Green World, but Brady had his homemade stills, and he checked that these were ready before the birthday parties. He was proud of his handiwork, and he was sure that his Pops would have approved. He took a snifter and gasped at its potency. What he couldn't do with PassengerFusionJets™ he would make up for by having the most fun party in the world. It made Brady feel young again, thinking about the fun they would have tonight. There had been a bright young party animal who had been flirting with him for the last few days. She was part of Debrock's crowd. Debrock might even have put her up to it, but he didn't care. He was thrilled at the prospect of getting lucky tonight.

By the early evening at the start of the party, he was already thrilled at the effort the partygoers had put into the evening's celebrations. His sons, Bill, Rocky, Wilder, Troy and Hawk, along with Lucy-Ian, and the mothers of his children, Amie and Helgarth, with the room, packed out with Debrock and his crowd of around forty Green rebels and freaky friends packed the room. Hawk had cranked up the volume of the old Trad Electro Dance tunes, and everybody began to party hard. Drink and Dabs were being consumed like there was no- tomorrow, and Brady danced away with his latest companion.

He had his own plans for the night. He would drink moonshine, dance for a while, as where he led his guests would follow. He had to remain reasonably clear-headed to give his speech to his birthday boys at midnight. Then he would have sex with this woman friend of Debrock's. Brady hadn't asked what her name was yet. And then he would have a couple of Debrock's super-strength dabs and then maybe sleep until lunchtime tomorrow. The New Green Year celebrations meant little to Brady Mahone, but he wouldn't stop his family from taking part.

Bodhi had asked, politely, for all Greens to sleep at their allotted time slots to ensure they were fully refreshed for the long process of receiving the UltraViolet™ at the New Green Year's celebrations, tomorrow, but the partygoers in Malibu had other arrangements, and sleeping was not part of their plans. It was 9:30, and the party was just heating up - there was zero possibility of anybody here retiring to their bed chambers at the preferred Green and non-UltraViolet™ sleeping slot by 10pm.

Hunter and his team of staff looked on from the edges of the party impassively. They stood to attention, waiting to attend to every need of the esteemed guests of Brady Mahone.

Brady was about to ask his companion her name when the music was turned up even louder. He smiled instead, and she twirled and danced suggestively next to him and then moved around him. Hawk raced into the centre of the makeshift dancefloor, and his brothers joined him. Brady guessed that it was Hawk who turned up the volume. The boys went into a jokey dance routine which clearly brought back some knowing memories for them. Brady laughed, but nobody could hear him within this din. He glanced at his watch as it just turned 10pm.

And then everybody collapsed.

Brady thought this was an elaborate prank at his expense. He looked around the room, and the only people left standing was Hunter and the staff. The music was still booming, but his boys, Amie, Helgarth and Lucy-Ian - he looked over the scene, waiting for somebody to jump up and cue the laughter on how they got Brady with this practical joke. If this was a joke, then they were incredibly well-disciplined. Even Debrock and his friends were utterly still. He looked down at his girlish companion at his feet, and then he knew that they were all dead.

He was frozen for a moment, and then he signalled for Hunter to cut the music. A staff member was dispatched, and without the music, it seemed eerily quiet. The lights went up, and a wrong switch had been pressed because the netting on the ceiling was released. Hundreds of balloons fell on the dancefloor. It was then that it hit Brady. He raced from body to body, checking for pulses or any other signs of life. He shook Bill and yelled at him to wake up, to no avail. One by one, he checked his family. He then cradled Amie in his arms and sobbed.

Brady looked up from the dead bodies and the balloons and into the face of Hunter. Hunter would have appeared expressionless, to most people, but to Brady's eyes, there was a definite smirk. It was an act of provocation, and Brady fell for it. He jumped up and hurled himself at Hunter.

Brady, deep down, knew it would never work, so he wasn't as surprised as he should have been to find himself doused in SecurityFilm™.

This is NanoRespect™, a trademark of Sattva Systems™. A crime against humanity has been committed. The welfare of our consumers is our highest priority. Please inform the nearest Disciple to remove Brady Mahone and dispatch xem to Sattva Systems™ with immediate effect. Thank you for using Sattva Systems™. Together, we save the world.

Hunter waited. He studied at the figure of Brady Mahone, suspended within the SecurityFilm™ with amused detachment. His Satt™ rang out. He fiddled with it and put it on the speakerphone. Brady guessed that he was supposed to hear whatever came next.

'Hello, Siddha. This is Hunter. Brady Mahone is captured and awaiting dispatch. Xe is technically under both our jurisdictions as I am the Malibu Disciple, and you are McFarland's. How do you propose we deal with this?'

'There is no need to instigate an Operation Clean-Up. The NanoPathogens™, which Brady had installed by persons unknown onto every File ever produced, will decompose the dead rapidly. I think it's appalling that he made a point of targeting our Green children with his free samples. I think it's xys revenge for the sterilisation programme of the Trads.' Siddha sighed mockingly.

Brady recalled his visits all over the world. He had given away thousands of free samples to children from Green Beijing to Green Cape Town to Green Quartiere Aurelio in Rome, he vividly remembered the young girl telling him that she loved him, and now she was dead because he gave her a File. He winced at the memory.

Siddha continued, 'There isn't going to be a trial. A Trad has no peers to judge xym. But the good news for Brady Mahone is that Bodhi will forgive xym, as it is part of the cultural identity of the Trads to destroy the things they don't understand. Is xe still there?'

'Yes. Xe can hear you. I'm not sure whether Brady Mahone has the intellectual capacity to fully comprehend the enormity of xys crime. Xe has murdered nine-hundred million in xys act of Green genocide. Even I struggle to digest such horror.' Hunter again looked into Brady's eyes with his subtle smirk taunting Brady. 'I know this man. Xe will deny it all and plead like a baby, but the trouble is, nobody will listen to the words uttered by a low-life Trad criminal. It's time Brady began to realise that xe has no friends and in addition, xe has zero credibility.'

It seemed strange to Brady that his mind was wandering and picking up on all the xe's and xym words in his time of utter despair - it was as if even language had evolved and left him behind.

Siddha said, 'Spoken like a true X™. Are you X™ as well?'

'Yes. My team have also taken the X™. We've earned it.' Hunter asked, 'What do you think will happen to xym?'

'Knowing Bodhi, I think he will let xym go. He knows Brady will travel the world trying to plead his innocence and throwing around baseless accusations, but these will be the ravings of a mad man. Bodhi will show mercy due to his extreme old age for a Trad, and I expect the X and the UltraViolets™ who survived his attack to shun xym. After all, those that are left are the Disciples and the Devout. They have always been wary of Brady Mahone, the Deceiver, and Corrupter. My guess is that xe will die alone. I'm presuming your service contract to Brady has been terminated?'

'Yes. We have served for more than a hundred years, but now we have been given a million years of life as our reward. We will now only serve Bodhi and Mother Earth. To tell you the truth, it's quite a relief to be leaving this den of iniquity.'

The Satt™ signal was silent for a moment, and then Siddha's voice re-emerged. 'Is there anything you need from me?'

'I would be grateful if you could tell Bodhi to expect the delivery of Brady Mahone, as I have our leaving arrangements to attend to.'

'Consider it done.' Siddha hung up.

Hunter took a deep breath, savouring the moment. He approached the SecurityFilm™ of the enwrapped, grimacing figure of Brady Mahone. He reached out his hand slowly, and then he touched the Film and Brady was sent away at high speed to Boulder Creek.

29: GHOST DANCE

The howls of the dead could be heard around the world. The decomposition of the Greenly Departed was swift, as there were no burials to be conducted. The recycling of the nine-hundred million NanoSuit™ layers had begun. As they emerged like husks, they saw the dead bodies of their loved ones, and they howled in the agony of their loss.

Many wandered in a confused state until they located their beacon. Some were thousands of miles away. Others found a stronger pull, as the genetic ties to Sattva Systems™ were strong, and they made swifter progress to join with their maker.

The screech of the death wails drove Brady crazy, and it even seemed to affect the progress of the SecurityProtocol™, which had captured him, as it strayed from its route as if a more substantial magnetic presence had interfered with its bearings. Brady wanted to scream to drown out the wailing, but he couldn't move a muscle in his filmy confinement. He watched the NanoSuits™ emerge from houses as the SecurityProtocol™ made its way tracking Highway 99 beneath him. The NanoSuits™ moved in their weird clockwork rotations as if they were driven by a system of cogs. Others flew like hatching flying ants moving straight up to the sky. He watched the sky changing colour to an unnatural shade of Electric Blue. And all the while, the howls of the NanoSuits™ got louder and louder.

Brady wondered whether he had died and was going to hell. He then saw an opaque NanoShell™ over the Sattva Systems™ HQ. It too was Electric Blue, and his SecurityProtocol™ slowed, almost to a stop. He watched the NanoShell™ open one at a time to let a single NanoSuit™ through to join with Bodhi. They were pressing against the NanoShell™, and now Brady could see that the smog of Suits™ had restricted his vision to no more than a few yards ahead. His SecurityProtocol™ merged with the NanoShell™ and then slowly slid through to the other side.

Compared to the chaos outside the NanoShell™ inside the Sattva Systems™ HQ, it was tranquil. The inside of the NanoShell™ had the usual forest scenes that a guest would have seen before. He was carried into the Main Hall. The people who were waiting for him were people he knew. Many of them he considered friends. They were in deep discussion, and those that glanced in his direction soon looked away either in disgust or embarrassment.

He tried to listen in, but a lot of the conversations merged into each other. *We should have known...It was a mistake to let him go about his business unchecked...I can't believe he could do such a thing...All those poor people...I lost friends, even children...And just a day away from getting their UltraViolet™...Life can be so cruel...I blame Bodhi...Brady must have had help, maybe it was a cell...We knew he was planning something, so why...*

He looked around. His heart sunk when he saw Samuel Beardon the Third in deep discussion with Lizzie and Siddha. To Brady's eyes, he looked like he was agreeing with them and not pleading on his behalf. Rhea and Glenarvon Cole were standing outside the main group. They were whispering conspiratorially as far he was concerned. He vaguely recalled the Regional Swedish Disciple, he knew her name was Bridgett something, but he also knew that she hated the sight of him.

Brady also made out the sounds of soft crying and commiserations, as some of their extended family members had lost loved ones who hadn't obtained the UltraViolet™ in time. It made him think of Tyrone and Raelynn and how they had only just escaped in time.

The loss of the sounds of the wailing dead Suits™ seemed to bring him back to his senses. He began to watch the room with a more strategic eye. He guessed Siddha was right that Bodhi might just let him walk out of here, but it made sense to case the joint for other potential escape routes. He eyed the group of Precious, Professor Pinar Dogan and Genesis Garcia suspiciously. He felt like they had a hand in framing him for this.

Cain wandered around alone as if he was deep in thought. It made Brady wonder if he wasn't wholly included in this inner sanctum.

Hours went by while the debates and discussions continued. There was movement from group to group. Brady thought his trial or whatever they had planned for him was about to start when Bodhi Sattva walked into the hall. He watched another NanoSuit™ dead soul merge with Bodhi. But all that happened was Bodhi had informed them that lunch was provided in the cafeteria. Brady watched in disbelief when they disappeared for another hour. The only thing of note that happened in this period was when Hunter arrived.

Brady assumed he'd left the packing to the rest of his staff while he made his way here. Hunter smiled at him and then placed an old antique pistol on the table near the suspended Brady Mahone.

At first, he was confused. Anybody leaving a gun for Brady Mahone in this predicament could be construed as trying to help him escape. However, Brady knew that an old gun couldn't inflict any damage on a Green. He looked around as best as he could from his confinement, and the Main Hall had nothing worth shooting at - even if he could shoot at a window or a pipe, he expected it to be Nano protected in some way. Also, he dwelled on the out-in-the-open placement of the gun. If Hunter was trying to help him, then there were plenty of places to conceal the weapon. He could have taped it to the underside of a table or a chair.

It then dawned on him. He was giving him the opportunity or the hint that he could commit suicide. Brady considered this option. He had no family; the world was full of dead NanoSuits™, and he would be made to be the patsy for a crime he didn't commit while he had to endure their sanctimonious crap about what a terrible person he was. He chewed it over and considered the speed at which his misery could be ended. Just one little squeeze on the trigger and bang - game over.

He knew for sure that he would have his opportunity. He knew how Bodhi schemed by now. Every Mafia hood he'd ever had the pleasure of talking to always spilt the beans on the foibles of their Godfathers. It was a way of proving their connections to the mighty and the powerful - the way they had their rivals murdered - there was always a little marker - the personal touch. He knew Bodhi would engineer a scenario where Brady would escape like a violent ex-con on the run. Brady could almost hear Bodhi saying, 'Oh dear, Brady has somehow got free, and look, he's got a gun. Everybody, stay out of his way. There's no telling what he's capable of.' Brady imagined the mock horror on their faces as he left and went into hiding, forever.

Another couple of dead NanoSuits™ wandered into the Main Hall, and they appeared like conjoined twins, and then another head appeared of a child merged with its two parents. Even from this vantage point, they looked like members of the same family. They were pulling in different directions, and they seemed to be attracted to Brady. They weren't wailing - they were still communicating with each other. *It's this way... No. It's over here... I was right about banding together to punch through the Shell™, wasn't I? ...The pull is coming from this direction... Are we nearly there yet? I want to go home.*

Brady watched the family move around the Main Hall like pieces on a giant Ouija board. Then they began their clockwork turning manoeuvre, one cog at a time, as one and then sped off in the direction of the cafeteria.

The gun on the table pulled Brady's attention back to his present problem. He determined that he wouldn't be a player in any game devised by Bodhi or Hunter. Instead, he wondered whether it might buy him valuable time if he got the chance to take himself hostage. He didn't know how they would react if he pretended that he was on the verge of suicide. They couldn't be seen to egg him on, but also, they wouldn't panic him. He knew they wanted to be free of any connection to this atrocity, and that meant that Brady Mahone had to take the cowards way out - by killing himself or running away. There had to be another way.

He relaxed. He let the SecurityFilm™ take the weight off. *Maybe, the biggest mistake they are making is giving Brady Mahone the time to develop a plan.* He examined the layout.

Another dead NanoSuit™ came into the Main Hall - again, it came close to Brady before concluding that he didn't smell quite right. It spoke to itself, like a demon communicating with hell. 'The families that bond together can puncture the Shell™. We will not be denied access to the Creator.' Brady shuddered at this sound of this twisted Suits™ voice and was relieved as he watched it glide away in the direction of the cafeteria where Bodhi was holding court.

There was the sound of murmuring and chattering, and then the selected Disciples and the Devout entered the hall. Brady knew it was no coincidence that these were the same people as logged on Professor Pinar Dogan's list. The surroundings were the opposite of grand, as each member of this caucus pulled up a simple chair made from recycled materials. There was no apparent hierarchy, but Brady noticed the little cliques that formed within the gathering. Even

Bodhi sat among them and not at the front and centre as expected of a Trad leader.

Out through the Main Hall, Brady could see outside to the interior of the NanoShell™, but everybody else had their attention firmly fixed on Brady Mahone. Faces fixed firmly forward.

Yet another dead NanoSuit™ found Bodhi, and as it merged with him, Brady thought it strange that the group no longer found this weird. Perhaps, it had happened so often in the past that it was no longer a thing.

In the meantime, he took comfort from the apparently bright Californian sunshine from within the HQ boundaries, but he hadn't forgotten that it looked markedly different from this from beyond the Electric Blue NanoShell™.

Bodhi made a lowering gesture with his hand, and the SecurityProtocol™ placed Brady on the ground, and the SecurityFilm™ around him melted away. Brady was physically in good shape. Although he was emotionally unstable, he was grieving for his family whilst at the same time simmering with rage at his treatment. There had been plenty of occasions like this in his life, where he had been judged for the crimes, he *had* committed, and he never felt anger towards the prosecution lawyers, the jurors, or the judge - he thought of Judge Audre Jefferson and how she became his friend in her later years - the post-Revolution years. He never saw himself as the good guy. He knew he was bad and that he knew the game of risk and reward he was playing. It was his job to get away with it, and their job to catch him if they could - and if they did, it was a fair cop. He knew the people judging him on those days were the good guys, and therefore, he had no animosity to them. But this wasn't how he viewed his current situation. Brady wasn't used to being the victim.

Brady inched toward the table and picked up the gun. It had been a century since he last held one. He couldn't remember for sure, but he guessed that the last time he held a pistol in his hand was when he escaped from the Modern Ridgecrest Supermax Penitentiary back in 2084.

He pointed it at Bodhi for a moment, and then at Siddha, he made a gesture pretending to fire it, but his audience remained silent and unmoved. He began to wonder whether he was on show for entertainment purposes. He looked at Samuel Beardon the Third, but he seemed to be reciting a prayer, and scanning past Cain and Lizzie, he looked at Rhea, trying to judge whether she loved or loathed him. Her face gave little away, but he drew comfort from the fact that her eyes had a hint of sadness.

Over the audience's heads, he was convinced that the NanoShell™ around the Sattva Systems™ HQ was distorting. And then he saw a writhing form of a massed group of NanoSuits™ creeping up behind the audience. He saw the heads protrude and retreat as if there was a battle for leadership to find Bodhi Sattva. The audience couldn't see them, but Brady could.

One of the heads emerged, and he recognised Bill, his son, and it wailed, 'I've found him.' The rest of the audience had long since taken no notice of the recycling of NanoSuits™. The mass moved closer to Bodhi. Brady was appalled at the sight of this monstrous mash-up of his family. He guessed that this was what they were waiting for. He couldn't stand it any longer. He raised the gun to his temple, and then he heard a howl of anguish. Brady saw the screaming head of Amie emerge. 'Brady. No!'

All eight heads protruded grotesquely from the conglomerate of eight dead NanoSuits™ in a muddy mess, and they leapt on Brady. The audience watched in utter confusion as they shouldn't be attracted to Brady. He heard the ghostly greetings from all of them simultaneously. It was difficult for him to home in on one voice.

Hey, Pops, you're still alive...Don't do it...What have they done to you? You must fight...We can help...Use our Suits™...

'I'm not taking the Green. I'd rather die...'

No...Please...We haven't got long...Bodhi is pulling us back to him...Don't resist...We will be your tool...We can't stay with you even if we wanted to...You must hurry...Tell them the truth...

'They won't listen to me. I've already been judged.'

Then be someone they will listen to...Speak up...We will become them...You must hurry!

He watched the figure of Hawk being stretched out of the formation with Wilder wrapping himself around his younger brother, fighting desperately to keep him with the rest of his family. He dropped his gun and began to speak.

'I had been through all kinds of tests. My eggs had been engineered to ensure I had a boy.' Amie's body moved to the front of the writhing mass, and she took the form of Libby Skye as she was depicted in the movie poster at her Malibu home.

'The doctors and nurses had been well rewarded for working on the Millennial Eve, but what I didn't know was that they were offered bonuses which would make them rich for life if they induced me to have the first baby in the world born on the Millennial Day. They even had a registrar ready. I should have wondered why I had to go to Tonga to deliver the baby. You could say that they were highly motivated. The only rule was that I couldn't have a Caesarion section. I must have a vaginal birth.'

Bodhi stared at her, and it seemed that he might have the power to extract the vision of his dead Mother from the clutches of the other NanoSuits™, but they resisted in this ethereal tug-of-war.

'They were brutal with me. As the clock ticked down, they tried everything to bring Xavier into the world, and then as the clock was about to strike twelve, the surgeon butchered me. He sliced me up, and they used a ventouse and pulled him into the world on the first second of the new Millennium. I cannot find the words to describe the agony they made me endure. I suppose I should be grateful that they stuck around for the emergency surgery I needed afterwards. If

I'd have known, what John's plan was, I would never have agreed to it, not even for this place. I have massive scarring to this day - even after the best cosmetic surgery you could buy back in those primitive times.' She wailed so loudly that it drew an echo from beyond the HQ's NanoShell™.

'Xavier's education began even before he was born. John had his teachers come and talk to the baby inside me. Can you imagine how weird that was, having to let complete strangers hover over my stomach and recite science and business lessons to a foetus? Every single day I had to let them do that to me.'

Bodhi yelled to drown her out, and Libby sprung back into the writhing forms. But she re-emerged. Amie was even more determined, and now she shone brightly in a stark white vision of Libby Skye.

'I talked to my unborn baby. He could hear me day or night. I used to say, "Xavier, this is your Mother. Whatever anybody should say to you, you must always protect your Mother." I must have looked like I was insane, but I talked to my unborn baby boy all the time, day and night. I had to keep my bond with my baby.'

She spat out, 'But he was Daddy's little science project, and he let me die. He could have saved me, but he didn't. He killed his own Mother.'

The gathered assembly began to murmur. The vision of Libby Skye turned spectrally clear, and, in her exhaustion, she fell from the mass and walked serenely over to the seated figure of Bodhi and merged into him.

Another ear-piercing wail went up, and this time it was from Helgarth. She emerged in the form of Tia Cassandra. 'We had a source from inside the FBI - she was on our payroll - and she gave us the crucial lead to Samuel Beardon the Second. He gave us the information we were looking for before he could give it to the authorities. Our source kept it from them. She was well rewarded for her silence.' Rhea shuffled uncomfortably and looked around for possible escape routes.

'John Kane despised humanity. He viewed them as worse than animals - actually, he loved animals, but that's hardly relevant here. He blamed humans for trashing the planet, and therefore he used humans for his experimentation. He was fascinated by nature, and he believed that humans were unnatural. He conducted little side experiments to understand the effects of nurture on virtually identical embryos.'

Rhea pretended to cough. She waved her apologies and stood up and headed slowly away. It was then that she saw the outer NanoShell™ stretching to breaking point. She couldn't see beyond the Shell™, but she knew it had to be a mighty force to be able to do that. She looked back at the distorted vision of Tia Cassandra.

'The first child he had was Xavier Kane, the person you know as Bodhi Sattva. He bred him to be perfect. From the moment he was conceived, he was hot housed to be the perfect heir to Sattva Systems™. The next child was born in the UK. He was indoctrinated with socialist values from before he was born. John Kane had people bombard the foetus with socialist doctrines and then raised by left-wingers. His name was Glenarvon Cole. Brady Mahone was his third experiment.' She answered a question that the audience couldn't hear. 'Closer to identical triplets. And Libby Skye is the mother of all three of you.'

The vision of Tia Cassandra laughed and howled at the same time. 'He strung her along. John Kane incentivised her and her friends to talk to you as a criminal while still in the womb. He had a script for them to follow, as they weren't particularly bright. This process continued until after you, Brady Mahone was born, and then your Mother, so to speak, died of a drug overdose.' She laughed hysterically, 'and then he placed you with a paedophile.' The exhausted NanoSuit™ of Helgarth fell as if there was nothing of substance for the others to grab onto. She completed her walk to Bodhi to recycle her Nanomaterials.

The NanoSuits™ of his sons and Lucy-Ian seemed to have lost their critical mass. Brady felt them fall away from him and sensed their utter exhaustion from their efforts to help him. They made one last effort to divert themselves away from Bodhi by leaping on Glenarvon Cole, maybe to confirm their story, or perhaps it was to apologise. Brady wondered if he would ever get to find out.

Brady saw Rhea pointing outside, and Brady watched the cracks appear in the outer Shell™. He remembered his conversation with Professor Pinar Dogan. He looked at her, and Brady raised his right arm high above his head. He clenched his fist so tightly that his skin turned white, and then he released it with a flourish in a gesture that suggested an explosion.

Pinar smiled, but she was obviously puzzled. She looked behind her. She seemed to be in shock for a moment until she threw her chair aside and fled for her life. Brady ran into the crowd, imploring them to follow her. Siddha and Hunter tried to restrain him, but Glenarvon Cole implored Bodhi to set him free. Bodhi didn't understand the sudden commotion. He watched with bewilderment as Professor Pinar Dogan raced into the building instead of away from it. Bodhi waved his hand dismissively at Siddha and Hunter, and they let Brady go free.

Bodhi's arm flopped back down by his side as if it was too heavy to hold up. Glen checked his own movements, and he sensed he was either getting weaker or heavier. Glen said, 'Where is Pinar going?'

'To the Sensory Deprivation Chambers.' Brady still wasn't sure if he could trust anybody here, but there wasn't time for assessing the motivations in an emergency. 'She's certain that Bodhi can't recycle nine-hundred million Suits™ within his body. He's Pure Nano now - he's not human, the whole things going to blow, and your NanoSuits™ aren't going to protect you.'

'Of course, they will. They have never failed.'

'I've seen it at Cima. If the same Nanomaterials are blasted at you. You will die. You must trust me. I'm begging you.' He added, 'Why do you think Pinar ran?' As if her actions were louder than her words.

The surge of black Nanomaterials began to ooze through the outer NanoShell™, and the California sunshine had turned to the black of night. The ooze moved like lava after an eruption, and it was all heading to Bodhi for recycling.

Siddha said, 'Don't listen to him, Glen. He's lying. Bodhi is going to be a God, and I will be at his right-hand side. You can't lose faith now. He's always kept his promises.'

Glen looked at the black mass and knew it was madness to stay. 'You do what you gotta do. For good or ill, my fate is tied to Brady's now.'

'Then, you are a fool, Glenarvon Cole.' Siddha turned away in disgust and moved toward Bodhi with Hunter alongside him. Brady kept his eye on Siddha. He never did trust him. Hunter whispered in Siddha's ear, and then Brady watched Siddha sneak away in the same direction as Pinar. He wondered if he was going to save himself, after all.

'I'll take as many as I can. Some will want to remain here. When I get to the Sensory Deprivation Chambers, I'll set the comms channels open. In case you didn't know how they worked.' Glen thought over the logistical issues. 'I'll tell the others to seal the Chambers for twelve hours, and then I'll be the first to check if it's safe to re-emerge. No point risking everyone.'

Brady said, 'What do the comms things do?'

'Obviously, once inside the Chambers, you are supposed to be isolated from external stimuli, but in this situation, we are going to need two-way communication. I will set this up, and then we can communicate with others secured within the Chambers and also communicate with the outside. We will need to know what's happening...' He felt pulled to the floor. 'I'm weakening.'

'Let's move.' Brady raced off. He yelled to the others, 'Come on. Go to the Sensory Deprivation Chambers...' He watched Bridgett dismissively wave Glen away, but he then saw that he had persuaded Precious to leave. Brady wanted to go to Rhea, but Glen had got to her first, and she was helping with the evacuation. He watched her arguing with Lizzie. He then saw the disconsolate figure of the Bear slumped in his chair. He was alone. Brady rushed to him.

'Hey, brother, you've got to go, y'know, save yourself.'

'My Alicia is going to die. How can I justify living if I can't protect my daughter?'

'I know, man. It's real hard, but she wouldn't want you to die as well. You know she wouldn't.'

'No. You go - save yourself. My time is up.'

'Isn't that for your God to decide - and what about Tyrone? Are you going to let me take the blame for not saving you when I had the chance? What kind of a friend would that make me?'

The Bear didn't answer.

'Look. Just save yourself today. For me, as a favour, and tomorrow you can do what you want. How does that sound? Couldn't we make a deal?'

The Bear didn't answer, but he did rise to his feet. Brady grabbed him by the arm. They started to race away when they heard a large crack, and the deluge of NanoSuits™ began to fill the Main Hall. Brady looked ahead and saw Glenarvon, Rhea and Lizzie make it to the corridor. He looked behind, and the only ones who were staying back were Bridgett, Hunter, and Cain.

'Hey, brother. You go on ahead. I'm going to try and persuade Cain to come. He's kinda been ok with me.' He shook the Bear. 'You promise you won't do anything stupid, old man.'

'I won't.'

Brady moved freely through the Black Goo, and he was surprised how light it was. It hardly impeded his movement. However, the Bear seemed leaden-footed and seemed to find it a struggle to move freely. Brady rubbed the dry film from his bare forearm. He expected his white T-shirt to be stained black, but the residue fell from it as if it was being repelled. He guessed that the thick clouds of NanoSuit™ materials were magnetically attracted to the Greens, and they were weighed down by the accumulations on their own Suits™. He checked out the condition of Bodhi in the distance, and he couldn't spot any signs of movement. He was alive, but he had the appearance of a man who had gorged on a massive feast of NanoSuits™. Brady felt static in the air raise the hairs on his skin, and he tingled all over. This latest addition to the evidence of his senses wasn't reassuring. He had to move quickly.

Cain seemed barely conscious when Brady reached him. 'Hey, man. Can I help a brother out?'

Cain gazed vacantly at Brady with his crystal green eyes. 'I'm ok. I deserve to die.'

Brady laughed, 'You can be a stupid fuck sometimes, but you've always been ok with me. Now come on, your friends are waiting for you. Let me help.' Brady tried to help Cain to his feet, but he didn't seem to have the strength to stand. 'I ain't got time for this, man.' Brady swept him up in his big arms as easily as if he was picking up a bag of feathers. He marched through the dead NanoSuits™ as if they weren't there, but he could hear them howling.

I can't move...I'm being crushed...He's here. I can feel him...

They tried to attach themselves to Brady, but they were repelled from his body and even his clothes.

That's not Bodhi...Where's Bodhi?

Brady resolved to ignore them as he carried the frail, white-robed figure in his arms. He wondered if he was running out of time as the air was thickening and the light seemed to be disappearing into the massed black souls. The screaming from the crush intensified.

Brady reached the storeroom, which contained the Sensory Deprivation Chambers. To Brady, it looked like the storage facility of a Funeral Home. The first line of matt black coffins were wholly sealed. He investigated the coated glass plate on the first one, and he saw Lizzie, who looked alarmed to see Brady peering down at her. 'No. No...' He readjusted Cain in his arms.

'Hey. I saved you. Talk about gratitude...' He peered into the gathering darkness and heard a fight within the wails of the Dead NanoSuits™. He went to investigate. He passed more sealed coffins, but then he found the broken ones.

Glen and Siddha were fighting but without any energy, as they were both utterly exhausted. Siddha grabbed the open lid of a Sensory Deprivation Chamber and heaved it back against the locks, and it fell to the floor, like all the others.

Brady muttered, 'Where the fuck are the SecurityProtocols™ when you need them?'

Siddha headed for the next of the last two undamaged coffins. Glen grabbed Siddha's ankles with the last of his strength. Brady quickly but carefully placed Cain on the ground, picked up a broken coffin shell and ran at Siddha. He knocked Siddha off his feet, and he put him under the lid like catching a bug in a glass. Brady piled more lids on him until he was sure he wouldn't have the power to escape the weight.

He went back to retrieve Cain, and he put him in a Sensory Deprivation Chamber. Cain was too weak to either protest or thank Brady, all he could do was stare at Brady like a helpless child. Brady closed the lid, and it sealed over Cain.

Glenarvon Cole was close to death. Brady picked up his brother.

Glen said, 'There's only one left. You take it, I should die like my GreenRev comrades...'

'Are you kidding?' Brady laughed and looked at Glen as if he was a dying soldier on the battlefield. 'I hate solitary. Brady Mahone has spent too much of his life being locked up. I'm damned if I'm going to volunteer for incarceration.' He scooped Glenarvon Cole in a fireman's lift and then dumped him unceremoniously into the coffin and sealed it before Glen could protest. He didn't have time for sad goodbyes. Brady shrugged as he muttered to himself, 'I may as well see out the end of the war. Let's hope they put on a good show.'

He heard a voice emanate from a speaker from a neighbouring Chamber. 'Your only hope is to get high...'

'Ain't that the truth, sister.' Brady joked.

He peered into the chamber, and he saw it was Professor Pinar Dogan. She said, 'It's theoretical but with a high possibility...'

'I don't think we got time for this...'

'Ok. Yes. You need to find a FusionPlane™, get as high as you can, but not directly above Bodhi. Go...Now!' She added, 'Hurry!'

Brady raced down the corridors through the black mist through the Main Hall. He tried to get his bearings in the deepening gloom. He saw the banner with the thirteen promises, and then he spotted the exit. He sprinted through the door, and he caught the sight of a FusionPlane™, but it was privately owned by one of the Disciples and, therefore, was unresponsive to him. He passed by a few other vehicles until he found Rhea's rental. He climbed inside. He took over the manual controls and vertically took off as fast as he could. He switched everything onto maximum power. All he could see was black as he ascended through millions of expired NanoSuits™.

He wondered whether he would ever see daylight again, but finally, he did rise above them. He set off due south just as day turned to night, and he watched the light being sucked into the Sattva Systems™ HQ. The hundreds of millions of Dead Souls were sucked away in a fraction of a second. This was followed by utter silence and stillness, and then there was a blinding flash of light. In a moment, the California winter sun returned, but it was eclipsed by a tower of light which reached to the skies and then spread in flashes all over the skies from horizon to horizon, creating a strobe light effect which lasted a few minutes.

Without even making the decision, Brady started to fly to McFarland. The sky had turned to an unnatural Electric Blue, and then as if the Hands of God had been placed on a Van Der Graff Generator, the electrical storms began. He saw thousands of people below him who had come out to witness the strange astral phenomena. He watched them all being eviscerated with unerring accuracy. Each lightning bolt was attracted to the identical NanoSuit™ signatures as the Dead NanoSuits™ coating the upper atmosphere.

The lightning bolts lit up a grid system about one hundred metres above ground level, which stretched to the horizon. The grid crackled and fired off millions of sparks, followed by mini-explosions, and although he had never seen one, and the only person that claimed that they had - Vance, who likened it to catching the picture at the heart of a Magic Eye puzzle out of the corner of soft eyes - Brady knew that these were the Security Protocols™ being wiped out by the storms of heaven. He fought the urge to whoop and holler at this awesome display of power, as instantly, he remembered that millions were being murdered in these same minutes.

He dwelled on why the Security Protocols™ were targeted. Until he made the mental leap that these were created from the same materials as the NanoSuits™. He also guessed that they had some cloaking mechanism that kept them from the sight of humans. If the Greens had been able to see the millions of these at once, they might have been more concerned. As it was, they only appeared infrequently, and at times of trouble, this gave them the brand image of Guardian Angels as opposed to mind-controlling machines. He vividly recalled being inside the goo they covered him in after the death of his family and friends in Malibu, and he thought that the goo was probably a kind of viscous version of the Nanoparticles the Suits™ were made from. He shuddered at the thought of this being a close relative of the dead NanoSuits™.

Brady thought of Alicia as he watched the thousands of people being turned to charred ashes beneath him in horror. It was only then that the enormity of what had transpired hit him. He slowed his FusionPlane™ to a slow glide, almost as a mark of respect to the dead. Everybody was dead. He reminded himself that this wasn't strictly true. Many of his chief tormenters and enemies might be alive in their protective coffins, but as the lightning strikes continued from all horizons, he wondered how long it might be before they could be released. This could go on for hours, or maybe years.

He headed to McFarland. His home in Malibu was the sight of the massacre of his family and friends, and it held no prospect of comfort for him. He became aware that although there were thousands of lightning strikes in the distance, they seemed to have slowed around him. Brady hovered over his ranch for a while. He didn't know if he was safe. He considered that the FusionPlane™ might be protecting him. As he lowered his vehicle, he noticed that there were birds, and then he spotted other animals behaving as if nothing had happened.

Over by the old bunker, he saw the doors move. He didn't land. He watched closely. The doors opened slowly, and then a couple of Greens who watched over the place in his absence emerged, blinking into the sunlight. One of them spotted Brady and waved to him. Brady waved back. He was concerned that they would be fried by the heavenly fires, but nothing happened.

Oh, man. If only Pops had been around to see that he was right about his bunker all along. He always said it could withstand anything mankind could throw at it.

Brady wondered who else might have survived - maybe in caves or onboard NanoSubmarines™...

He manoeuvred his FusionPlane™ to head back to Boulder Creek. He flew quickly, and he kept checking the skies for lightning and the ground for any other signs of Green survivors. He didn't see any. Finally, he landed at Sattva Systems™, and he was surprised at the lack of damage. *It must be one of those death by electrocution kinda deals like they used to do to us good 'ol boys in the old days.*

There wasn't a single sign of the black NanoSuits™ of the dead. He went over to the resting place of Bodhi Sattva and if Brady expected any precious metals to be left behind. Something he could have made into a manly piece of jewellery, then he was to be disappointed. All that was left was dirt. He moved his fingers through it. He sniffed it on his fingers, which reminded him of coal dust.

The height of Green technology and it's turned to coal dust.

Brady removed his Sattva Ring on his Pops' silver chain and placed it on the black dust.

30: ELECTRIC BLUE DAY

Brady opened each of the Sensory Deprivation Chambers and helped them climb out as they were still feeble. It wasn't a coincidence that the first one he rescued was Rhea Laidlaw.

'I suppose you're going to arrest me now. That'd be just my luck.'

She laughed, 'No. You're free to go. Brady Mahone.'

'But what if I don't want to go?'

She dug him weakly in the ribs. 'Maybe, I'll bring you in for questioning later.' She looked around at the other Chambers. 'I think we should let them out. They will all want to know what happened, and then we need to plan for the future.'

Rhea didn't have the energy to release anybody, so Brady helped to lift them out. At first, he put them on the floor, where they sat with their backs against the wall. He went to the Main Hall to bring them all chairs, but the air reeked of coal dust, and even though it rolled off him like water droplets off his old, waxed Poacher's coat, he wondered whether it was potentially dangerous to the Green survivors. He returned empty-handed. Glen asked, 'What happened?'

'It's bad. I don't think many survived. I'll tell you later. You all need to get outside as I don't think it's good for you in here. There's a lot of dust in the air - I think it's the same stuff that's making you real weak.'

Glen struggled to his feet and started to help the others to their feet. He hadn't the strength to assist the Bear, so Brady went to him, and he needed all his power to raise him, as he was almost a dead weight now. 'Any news about my Alicia?'

'She's gone, like nearly everybody else. I'm really sorry, man.'

'You're not one for doling out false hope, brother.'

'Words were never my strong point - you know me. Now come on, you're going to have to be strong for the others.'

The Bear smiled knowingly; he knew Brady was trying to instil a sense of purpose in him. He appreciated the attempt. Brady made several trips to carry a survivor and place them in the fresh air of the Californian winter sunshine, which had re-established a semblance of normality. Brady looked up curiously at the Electric Blue sky. Professor Pinar Dogan followed Brady's sightline and was puzzled and then profoundly concerned.

Brady Mahone, the last Trad on Earth, looked over his exhausted Green survivors - Rhea, Precious, Lizzie, Professor Pinar Dogan, Genesis Garcia, Cain, Glenarvon Cole and Samuel Beardon the Third. Those that found sufficient energy grieved for their lost loved ones. He was surprised to see Genesis Garcia weeping so openly as, for some reason, he thought that politicians didn't cry real tears.

'Cain?'

He roused from his inner thoughts. 'Yes.'

'Are you X-Ray™?' Brady added, 'Bodhi, Hunter and Siddha were. I'm guessing, as part of their crew, that you would be as well.'

'No. I hesitated and asked for more time to consider.'

Brady turned to the group. 'Anybody else?'

A few hands went up hesitantly. He studied them. Professor Pinar Dogan, Glenarvon Cole, and one that took him by surprise until he revisited the connections - Lizzie.

'And yes - we still can issue X-RaySuits™.' Pinar answered before Brady even thought of asking. Pinar scanned the scene. 'The facilities are untouched.'

'From what I witnessed, massive electrical storms produced millions of lightning strikes which seemed to seek out the Greens. It didn't touch me, the FusionPlane™ or even the wildlife.' Brady knew he was removing any last vestiges of hope for them with this statement.

'And Moses and Aaron did so, as the LORD commanded; and he lifted up the rod, and smote the waters that were the river, in the sight of Pharoah, and in the sight of his servants, and all the waters that were in the river were turned to blood. Exodus 7:20.' He had used his reserves of energy to relay his sermon with as much power as he could, but his breath was laboured, and then he lay down on the grass verge near the Main Entrance of the Sattva Systems™ HQ. The Bear visibly wilted.

Brady shook his head. He was as interested in Religious Education lessons as he was in Science. He only had one thing he desperately wanted to know, and that was whether these Greens would clear his name and accept responsibility for the deaths of their own kind. 'You know I had nothing to do with these deaths, don't you? Does anybody actually believe that I would kill my own family and friends?' He studied each of them. 'Look. I know, I ain't no saint. I killed people, bad people in my eyes, but I didn't have anything to do with this.' He raised his arms as if to indicate the world. 'Come on, people. Put a guy out of his misery, here.'

Pinar said. 'One of the side projects which John Kane instigated, decades before the Revolution, was developing Nanoparticles as a pathogen.'

Brady wasn't going to stop Pinar talking by asking what a pathogen was.

'It had a working title of NanoTaint™. It was a method of transferring Nanomaterials to the centre of the brain. These particles were inert and undetectable unless we activated them. John had a twisted sense of morals and would not conduct these experiments on animals, but humans, especially children, were fair game. I won't lie, I knew everything, but I was gaining an insight not afforded to other more regulated branches of the scientific community.'

Rhea interrupted. 'I was working for the FBI at the time, and Marjorie was with Military Intelligence, while her husband was with the CIA, we were investigating the deaths of children, and he had put together a case on the mysterious deaths of children in Pakistan. We had links to John Kane.'

Sissy said, 'I didn't know you were in the FBI...'

'Why would you? There was no FBI. It gave me a sense of purpose - I enjoyed my old life, I wanted to know how you did it.'

'I've still got those files.' Brady stated. The others were puzzled, but Rhea was intrigued. 'I stole them from the Los Banos Police Department. I've seen those dead kids. Judge Audre Jefferson went through them all. She made me a summary that even I could understand. However, I never saw anything in there that mentioned this NanoTaint™ crap.'

Glen looked over to Pinar, and it was a look of a colleague who'd been kept in the dark. Pinar said, 'With a complex magnetic switch, we could instantly but painlessly terminate a subject. He was keen to try it out on the Files used by his paedophile ring if they ever tried to blackmail John Kane. Each file was coated with NanoTaint™, and it was ingested through the fingers. It was a prototype technology which was eventually used in Distors™.'

'That actually makes sense. I tried to give one of these Files back to Bodhi - long story, I was blackmailing him.' He waved away any attempts to get him to continue. 'That's a story for another day.' Brady was puzzled. 'So, why didn't I die? Nobody handled them more than me.'

'Bodhi was a natural birth. By the time you and Glenarvon Cole's conception in the lab, you were genetically engineered to repel NanoTaint™. The last I saw of John Kane; he was going to bring you back for tests. There had been a memory distortion as a child with Bodhi, and John wanted Xavier, Bodhi to be perfect. You were one of two perfect donors. You were the most dispensable due to your conditioning.'

'Thanks for reminding me.' He peered into Pinar's face with her brown eyes. He wasn't sure whether he was talking to a machine or a human. 'If I was to take responsibility for all these deaths, and it was designed to keep Bodhi Sattva's impeccable reputation intact - then he couldn't have got somebody else to do it for him, say Siddha, for instance...'

'Bodhi did it. And I was the only other person in the world who knew he had the means. Bodhi thought he was doing it for the right reasons. He was saving the planet, and he wasn't going to waste *Her* resources on Greens, who were unwilling to work for a thousand years. It was simpler to blame it on you.' Before anybody could comment, Pinar raised her hand, 'I may as well tell you how it was done with the final details. Bodhi grasped the opportunity for the disloyal to self-select themselves for elimination when he watched Brady grow his business - all he needed to do was take over the manufacturing to enable worldwide distribution. The NanoTaint™ was placed on the head of every Diamondback Rattlesnake.' She looked only at Brady. 'We didn't concern ourselves with your original homemade sales, as you were utterly persuasive at making your customers want more.'

Pinar looked back at the group and raised her hands. 'I know what I've done - I'm guilty. I never believed Bodhi would be so decisive.' She looked up at the sky and pointed, 'This is an extinction-level threat. I will try and make amends by helping to solve this.'

Genesis Garcia had been reflecting on how she helped design the BMEE logo with the snake twisting through the letters. 'Ruthless - not *decisive*. He instilled into each of us here, never to touch these files, as he would consider that as an act of giving in to the temptation of nostalgia for the Trad world. We now know why.'

The others muttered in agreement but were interrupted when a Satt™ rang out with an unfamiliar tone to everybody but Rhea. They all looked at her. She answered and then put it on speakerphone. 'Hi, Tia. You're on speaker. There are only a few survivors. You can talk freely.'

She said to the others. 'There will be a short delay. Tia is on Mars, but one thing she is a genius at is communication technology. The delay in transmissions will make regular conversations tricky, so I'll resort to using the term *over* when I have finished my sentence.'

Tia said, 'Our observatories witnessed the Earth appearing like a pulsar for a few minutes. Of course, I know it wasn't a pulsar, but I'm using the terminology for descriptive purposes. This was followed by a worldwide thunderstorm, and we tried to communicate but received no answer. It's good to hear your voice again, Rhea. Over.'

Rhea was about to answer, but Pinar pleaded with her to let her speak to her first. Rhea gestured, *ok*.

'This is Professor Pinar Dogan. We need your help. In the aftermath of the quantum mechanical black hole's rapid evaporation, it has created a layer of carbon particles in the stratosphere. The amounts are significant enough to change the quality of light reaching the Earth's surface, damaging vegetation. I'll continue with my work here, but it would help if you can get some of my old colleagues working on the problem at your end. To use round figures, there were approximately one billion people, each with eight NanoSuits™. These are polluting the Earth's atmosphere. The sky has changed colour substantially. Over.'

They all looked up at the Electric Blue sky. If they had noticed it before, they put it down to becoming accustomed to the light after their trauma, but Pinar was right - the colour change was unmistakable.

Glen said, 'We haven't done this for nothing, have we? I don't believe this.'

'You shall have no other gods before me...' Samuel Beardon the Third muttered his response in reproach to his own sins.

Pinar said, 'Science and humanity are strange bedfellows, with every new discovery comes the means of man's salvation and destruction. Science has given us this problem - fortunately, it may also have the solution...' Pinar muttered, 'Science will help fix up what its users fuck up.'

The Satt™ caught up with the transmission. 'Our Laser-Induced Breakdown Spectroscopy has confirmed your analysis. We will send whatever resources you need. I'm in the observatory with the man who first observed the Earth's disturbance. He claims he heard his uncle's voice on the speakerphone. I'll put him on for a moment...'

'Was that you, Uncle Sam? We are ok up here. Raelynn and I are having a baby. I'm going to be a Dad...sorry...over.'

'The bad news can wait. Let him have his moment.' Brady shook his head and pointed up to the heavens.

Rhea said, 'You can talk with him in private afterwards. You can use my Satt™ for as long as you wish.'

The Bear nodded and whispered, 'Thank you.' He then shouted as if he had to physically make his voice carry all the way to Mars. 'That's wonderful news. Pass on my love and congratulations to Raelynn.'

Brady shouted, 'Way to go, man. You tell Raelynn that I'm mighty proud of her.'

Rhea smiled and spoke into the speakerphone. 'Over and out.' She said to the group. 'I'll leave the Satt™ on the reception desk. Anybody can use it, but I suggest we take turns monitoring it for incoming calls.'

'I think we should take a bit of time to recover...'

Brady looked at his watch and said, 'What the fuck is the time? My watch says 75:10.'

'I'm sorry, Brady.' Pinar shrugged. 'Everything's been set for the GreenMetricTime™. It's the least of our worries. You'll just have to get used to it. In old money, it's just after 6pm.'

'Ah, for fuck...'

Rhea took hold of Brady's hand, 'I don't mind teaching you...unless you don't want me to...'

'Yeah. Ok. Deal.' He laughed.

'Let's say we get out of here.' She said to the others. 'Shall we all meet back here in a couple of days and make some plans for the next steps. The old Satts™ should still be working if we need to contact each other.' Rhea led Brady to the FusionPlanes™, and she opened one.

Brady said, 'Hey, that was your rental?'

'Yes.'

'I might not have got out of here in time if it wasn't parked up. All the others were Private...'

'So, are you telling me I saved your life?'

Brady laughed, 'I wouldn't go that far...' She gave him a look of mock disappointment. 'Ok, yeah, you saved the life of Brady Mahone.'

'And what's your life worth?'

'What do you want?'

'Let's start by letting me have a look at those Los Banos Files of yours.'

Brady laughed, 'There are dozens of boxes of them. You might have to stay over to get through them all...'

'That's fine by me. I don't mean to impose.'

The FusionPlane™ lifted off vertically, and Brady set the autopilot to the Mahone Ranch. 'On one condition...'

'And what's that?'

'That you read them slowly. I wouldn't want you to miss anything.'

She held his hand, smiled, and then kissed him. As she pulled away and sunk comfortably into her passenger seat, the sky's Electric Blue colour caught Brady's attention.

He said, 'The sky looks kinda cool.'

'Yeah, if you discount the tons of carbon dust threatening to destroy all life on Earth.' She teased. 'Hey, Brady-kins...'

'Brady-kins!'

They both laughed. She asked, 'What are your plans?'

'What do you mean?'

'Well, as far as I can tell, you've only got a few Brady Mahone Entertainment Enterprises customers left, and I don't think your millions of Green Credits are going to be of much use anymore.'

Brady shrugged, 'I suppose I'll just have to retire.'

'So, you wouldn't be interested in going back to work, then?'

'I dunno. What could I do?

'Is that modesty I hear, Mr Mahone?'

'We both know I'm not cut out for Green work...'

'What would you say if I told you that a certain Fleet Captain Marjorie Hampton is planning to return, and she thinks you would make a great LeviathanLifter™ pilot?'

Brady gasped, 'Oh, man. That would be cool.'

'Marjorie believes that the LeviathanLifters™ will be called into action to spray the dust clouds from the stratosphere. Do you want the job?'

'Hell, yes.'

Rhea laughed, 'If I was still an undercover TV reporter - I think my intro would run something like: Brady Mahone saves the world!'

Brady roared with laughter. After a minute or two, he calmed down, and he remembered those he had lost along the way. 'You know what's real funny?'

'Go on.'

'If my Pops were alive today, I would have to have told him that we've just invited a bunch of Martians to invade the planet.'

THE END.

ACKNOWLEDGEMENTS

I'd like to give my heartfelt thanks to my family, Cathy, my wife and my daughters, Beck and Katie, for their love and support while writing (and recording) this book.

A Small Request...

If you have enjoyed this book, do please help to spread the word by putting a review or a rating on your favourite bookseller or Goodreads; by posting something on social media; or in the old-fashioned way by simply telling your friends or family about it.

Book publishing is a very competitive business these days, to a saturated market, and independent publishers such as ourselves are often crowded out by big business.

Support from readers like you can make all the difference to a book's success.

Many thanks.

MORE FROM JIM LOWE

Previously published by Jim Lowe: The New Reform Quartet

B ook One: New Reform
Tatum had learning difficulties and had a brutal home life, but one thing to emerge from her living with a family of gun runners was that she learned to shoot with unerring accuracy.

When she finally escaped her family, she found friendship and camaraderie with a sisterhood of feminist activists until many of her friends were killed in a deadly terrorist attack.

It was then that Tatum spiralled into a state where the only solution was to take revenge on their killers...

The New Reform series was conceived in 2013 (before Brexit and Trump) and was a darkly satirical look into future political influences.

Not only did it play with the idea of corrupt populism, but also militant feminism, marketing, hacking, viral content, social media influencers, new money combined with dark desires - and even what could happen to the latent power of the aristocracy and the liberal elite if their power was turned inwards to ignite a potent force.

The four books have different themes but are interlinked, and by the end of the final book, all the plotlines are neatly gift-wrapped and presented with a tightly knotted jet-black bow.

Set in the fictional city of Arlington, this alternative history spans decades beginning in the eighties.

The story begins with Tatum waiting and watching - something she is exceptionally good at. In fact, she could watch and wait for England - and beyond...

Book Two: The ODC (The Online Death Cult)

Denise was a soulless sociopath with money to burn and urges to satisfy, and then she met Brandon. He was a celebrity seeker with a love for her, but with no regard to the trail of destruction, he would be willing to cause to make her his own.

Book Three: With Two Eyes

Nadie was only seeking the truth for the family of the man she had loved, but instead, she found herself treated as a travelling freak show. But as she doggedly continued in her lonely quest, little did she know that she was changing the world one step at a time.

Book Four: Fourth Room.

Bob had all the power and money he could want, but all this gave him was boredom and frustration at his perceived lack of freedom. Would he stand in the way of those who would use his position to start a new world order in his name...

All titles will be available, wherever possible, on eBook, paperback, hardback, and audiobook.

If you want to know more about my writing and recording, please visit my website at **jimlowewriting.com.**

THANK YOU.

Don't miss out!

Visit the website below and you can sign up to receive emails whenever Jim Lowe publishes a new book. There's no charge and no obligation.

https://books2read.com/r/B-A-KPCR-KNTVB

BOOKS 2 READ

Connecting independent readers to independent writers.

Did you love *2184 - Twenty-Second Century Man*? Then you should read *New Reform*[1] by Jim Lowe!

[2]

Tatum had a brutal home life, but one thing to emerge from her living with a family of gun runners was that she learned to shoot with unerring accuracy.

When she finally escaped her family, she found friendship and camaraderie with a sisterhood of feminist activists until many of her friends were killed in a deadly terrorist attack.

It was then that Tatum decided that her only meaningful solution was to take revenge on their killers...

The series covers a wide spectrum of social forces all vying for supremacy, from corrupt populism, social media influencers, hackers, and gangs, through to old money and faith.

---

1. https://books2read.com/u/4DKOqk

2. https://books2read.com/u/4DKOqk

All of this is viewed with a dark satirical eye and the series resolve all the plot lines and is neatly presented with a jet-black bow.

But for now, the New Reform Quartet begins with Tatum, who is watching and waiting, something she could do for England and beyond...

Begin the journey into this far-reaching dystopian world today.

Read more at https://jimlowewriting.com/.

About the Author

Jim Lowe was a bookseller for a UK retail chain for forty years but has now taken early retirement. He loves books and the creative arts.

He is married to Cath and has two grown-up daughters, Beck and Katie.

Jim is an active - some might say, an over-enthusiastic - member of his local community in the Worcester area and runs Facebook groups for musicians and writers of all backgrounds and levels of experience. He has also worked closely as a volunteer for BBC Introducing as a filmmaker, and his niche YouTube channel for local artists has had over 300,000 views.

He has lived and worked in many locations in England including, Ashbourne, Braintree, Burton-Upon-Trent, Bury St Edmunds, Chelmsford, Derby - where he was born and remains a lifelong Rams fan - Great Yarmouth, Lowestoft, Tewkesbury and Worcester, where he has lived for more than twenty years.

Read more at https://jimlowewriting.com/.

Lightning Source UK Ltd.
Milton Keynes UK
UKHW012116020123
414514UK00016B/69

9 798201 535995